PENDULUM

Kent Lauder

PENDULUM
by Kent Lauder

FIC045000 | FICTION / Family Life / General
FIC019000 | FICTION / Literary
FIC008000 | FICTION / Sagas

Library of Congress Control Number: 2023912116

ISBN: 979-8-88636-033-2 (paperback)
ISBN: 979-8-88636-034-9 (ebook)

Cover design by
Lewis Agrell
Cover art by Julie Trail, JulieTrail.com.

Printed in the United States of America

Authority Publishing
13389 Folsom Blvd #300-256
Folsom, CA 95630
800-877-1097
www.AuthorityPublishing.com

Contents

Prologue v

1. Sam 1

2. Charles 17

3. Breakdown 26

4. At the Ranch 41

5. The Mine 62

6. The Gathering Storm 85

7. Reunion 93

8. Sally and Robin 110

9. The Meeting 119

10. T. Bob 135

11. Unease 146

12. Riding Herd 154

13. Confrontation 163

14. Grit 174

15. Family Council 180

16. Retreat 190

17. A Great Dynamo Silenced 213

18. Negotiation 218

19. The Storm Abates 232

20. Renewal 239

Prologue

Tucked away among the dusky shadows of the old house, the great clock chimes its course through irretrievable time. Chopping arbitrary bits of space into measurable intervals, this mechanism was designed to satisfy the need for organized life. Central to a culture captivated and consumed by time, this manmade contraption also leaves in its wake regrets, and the promise of an uncertain future. To its subjects, it is a standing reminder of the ghosts that once were, and by extension, the anxieties of what may be. What it fails to suggest is the eternity of the present.

Beneath it all, and driving it all, is the pendulum; its slow, oscillating arc a suggestible mimic to life. Some would see only upheaval within its undulations, but for others, it could be seen as a metaphor for the new and renewal of life.

Its inevitable alternations also guarantee entropy, as sudden events invariably occur to upset the status quo—disturbances for which man's best-laid plans became secondary to what circumstance, what some might call destiny, had in mind. Analogous to the slow process of mountain-building, the raising of the land will, at periodic intervals, cause portions to suddenly collapse to its angle of repose—to its point of equilibrium. While periods of stasis between these upheavals may seem calm, the uplifting continues unabated and undetected, carrying with it the certainty of future disruptions. So it is in the lives of men. Intervals of peace only give the illusion of stability, but all along, the pressure toward instability continues.

Whether fueled by hope, or just plain naiveté, our players are about to embark upon their own unpredictable paths.

I

Sam

Sam Ellis glanced down through his steering wheel to find that he was doing only forty-five. The safety bumps on the roadside jolted him out of his daydream, adrenaline shot through him, and he instinctively turned the wheel to the left to get back onto the highway. Overcompensating, his truck began to slide on the sandy berm and spin around in an almost perfect circle before stopping.

Fortunately, he was traveling on Nevada's Highway 50. It had acquired the moniker "The Loneliest Road in America" for good reason, as he hadn't seen another vehicle for the last ten minutes. He pulled over, got out, and leaned against his truck to allow his pounding heart to calm down.

He sensed that it wasn't so much tiredness that caused him to be so distracted, but something else. His sudden return to alertness had closed the door to his silent rumination, and try as he might to recapture it, it only grew that more elusive. He couldn't recall why he had been so mesmerized. As a younger man, he would have burned through a desert road like this with no problem—and no weighty thoughts. But now sixty-three, with a paunch to his midsection and thinning hair to match, that young man had long ago disappeared in the rearview mirror. But that younger Sam had also grown up in this land, this great expanse where people measured distances not in single miles, but in tens of miles.

It had been forty years since Sam had left this area for good to move back east to pursue his high school and community college teaching career. Even though he was now retired and had time on his hands, coming back to the family ranch in western Nevada that his brother ran was rare for him to do. The last time Sam had seen Charles and his wife Sally was five years ago, when they had flown to his home in St. Louis for his wife's funeral. Before that, it must have been eight or so years since he and Helen had traveled to the ranch.

Then his rumination returned—Charles. His older brother was the very reason he had decided to make this westward journey. The ostensible reason for this trip was Charles's recent angina attack, and though less than a full heart attack, coronary artery disease is still serious. Sally called Sam to let him know that, while he had recovered, he was still working as hard as he had been before, and she asked him to come and perhaps urge him to slow down his workload.

He was feeling anxious about how he would be received. He sensed that Charles might still hold some latent animosity about him moving back east so long ago and leaving him to run the ranch. In any event, he figured that it was certainly time to make a reconnection, perhaps even a reconciliation, with his brother. Because of Charles's condition, Sam wondered if he would be needed to stay longer than anticipated. Would he be stepping on any toes just by being there? Finally, he decided, or at least hoped, that it would work itself out when he got there.

Sam's journey from his home in St. Louis would normally take a long day and a half traversing the prairie and the Rocky Mountains, and an equal amount rolling through the vast sunken landmass of the Great Basin Desert beyond Salt Lake. Sam had now entered this area that stretched all through Nevada before reaching the Sierras. It had been variously called a depression, an emptiness—even a wasteland. It was also called a sink, because what little rain it received had no outlet, trapped as it was by the surrounding and imposing mountains.

Because the subduction of the ocean floor off the Pacific Rim had caused the land to buckle eastward and upward in a continuous wave set of valleys and mountains, Sam was forced to traverse a dozen or so of these north-south ranges, and to experience a series of elevation changes as he went from valley to pass to valley again. The few communities in the region had developed only where sparse water accumulated, meaning that they were small and separated by miles of dry, isolated expanses. For most people, this segment was no tourist destination, but for Sam, it was what he most wanted to revisit. He could have continued to drive for the next six hours to reach his destination, but he wanted to take his time to see the land he had been away from for so long, and do what he hadn't done in ages: spend the night camping out.

Leaning against his truck by the roadside, and now somewhat calmed, he had a chance to look around. He was following the same wagon trail his great-great-great-grandparents had trekked a century and a half earlier. He held great admiration for the stubborn determination all immigrants had, but he also knew that desperation and ignorance had a lot to do with it—the desperation of a people who knew they hadn't any better chance had they stayed back east, and the ignorance of just how difficult the trek would be. If things had been reversed, and the pioneers had been forced to begin crossing the western mountains and desert first, then, according to one old sage, "They would'na went." But those who survived the harsh gauntlet must have felt like they could accomplish anything because, for the most part, many had succeeded in their newfound enterprises, their potential seemingly as open as the land they ventured through.

Deciding to take his ancestors' route allowed Sam to see what they had seen, and maybe feel a little of what they must have felt. It was a less-traveled route for those pioneers. There must have been some reason they had deviated from the well-traveled Northern Humboldt Route. *Disputes with other immigrants in their wagon train?* That answer had been buried with them long ago.

Sam stretched and breathed in some clear air. Certainly no longer in need of a wakeup, he strode up a small hill, attempting, unsuccessfully, to skirt the sagebrush and sharp, thorny bushes that grabbed at his clothes. He knew that the original route, which was to later become part of the Pony Express Trail, had to be around here somewhere, but he could see no evidence of it. This somehow made it all the more compelling. A great spectacle of high drama from the most common of people passed through here, all risking their lives in search of a better one. Since few remnants remained, their stories could only be left to the imagination.

A century and a half later, other than the paved highway, little had changed. The pioneers would have had no difficulty recognizing the landscape that lay before him today. He climbed back into his truck and continued on, as did his ruminations.

Sam stopped for gas in the Nevada town of Ely. Then, driving toward the end of town, he came upon a hitchhiker, a nicely dressed, dark-complexioned young man sporting a small backpack. On impulse, he decided to give him a lift, thinking that it might be a good idea to converse with someone other than himself.

Turning off his radio, which was broadcasting mostly static anyway, he opened the passenger window. "Where you headed?"

"California—eventually."

Sam activated the door locks, and the young man tossed his pack into the back seat, adjusted his cap, and got in.

Sam glanced at his new companion. He was feeling a bit unsure of his decision to stop, but his rider seemed somewhat reticent himself.

"I can take you about a hundred miles or so. After that, I'll be camping out for the night past the next town."

"Fine by me," his passenger said as he fastened his seatbelt. "The closer I get to California, the better. And thanks."

"Where are you from?" Sam asked as they pulled away.

"Michigan. On my way to Sacramento. I'm Vihaan, by the way."

"Sam here. That's an Indian name, isn't it?"

"I was born and grew up in Michigan, but yes, my parents are from India. Never been there myself. I got a good job offer in computer software. Pays better than back in Detroit," Vihaan said as he removed his cap and readjusted his seatbelt.

"Don't forget, California prices are also better—meaning higher. Might more than offset that raise you're looking for."

"Yeah, I heard that," his rider said with a grin. "But I'm staying with a friend at his apartment, and I think the opportunities will be good. I also needed to get away. My name means 'new era'—or new beginning," he added, laughing, "so I guess starting over is something I'm supposed to fulfill. I can always go back if it doesn't work out. Could have flown, but one-way tickets are expensive. It's my first time out here, and I wanted to see a little of what it was like."

"You're seeing a lot of it now," Sam said lightheartedly.

Vihaan turned his gaze away from Sam and back to the scenery. "I'm used to green trees and lakes. This is really desolate. There's not much to see, is there?"

"Depends on your perspective. I spent the early part of my life here and the last in St. Louis, but I know what you mean. It can be unnerving, certainly when you see it for the first time. I'm going back to the old family ranch outside Reno that my brother runs. Actually, the ranch has been in the family since the late 1850s. Right now, we're following the wagon trail my forebears took."

"Wow, you have a real history here. You returning for good?"

That innocent question got Sam's attention. "No," he said, and paused. "When I moved back east forty years ago, my brother took over the spread. But he had a mild heart issue a while back, so I'd like to see him and maybe help out a little if I can. I'm retired, and my wife died some years ago, but I'm not looking for any permanent move. I do have an ownership in the spread, but my older brother, Charles, is the one who makes his living from it. I don't know how much longer he can keep going, but," Sam paused again, "I don't plan on staying any longer than I have to."

Vihaan sensed apprehension in Sam's voice and decided not to push the question, then he asked: "How old is he, if you don't mind my asking?"

"Let's see…sixty-eight now, I think. Anyway…" but Sam decided to pivot here, not wanting to continue that line as well.

Sam was beginning to warm to his companion, and since Vihaan was willing to open up about this raw land he was experiencing, Sam decided to follow through with his own thoughts on it, and returned the conversation back to that topic.

"Now, if you live out here long enough you get used to it, and you might even come to appreciate it. For those who live in urban areas, all this vastness, this desolation, as you call it, can seem threatening."

"Just looking at it, I don't think I could ever get used to it."

"Well now, look at the other side. Your cities have a lot of artificial authority that only gives the appearance of security. There, that threat is more from people, but you're used to that. The threat here is more from the environment, which you aren't used to."

"But don't most people live in the cities around here? Reno and places?"

"You know, you're right. Hadn't thought of it that way. Except for a few ranches, like the one my brother owns, most do live the urban life. But civilization has been imported to the outback as well, and a lot of this emptiness you're seeing is slowly disappearing. They call it progress. I'm not so sure."

"I guess living in Reno would be the same as Sacramento," Vihaan offered.

"Definitely, but so far, it's still surrounded by all this," Sam said as he stretched out one arm. "For some people, there's something comforting in that."

"Are you one of those people?"

Sam thought for a moment. "I suppose you could say that. But I look at the contrasts: openness instead of congestion, silence instead of noise, the natural instead of the artificial. There's danger here, to be sure, but it's indefinable. You're feeling that now. If you go into it, you go in cautiously, not casually. To some, it feels like some unknown entity is in control. It's just that it can't be put into words—only a vague feeling that's hard to dismiss." Sam took a quick glance at his passenger. "I did grow up here, so maybe it is ingrained in me. You don't have that history. The one good thing about the desert is that it can give you a sense of freedom, of liberation. That's what I meant by comforting."

His passenger continued gazing at the dry landscape, and mused: "I feel like I'd just like to be away from it. Anyway," he added with a little more vigor, "you said that your ancestors came through here. I bet they wanted to get out even more. How long did it take them?"

"I think, overall, about five months or so. My own ancestors came by wagon train that started from St. Joseph. We don't know what prompted them to do it, but only when they struggled across the plains and the Rockies did they realize that the harshest part lay ahead of them. Then they would have had to climb the Sierras before their final descent into California. For whatever reason, they may have arrived too late, and with the threat of snow in the mountains, probably decided to stay on this side. They all knew what happened to the Donner party a decade before. Our trek is a lot easier, of course. Three or four days on asphalt roads. And by the way, you're hitchhiking all this way yourself," Sam said energetically. "That's pretty gutsy in itself."

"It's a new experience for me, but I've been staying in motels; haven't been forced to camp out yet like you plan to do."

After cresting one range, Sam caught sight of a brilliant light emanating from the base of the next. Sharp and penetrating, there was no doubt as to its origin. In all this open expanse, only the unnatural could give off such a concentrated glare. The laser-like reflection was the next town, with the sun glinting off its glass and aluminum. Compared to its surroundings, it seemed an inappropriate, alien thing. But like all things peculiar, that light fixated their attention to the exclusion of most everything else, and they were still fifteen miles away.

It took a good ten minutes before the reflections resolved themselves into distinct forms—power poles, signs competing for height, and a few low-slung buildings that refused to meld into the hills behind. As they came closer to what seemed to be a very small township, the speed limit signs appeared: fifty-five, forty-five, thirty-five, and finally, twenty-five—all of them slower than necessary. Sam wondered if these people were so insecure that they needed to force drivers to slow to a crawl just so they could be acknowledged.

In any event, Sam didn't need to get caught in some speed trap, so he dutifully obeyed the rules.

The main artery cleaved its way through the town's short midsection. There seemed nothing to serve as a kind of gathering point that could be found in most larger communities. Sam noticed a small, decrepit-looking fenced-in lot that might have at one time been a park. Two small, dead trees stood in the center, surrounded by scrub brush, dirt, and the hint of what may have once been grass. Several aging buildings indicated that this "town," which was little more than a traveler's stop, had once seen more prosperous times. This was not unusual in this part of the country. When mines played themselves out, most miners moved on, leaving only a few survivors that now cater to the needs of those passing through. Among the structures were a small variety store, convenience store, motel, and an auto repair shop and gas station. Sam surmised that because there were a few buildings and residential trailers on the outskirts, there must be some miners about still looking for that elusive paydirt.

"When I talked about the beauty of the desert, Vihaan," Sam said, "I wasn't talking about places like this."

"That's good to know. Looks more desolate than its surroundings. Sure seems like a soulless place," Vihaan said. "Each building looks wildly different from the one next to it, like they were thrown down from above to land *wherever*."

"As long as it wasn't in the road, I guess they deemed that sufficient urban planning." Sam chuckled. "This isn't your typical small-town America, but I think it's the road itself that gives off that feeling. It's like a river without sustenance, taking out as much as gets sucked in. I'd bet you could depend on its people being tightly bound, more out of suspicion than pride."

"Now you've got me spooked about these people," Vihaan voiced with concern.

"Sorry about that," Sam said hesitantly. "That's just a prejudice showing through. You really never know how people are until you get to know them."

Sam pulled his Toyota pickup in front of the convenience store, a mid-1960s structure that looked like it had once tried to pass itself off as something modern. It seemed to Sam that its disheveled appearance of peeling paint and bent aluminum might also be a reflection of the town's occupants.

"I wonder if these people feel like they've been stuck on the wrong side of the fence."

"Well, the grass has to be greener on the other side, since there doesn't seem to be any on this," Vihaan joked.

"This is where you get off, Vihaan." Sam laughed. "Since I'm going to be camping out pretty soon, you'll have a much better chance getting a ride from here, at least to Reno. If not, you'll at least have a place to stay tonight," Sam said as he pointed to the small motel across the street.

"Thanks for the lift," Vihaan said as he climbed out of the truck and opened the back to retrieve his pack. "And the talk. It's something I'll have to think about. Hope you have a good visit with your family." He closed both doors and started to walk away. As Sam was getting out himself, Vihaan turned back. "Hey," Vihaan said, laughing, "when you go camping out there tonight, don't be casual about it." Then, adopting a more reflective tone, he added: "After hearing you talk so much about this place and your brother and his ranch, maybe you'll be making a new beginning too. Take care."

Sam smiled as he waved him off, then went into the store to get what he needed: ice, bacon, eggs.

After gathering the items off the shelves, he asked the girl at the checkout counter, "You have any milk?"

She silently pointed to the dairy cooler.

Given his own somber mood, Sam thought the girl seemed as sullen and depressing as the surroundings. Oddly pale and overweight, she sported more than a hint of the rebel with her spiked and bleached tuft of hair. Sam figured that she hated her job, along with the town she was forced to live in.

Sam caught himself generalizing again. *She's sullen because she's young. Sex, drugs, and rock and roll are just as common out here as in any city.* The only thing the girl lacked was a more outlandish outfit. The store owner, probably her father, must surely have made her wear that cheesy apron with the cheery lettering: *Robert's Groceries, Best in the West.* This, most likely, only served to piss her off further. *Or maybe she doesn't bother to dress more outrageously because there aren't enough people around to notice,* Sam thought. *What's the point of personal insurrection if no one pays attention? Defiant self-righteousness does need its audience.*

He wanted to tell her that the real world was no better in the city, that it was just a trade-off of one set of problems for another— boredom for anguish and all that. But he knew that nothing would dissuade her any more than the pioneers would have been dissuaded from their purpose, even if they had known about the harsher road ahead of them. Maybe the grass was greener.

"Will that be all?" the girl asked under the flickering of the few working fluorescent lightbulbs.

"That's fine." Sam paused, then thought he would try to force some civility from her. "Do you go to school here?"

She looked up in surprise. "Yeah, I graduate in June," she offered curtly, as if hoping that would end the inquisition.

"That's great. Where do you go to school? I mean, with a town this small, is there a school here?"

"Oh, no, we're bussed over to Austin. They have a K-to-twelve school there, about sixty kids." The scowl was beginning to melt.

"I've always wondered what it's like to be in such a small school. How do you like it?"

"It's okay, I guess. I have cousins in Reno and stuff. They go to these huge high schools with thousands of kids. I'm going to move there when I go to college."

"College?" Sam asked, caught off guard.

"Yeah, got a scholarship to UN Reno. It has a good two-year course that could set me up for law at Cal, but I'm not sure."

There's gotta be a lesson in there somewhere, Sam thought. *Maybe keep your mouth shut and your mind open.* He left his prejudices, along with his change, on the counter.

Sam drove across the street to the one gas station in town. He had over half a tank, but he didn't plan to let it get below that out here.

His imagination returning to overdrive, he pictured the station's overinflated gas prices run by a blind banjo player. Instead, a young attendant, wearing relatively clean overalls, came out. Wiping his hands on a towel, he rounded the hood, brought his head down to Sam's eye level, smiled, and asked, "Fill 'er up?"

"Sure," Sam said as he pulled the hood latch and got out. "I want to check the oil, too."

"I can check it for you. Where you from?" Then, noticing the Missouri plates, added, "Not from around here, I take it."

"St. Louis."

"Well, most who come through aren't from around here, that's for sure. Where you going?"

"To visit my brother's family on their ranch outside of Reno."

"No kiddin'?" he said as he unholstered the gas nozzle and started pumping. "I worked in Reno for a while. What's the family name?"

"Ellis. It's the JE Ranch. Grandfather Jacob Ellis started it in the late 1850s."

"Doesn't ring a bell. Then again, lots of things don't ring my bell." He then went to the hood and pulled out the dipstick. "Almost a quart low. Want to add some?"

"Sure. I think twenty-forty is what it takes."

"I never remember, either," he said lightheartedly. He proceeded to check the door sticker. "That's about right. I'll check your tire pressures too." As he poured in the oil, he said, "My dad owns this station. I tried the city life, but it was too fast for my liking. Came back to work for my father. He's going to quit in a few years, so I'll take over. It breaks even, and that's good enough. I like it out here. Peaceful. Go hunting. A few fishing holes around."

"I was talking to that girl across the street. I think she wants the city life. Said she's going to the university in Reno."

"That's Claire. Yeah, smart girl. She's tired of this place. I think she'll make it."

"I'm going to camp out tonight. Do you know of any good spots nearby?"

"You can camp anywhere out here. I'd continue down the hill for a while, maybe even past Austin, and when the road flattens out, you can turn on to any one of the dirt roads you see. Not much water or trees out there, but for one night, you should be good. Tire pressures are okay," he said as he recoiled the air hose.

"Thanks."

As Sam left the station, he thought about how funny preconceived stereotypes can be blasted by a single encounter or two. On the road out of town, he didn't see Vihaan, and figured he must have gotten a lift quickly.

The sun was still high but starting its early spring descent. It would be glaring through the windshield in an hour, and Sam wanted to look for a side road and pull off to some secluded place. Tomorrow's ride to Carson City, then northward through Reno and out to the ranch, would take him only three or four hours. He had stayed in motels the last two nights, but once out of Salt Lake City, he felt free to stay anywhere, and was looking forward to it. Just having some simple camping gear helped reinforce his sense of liberation.

Within several hours, Sam had gone from the highly populated, tree-lined city of Salt Lake to a nearly waterless expanse. The first obvious thing people would notice was the sparseness of plant and animal life. Sam felt more aware of this than when he had lived here years ago.

Sam had a good imagination, and he loved a mystery, but he also knew that when you tried to analyze the mysterious, when you tried to get down to the nuts and bolts of it, the mystery would dissolve. He thought about how fragile a thing this place was. Disturbed, it could transform itself from the transcendent to the commonplace in the time it took to encounter a discarded beer can, or wherever the hand of man had probed, prodded, and left its calling card.

Once past Austin, he pulled onto a bumpy, rocky, dirt road and went about eight miles north, then parked his truck beside a dry wash. Not much of a place, but it would do. No water, just a few mesquite trees for shade and mental comfort. Nature's authoritative hand made him conscious of his physical wellbeing, and he made it a point to never go too far out if he found he had to hoof it back to the road. He had all the emergency needs: backpack, water, food, warm clothes, good boots, everything he would need for a day's hike out—if necessary.

It was now six thirty, and the sun would be touching the horizon soon. He turned off his engine, and immediately a weariness set in. The hum of the motor had been constant since St. Louis. There was always noise of some kind during his journey: people, cars, radios. It had been everywhere, so much so that its lack out here was striking. From sitting in his truck for so many days, his muscles felt atrophied, and he had to struggle out. Once unbent, he had a chance to look at the vastness of the scene. There was visibility for twenty miles around. Flat sagebrush nearby, rolling hills at various points, some snow still on the distant mountains to the west, and not a peep. It was extraordinary.

Sam scrambled up a small sandy hill and paused. Even the noise of his pounding heart was intrusive, and he had to wait for it to calm down before he could feel the silence's full effect. But if the desert invoked feelings of liberation, it could also spark uncertainty and fear. Back in St. Louis, there was always someone around to elicit a sense of security—if not friends or neighbors, just the presence of people and the protective feeling of an authority in control. Forty years in an urban environment would do that. As much as he had gone on to Vihaan about the attraction of this place, the alluring aspect could also evoke a foreboding one. For now he was alone—really alone. He may as well have been the last man on Earth. Even his cell phone didn't work.

Sam considered himself to be a practical man, and that life was a jumble of contradictions, that if there was an answer to it all, it would have been found out by now. But the irrational was now fighting for his attention. He could sense the sentiment-driven, fearful part welling up and tried to put that out of his mind, or at least his conscious mind.

Nevertheless, the expansive view he witnessed as he stood on the knoll was picturesque. Looking west, he could see miles of open desert that eventually enfolded under improbably high snowcapped mountains beyond, with colors of every imaginable shade melding into each other—or at least every shade of brown, yellow, and the increasing redness from the setting sun. Little green was in evidence.

He thought about how life interacted—or better yet, minimally interacted—in desert areas. A lush environment might seem healthier than an austere one, but the fight for survival was just as intense. Where resources were plentiful, the struggle occurred between the organisms themselves, whereas the struggle in arid regions was primarily with the elements, and this resulted in a more symbiotic relationship among living things. *So it goes with people*, his thoughts continued. *Having prevailed over the elements, human-generated anxiety took over. Maybe that's why some have described the desert as "clean."*

Then it occurred to him that what he was really thinking about was his own role in this, and he wondered where he stood within this scheme. Having grown up in this environment, then living and working in a societal one, Sam could see the difference. Simple life-and-death clarity in one, and angst, alliances, and betrayals in the other. He wondered if he was about to be pulled back into the first one just as easily as he had been pulled out of it so many years ago.

A chilly breeze was coming on, and in this high desert, it would get cold at night. Sam found a used fire pit and some sage for fuel. He wasn't the only one to have camped here. These dirt roads, no matter how rugged, had to be made by someone. *There don't seem to be many pristine places left*, he thought. He found it depressing to see the human element strewn about: broken beer bottles, plastic, and the inevitable spent shell casings.

He could envision the whole process being worked out. Thwarted by lack of water, humans could do only so much here. If they couldn't dig food up out of the ground, they would pull out its guts—gold, silver, and anything else of value, then leave the landscape scarred. There was no cycle of renewal for humans here. No beginnings and endings with the promise of new beginnings. There was little to keep anyone here once the resources ran out. It was the grabbing and the getting that left these places culturally and ecologically deprived. The only thing left was resentment, and an insult to a place that could give no more.

Sam tried to put an end to this foreboding and went to work. After a quick dinner over his Coleman stove and some coffee by the fire, he set out his sleeping bag in the back of his cab-over truck. He wanted to read but was tired after the long day of driving, and it was already starting to get dark. There was no life out here except for the nocturnal, and he wasn't one of them. But he couldn't settle down.

When doing busy work—cooking, cleaning up, preparing to bed down—his mind had been occupied. It hadn't had the time to dwell, but now that he was just sitting by the fire and relaxing, the excitement at arriving began to dissipate. Then the old ghosts began resurrecting themselves again. Being alone in the enveloping blackness stood in sharp contrast to the bright, unlimited scene of just a couple hours ago, and it prompted his imagination to invent primitive, irrational fears.

He thought back to the original settlers of over a century ago. *How could they have done it?* he mused as he settled into his sleeping bag. *They seem to have been so different.* They lived right on the edge. Hardships were accepted because that was all they knew. Starting out across the country with a pregnant wife was not uncommon. There was always a good chance that at least one child would die in any family. But they persisted. By the time they had reached this far on their walk to California, they were tired, hungry, and once in the desert, thirsty. Given that they were just trying to get through without dying, they would not have appreciated the stark beauty of this place. To them, it was an obstacle, not a source of wonder. The glorious mountains ahead were nothing but barriers.

The desert was still an obstacle to those trying to make a living in it now. *This may explain why many here seem to have contempt for it,* Sam thought. This trip could become a horror in an instant if, say, the truck wouldn't start, or maybe the twist of an ankle if he had to walk out. So, the obstacles were no illusion. *I could starve and die.* Nature out here really was frightening. Of course, that was also its attraction.

It had been five years since the death of his wife, and Sam had spent much of that time sheltering himself more and more from the outside world. *I guess I thought this journey would be another way of protecting myself from those nagging currents welling up inside.*

But this barren landscape had the opposite effect. His senses were more heightened, becoming as clear as the air itself. Attuned to the surroundings, he began to accept that whatever wisdom he was attributing to his senses were his own thoughts being reflected back. This place was the medium, he merely the receiver.

But he wasn't finding that peace he sought, nor had he yet experienced the stillness of open space that would allow him to hear what his mind had been trying to tell him. Maybe it was something important.

Charles and the ranch. He hadn't been back to the old homestead since long before Helen died. Then came Vihaan's comment, after hearing Sam go on about the glories of the desert, that maybe he, too, was looking to make a new beginning. Life is a cycle, they say, and he wondered if that included his return to the ranch.

After finally settling himself into his sleeping bag, one final thought came to him: that this might be more than a casual visit.

2

Charles

Perched on horseback atop the highest of the surrounding hills, Charles Ellis had a difficult time seeing what lay before him. Then, but only if he stared long enough—movement. There wasn't much to see from four miles away, only tiny images that seemed to shift positions over time. Against his better judgment, he found himself drawn to this spot every so often, just to see the action. This troubled him, but he couldn't put his finger on exactly why it troubled him.

Earthmovers, they were—impressive wheeled giants crawling to and fro across the earth, fulfilling their namesake by cutting away the hills and filling in the valleys.

"Well, Dave, you think they're getting anywhere?" Charles asked his foreman as he moved his horse around to allow him a better view.

At six foot four, with a husky (though not portly) build, Sam's older brother was a physically imposing figure with an equally impressive personality.

"They seem to be working on that same dirt pile they were last week," Dave responded.

"But they are making progress, right?" Charles said, baiting Dave as he always had over the last twenty-plus years they worked together.

"Well, ten years ago, this infestation was limited to just a couple miles out of Reno. Now, the developers have moved fifteen miles out, and four from us. But if progress means the destruction of our ancestral lands, then yes, they are to be commended."

"Now, hell, you can't even dig a post hole around here without some tribal council claiming exclusive rights over it. Is every place here ancestral, or can't the Irish in you see all the improvements we've made?"

"That Irishman was my great-great, whatever grandfather, Kemosabe," Dave insisted. "Most of the rest of me is authentic, homegrown Paiute material, as you well know. Besides, if I'm not mistaken, now they're the ones beginning to intrude onto your ancestral land, if you get my drift. The one your own brutish ancestors stole from us. Isn't turnabout fair play?"

That comment hit a soft spot in Charles's uneasiness.

Charles's foreman did have a deep history in the area. He may have been slight of build and wiry compared to his boss, but he was no Sancho Panza to Don Quixote. Quick-witted, he could outsmart his boss when circumstances called for it.

For some time, developers had been buying up farming and ranching lands in the outskirts of the Reno area, converting them into housing and businesses, and radically changing the landscape in the process. It was beginning to intrude into Charles's own self-assertive opinions about progress. He never used to have a problem with development, nor was he ever concerned about population growth. After all, newcomers brought in the money and made everyone better off—didn't they?

"Let's get back, Dave," Charles said. "Sally will have supper ready, and you've got work to do. I want to get the last of the cattle in."

"I'll check the cows in the south forty. Shouldn't take long."

"Cattle, not cows, Dave, and we don't have no forty nothing!"

"Oh, sorry, boss. I'm sure I'll figure this job out pretty soon."

The two turned their horses around, and now side by side, started back down from the sun- and wind-exposed rounded hill that grew nothing but sharp, lichen-covered rocks, and the occasional sage scrub for variety. Except for its sentinel attributes, it had no other function.

"Well, it is progress," Charles repeated, more to himself than to Dave. "It's going to be a while before they get much closer—don't you think?"

"What? Yeah, I suppose so. But they're just like a bunch of ants. They'll be sending scouting parties our way pretty soon, clearing the way for more of that goodness."

"Come on now, Dave, how long have we been at this? Look at what we've accomplished, and what you've gotten out of it. Indians here live a longer and better life than if this had never come along. You'd still be riding horses instead of a pickup."

Dave paused, stared down in bewilderment at his own horse, and answered in mock slowness, "What's a pickup?"

"You know what I mean," Charles said, laughing. "All this modern technology has made life easier for all of us."

"I suppose you're right, at least for those of us that survived." Dave often had a way of sounding like he was agreeing with you while still getting his digs in.

Not appreciating Dave's sarcasm, Charles continued, "All those government restrictions and their choking rules keep the small guy down. Know what I mean?"

Dave said nothing. Charles's habit of dropping non-sequiturs never seemed to be a concern to him. Charles just thought them logical continuations of his own thought process. If others couldn't keep up, that was their problem.

Charles pulled out one of his well-concealed cigars he thought his wife Sally didn't know about, bit off the end, and fired it up.

"Those city folk have no clue about how hard it is just trying to make a living out here. Not that they would give a shit. They wouldn't be here if it weren't for us, and now they're telling us how to run our business: raising taxes, interfering with our water rights. And don't talk to me about environmentalists. Do-gooders sticking their noses into everything, telling us what we can and can't do, then pushing for more regulations. What's happened to our freedom, anyway? We've been doing this for generations."

"Five, anyway," Dave quipped.

When Charles began to ramble, his thoughts tended to run into each other, like waves rushing against a seawall and bouncing back.

With Dave leading the way along the now-narrowed path, the two continued their descent down through an aspen grove tucked in one of the few flattened creek beds that dotted the hills. The canopied trees changed the atmosphere dramatically. Wet earth instead of bone-dry rock, green instead of brown, and filtered sunlight instead of hot, windy exposure. The riders stopped to let the horses rest in the shade.

"Talked to Bob Whitney yesterday," Charles said.

"Yeah?" Dave said cautiously, turning his horse around to face him.

"Told me—confidentially, mind you, but he'd trust you—he's not going to go on after this year. The costs are too much for him to get more help, like for everyone else around here. Unless he can get a buyer to run it as a ranch, he'll have to sell to developers, although his small spread may not be big enough even for their interests."

"Big Bob's been talking like that since we've known him."

"I think it's different this time. He's in his mid-seventies with no one to inherit his place. He sure can't work any harder than he is now, and for what? Just to make ends meet? He's tired."

"Big Bob Whitney." Dave drawled out the name as one would a legend. "One of the stalwarts. Didn't he survive a bunch of wives— three or four?"

"He didn't survive them; they left him. He used to get a hotel room for a weekend and prowl the bars in the casinos for some dame. He'd buy them drinks and lay on the patter about how he owned one of the biggest and richest spreads in the area. They weren't the smartest bunch. Sometimes he would get all worked up from the drinking and want to marry them then and there, usually at the 'No Questions Asked Elvis Chapel,' or some such place."

"That must have cost him."

"Yeah. Alimony. But no kids—all his wives were beyond those years. The first one lasted a good two years I think. After they found that his servant-run 'mansion' wasn't a mansion, that he wasn't rich, and that they were to take on the role of servants themselves, they left. Some people never learn. Probably that triumph of hope over experience thing."

"I would have thought he'd be the last to admit to being mortal."

"Well, he won't be the last. What do you think? I'm sixty-eight myself. Do we all have to die with our boots on? It's just hard to know that life is temporary, especially now with this damn heart thing. It's not always easy trying to keep up this cowboy image, you know."

Dave nodded at the familiar rehashing of the rancher's mantra—tough guy posturing. When Charles took over the JE Ranch, he had found himself forced to adapt to the ranchers' closed way of thinking. It wasn't hard to do.

But for all his posturing, Charles wasn't really one of them. Owning one of the oldest family ranches in the area, and possessing a more tactful disposition (when he didn't rile himself up), he held a somewhat prominent position in the fraternity. This allowed him some latitude in his thinking and he didn't always have to affirm someone else's boilerplate pretense. Still, just the same, he could be as hard-nosed as the rest of them. "It's all business, Jack," he was fond of saying.

"Newcomers and these developers," Charles continued. "Who do they think they are? People are coming in by the carloads, and staying—not working the land, mind you, but working at jobs that don't depend on the fickle nature of . . .well, nature. Now, I didn't mind the gambling casinos when they came, but now it's industry and business, and those damn lawyers right on their heels. The people are covering the land with their houses and their streets and their kids, and God knows what else."

Like most ranches in the dry west, only a small portion of Charles's land could produce any kind of return, and until a few decades ago, there was no other use for it. Typically, the productive areas were near the arroyos where most of the water flowed. Cattle could graze somewhat on the poor vegetation in the dry outlying areas, but they still needed the few oases that dotted the lower patches.

For much the same reason, humans needed these green spots as well. Charles's ranch lay in the lowest, and wettest, eastern portion, below the hills to the west and the still-taller mountains further west. At the center of it all were sixty or so acres of farmland for feed and crops, the barn, stable, house, and not a few aspen and towering cottonwoods. All were framed by the surrounding vast, dry wildness that gave the incongruity of contrasts a significance as a single thing. That contrast was reflected in Charles as well, and for that matter, in anyone who had a past here.

The ranchers here could be counted on to be opinionated, stubborn, cantankerous at times, and close-knit when threatened. *At least they used to be*, Charles thought, reverting to his original thinking. *But things aren't the same as they used to be.*

"Newcomers, they think they own the place."

"The problem is, they do," Dave piped in. "You don't know what you've got till it's gone," he sang. "All right, guess I'll cross over here. I'll open the gates so's I can get them—what—*cattle?*—herded. See ya' tonight, Charles."

"Don't forget, I have a ranchers meeting to run tonight, may be gone when you get back."

"Got it."

Dave descended down the gully and up the other side. Charles admired Dave's exceptional lightness and ease with horses, attributing it more to his Paiute heritage than to mere experience.

"Oh, I forgot," Dave yelled from the top of the next hill. "Sally told me before she left for town: your brother's coming in. Driving from St. Louis. Be here tomorrow. Maybe."

Dave pulled his reins sharply to the right and disappeared down the other side of the rise, denying Charles any time to respond.

Charles never reacted quickly to situations. It always took him time to absorb information before it formed a cogent whole in his mind. Initially, though, he felt that the appearance of Sam might be more than just a brother's informal visit—that consequences might come of it.

I bet Sally urged him to come. One minor heart problem and everyone goes into a tizzy. Even the doc said it was minor. A few pills and I feel fine. And what could Sam do here anyway? Tell me to slow down? He did work here before he went back east, but he's not so young himself. Probably out of shape, too.

Charles veered down the canyon trail east from the one Dave had taken. It was a longer way, but he didn't feel in any rush. Now that he was out of the irritation of the wind, the cool breeze and warm sun made for a comfortable ride. He had felt restless pretty much all day and needed a respite from all this thinking about the changing landscape, and now about his brother arriving. He was already feeling resentment over Sam's arrival, which caused him to fall back into a funk.

The trail that he had taken thousands of times before felt different somehow. He wanted to take comfort from everything that was familiar, a reassurance that everything was where it was supposed to be. That ten-ton rock at the turn of the familiar path had been there for thousands of years. It was right and proper that it should be where it was.

But what had seemed permanent before was beginning to feel fleeting.

There they were, those giant machines leveling the reluctant land, filling in the valleys with the hills as though trying to level lives and lessen anxieties—and all of it for the addition of new homes, shopping centers, and high-speed roads. Developers were lowering the playing field for external comfort, as if getting somewhere faster would somehow bring contentment. But all they were developing was gridlock and stress, which made them build even more of the same in order to alleviate that for which they were the cause.

Charles was beginning to detest it all. Despite going on to Dave about how great progress is, doubt had entered his mind, revealing things he didn't want to acknowledge. The relentless nagging forced him out of his comfort zone by questioning his own beliefs, with the hint that alternatives just might have merit. For Charles, the foundation of principles he depended on was integral to his struggle to maintain his own self-esteem. Doubt was exposing that bedrock as something other than the solid foundation he wished it to be. *You want progress? Well, there it is at your doorstep, but it'll destroy what you love.*

Having to accept conclusions that went counter to a lifetime of cultural biases, personal resentments, and impulses had him feeling bound up. He wanted to fight back and deny the contradictions, and to fabricate rationalizations that would fit more comfortably in his thoughts. It wasn't working.

But for a scarce few people like Charles, times like these could bring a questioning and a fermenting that ran counter to those stubborn biases. Charles was well-read, college educated, and understood that there were several versions of reality. At times, he could display a line of insight that ranked him a notch above his contemporaries. Dave had mentioned turnabout being fair play when he compared this new development to the demise of his own culture. *Maybe there's something to that.*

Charles never felt the need for words to express his surroundings, or his place in it. The land made the man in its own image more so than the man tamed and tweaked the land to his advantage. Over Charles's long years in this one place, he was more concerned with how effective he was, not how he was affected. Without his knowing it, Charles had woven his roots throughout the land and water and trees and sage and rock and sky—"bonding," as the trendy would call it. But they were not so much roots as nerve endings, sensitive to the slightest disturbance. He could no more be pulled from this land, and live, than an aged tree could survive if yanked up by its roots. Though he was integral to it all, he did not know this. Not yet.

But why would he? He would have had to be a detached observer to see it, which he wasn't. But an outsider could. They would be able to see things as they were because they were disconnected from the process. And Sam was an outsider.

Now there were two significant things weighing on his mind: the changing landscape and his brother's impending arrival—two separate, though perhaps not inseparable events.

Charles made one last turn out of a grove of cottonwoods that edged his meadow. It revealed a postcard panorama of the house, outbuildings, barn, and equipment. His whole life lay across the field before him. The thought of being able to dismount at his own back door, walk a few steps, and have a beer lifted his spirits.

Before he had a chance to spur his horse onward, SOB, sensing the final part of the journey near, was way ahead of him and took off at a gallop. With Charles surprised but secure in the saddle, they made a beeline—for the barn.

3
Breakdown

The cold, crisp morning found the sun skulking behind the nearby range. Sam awoke at a late hour under the camper shell of his truck, and found himself confronted with that troublesome dilemma of whether to stay in the warm comfort of his sleeping bag *in here* or get up and try to dress in the bone-chilling cold *out there*. He could have waited out the sun behind the high hills, except that he had to pee, so he turned over. That didn't fool his mind one bit. Finally, he forced himself to make the effort. Once begun, there was no going back, as speed was of the essence. If you want to set records for dressing, you need only be in the freezing cold for motivation.

Once bundled up, with the Coleman stove cooking bacon and eggs, and with coffee in hand, he had the luxury to pause and look again at the scenery. Unfortunately, even the smallest nagging could shatter the beauty of the great outdoors, and that nagging was welling up again. He wasn't that eager to see his brother. Silences over the phone at Christmas or birthdays only bore out the needlessness of personal contact, and the considerable distance between St. Louis and Reno was enough of an excuse to squash routine visits.

But Charles's health problem, though apparently mild, was at least serious enough to kickstart him into making the trip. *What is it about family connections that's so tenacious?* he mused. *The blood-thicker-than-water thing with all those social constraints and expectations?* He felt the ties that bind everywhere, like being entangled in a web strung out over the land. To Sam, it was like a bunch of interconnecting strings of varying tensions pulling him from different directions at once. The relaxing of the one he felt at getting out of St. Louis only led to a greater tugging from the other end; he knew that he was caught in the same old web as everyone else. He then thought, *I guess we're all chained to constraints; if it isn't family, it's all the customs and rules that can be as strong as gravity.* Sam understood that knowing and reconciling were different breeds of cat.

Charles and Sally were the only family he had left. He and Helen had no children. In the era of the seventies, they would have been considered "barren"—a tactless enough label. No matter how subtly conveyed, it branded them as outsiders. Families, especially in the Midwest, were the quintessential center of community life. Couples with children naturally congregated together, and most of their conversations revolved around their children, often little more than civilized boasting matches.

Now that she was gone, many of their connections had disappeared, and he felt that he had better pick up this last thread before it, too, was torn from him.

So here he was, finally making the effort. Because he was less tied down than Charles and Sally, it was he who would come to them.

The sun had finally peeked above the rim of the nearby hills, and within minutes, the temperature rose high enough for Sam to shed his heavy coat. But he couldn't shed his anxiety. He finished off his breakfast with some Cheerios and a pastry purchased at the store, hoping that its manufacturing date fell somewhere within its multiyear shelf life. Then he began organizing his stuff. *If Helen were here,* he thought, *she would have already had all this organized and in its rightful place.* But she wasn't.

Before her death, Helen never would have let Sam's family relations deteriorate. If she couldn't nag him to call his brother, she would do it herself. She and Sally got along fine, probably because they both had to contend with stubborn husbands. Sam and Charles, separated by almost five years, were far enough apart that each grew up in different eras populated with different people. Helen's death only shut the door tighter. Occasionally, Sally would call Sam to try to keep the contacts open. Sam knew what she was trying to do, and he resisted. He was always polite but curt—a stubbornness for which he now felt ashamed.

He could have flown, of course. Driving all this way was ridiculous. But having his own vehicle gave him control, and the ability to leave quickly if things got awkward. It was a symbolic hidden knife that he could use to cut those cords at a moment's notice.

Strangely, he was uncertain why he felt such uneasiness. Then he realized that it might have been a bit of resentment toward Sally for pulling him away from his well-structured and comfortable life. Or was it a stupor?

He wanted things to be simpler. Advancing age meant that there was less tolerance for pretty much any disturbance to that sedentary life. *Maybe that's why old people disintegrate and disappear from society,* he thought. *Give up responsibility and you give up that respect you spent a lifetime trying to promote, protect, and pamper. Don't mean squat if you built an entire civilization with your own two hands. You get replaced by a younger crowd who want no part of your outdated ideas. They say old age is a return to childhood—a patronizing statement to be sure. All that's left is the whining.*

So there he was in the middle of this exquisite isolation, and his thoughts turned to the mundane. He was tense and impatient. *Time to shove off.* Sam continued his packing. Food, pots, and cooking paraphernalia were thrown haphazardly into the back of the pickup.

After slamming the tailgate closed, Sam decided to traipse back up the rise he had visited the night before for one last look around. When he got there, he found that he wasn't as inspired as he had been the day before. He turned back to his truck, then hesitated, wondering what sort of object could cast such a dark shadow beneath it. *An animal?* No, it wasn't an animal, or even a thing. His stomach took a turn when it occurred to him what it could be, hoping against hope that it wasn't true.

It was. An oil leak, doubtless caused by a puncture from a rock or boulder. Bad news. Sliding under, he noticed that the skid plate meant to protect the oil pan was missing, and he could see the gash where the oil had drained out.

When a car wouldn't start, or a fan belt broke, or a tire went flat, there was always a chance that a repair could be made, at least something to allow the car to limp back to the main road. But here, Sam was stopped cold. The lifeblood of the truck was gone, and there was nothing to be done.

Maybe I could plug the gash, he thought, but then he would need more oil, which he didn't have.

Now the desert he so wanted to be in was something he wanted to be out of even more. He knew it was futile, but he again tried his cell phone. And again, nothing. He would have to walk seven or eight miles to get to the main highway where hitching a ride would be no problem. *Just a long walk, so stay calm. Five, six hours, no problem.* He knew that he should stick to the dirt road going back, even if he spotted a shortcut along the way. Having to zigzag around sage and shrub in this sandy soil would take more out of him than going the longer way on the hard-packed dirt. Less chance of spraining an ankle, which was critical, and a lower probability of running across a rattler. Plus, he wouldn't get lost that way. Dirt roads did have a habit of disappearing when they ran crossways to your line of travel. Even from only a few feet away, they could show no sign of themselves until you were right on them.

He thought about what he should carry. Having been brought up in this land, he was fully aware of the necessities of desert survival. First, the daypack, with as much water as possible. That load would lessen during travel. Food wasn't the most important, assuming he could get out by the end of the day. *Bring enough, anyway.* Warm clothing—lots of it—for layering, and sleeping in, if need be.

He made sure his boots were in good shape. Hat, all-purpose knife, plastic for a makeshift tent, cording, matches, and some starter fuel. *Sleeping bag? Heavy, but absolute warmth guaranteed. Not sure about that yet. Stove? No. First aid kit, of course. Medicine. Map. Compass. A lightweight walking staff that a piece of cloth could be put on to flag for help. Wallet! Going to have to pay for repairs. Car keys. Flashlight.*

"Am I going back the way I came in?" he asked himself aloud. Then, trying for some self-induced confidence, he added, "Yeah, okay. Lock it up. Let's go!"

He was nervous, impatient, and anxious. "It's not a desperate journey," he kept telling himself. *Eight miles maybe? Why am I so anxious? Just go for it. It's not like I have another choice.*

This didn't ease his mind one bit. Having gathered what he thought were the essentials, he unlocked the truck and combed through once more for anything that might seem useful. He had better thoughts about other nonessentials: too much clothing, extra shoes, anything that would weigh him down. At the last minute, he decided against the sleeping bag and threw it inside. With his daypack overloaded, he was off, with not a single positive thought in his head.

His steps were quick as he hurried along the road. Rushing this way would use up energy, but he kept pushing despite his commonsense reasoning against it. Finally, about a half-mile out, he began to relax, looking up from watching his own boots for a change, and taking in the sights.

The way back was hilly and twisting as he crossed many small, dry washes. The up-and-down twisting road would take him longer than he'd counted on. It also made it impossible to see far enough ahead to tell where the highway could be. But he had his map, compass, and the knowledge that he was going in the right direction. Of course, it also helped that he was following his oil leak.

He hoped that maybe someone might come by this way, then reconsidered that they would be coming in, not out, and would be put out to go that far back. *Just keep trudging on, Sam.*

There was little breeze in the air, and when he stopped, the quiet engulfed him as it had the night before. Like in some old science fiction movie, everything around him seemed frozen in time. No movement of any kind. They were out there, of course: lizards, snakes, rabbits, insects, antelope, wild horses. But they had evolved to be inconspicuous in their surroundings. The only noise he might hear, other than his own clumsy footsteps, would be that of an animal going after or escaping from another. But Sam did not feel privy to this stalking and hiding environment. The day before, he had the feeling of being an integral part of this landscape, and everything living in it. Now he felt alien and vulnerable, as though his own species no longer belonged.

The weather at midmorning was comfortable, but as the sun rose, the shortening shadows began to dissolve those once-sharp, well-defined features. This was when the desert began to conceal its own brilliance. The lengthening day was blurring those lines. Midday was not alluring. Morning and dusk were the desert's best-kept secrets, and when most travelers encountered it the least.

His oil trail finally ended, and he saw a sharp, protruding rock a few feet further on that must have been the cause of the gash. "Can't do anything about it now," he grumbled aloud.

He continued to follow the road south past an escarpment of hills to his left. What had been one kind of scenery from behind the windshield looked totally different when walking on foot in the other direction. He saw much more this way, and that included a sidetrack, overgrown and almost hidden, that led eastward toward a deep canyon a few hundred yards beyond. After having already covered over a mile, he felt better about his prospects for getting out, and seeing plant growth up ahead, decided to follow it, hoping to replenish his water supply.

Pushing through the high scrub brush brought him to a near-tumbled-down shack and a litter of rusted tin-ware, and just beyond and a little to the left and up from the narrow canyon floor was the telltale rust-colored rock mounds that signified the tailings of a mine. He then came to the mine, which was near some healthy-looking mesquite bushes. This indicated the water source, something the miners could not have done without. After filling his water bottles, he had a chance to look around. As for the mine itself, a two-foot diameter hole was all that remained of an attempt to plug it up.

Mines were everywhere in this part of the country. For miners, it was a common practice, if the mines were still active, to seal them up in such a way as to discourage others from getting overly nosey about your claim. It was always wise to take precautions if you had a hankering to return. But over time, wind and water bore into the plug, exposing a hole large enough for a person to fit inside—that is, if a person wanted to.

Sam returned to the shack. It was something on the order of a single ten-by-fifteen-foot room. As he entered, he was careful not to step on the protruding nails sticking out of the jumble of boards. He dug through the rubble, and guessed that it had been a long time since anyone had been there. The room contained two rusted bedsprings and more empty tin-ware on makeshift shelves, which required an old-fashioned can opener. It all hinted that the last prospectors had been here probably no later than the 1940s.

He thought that if he snooped around long enough, he might have been able to piece together a story of the people who had lived here. He lifted a few boards and discovered information he hadn't expected. Pieces of linoleum on the floor and scraps of wallpaper on the sideboards suggested that the occupants had attempted some level of normalcy in their living space. He found a few hooks for curtains over what was once a glass window. It all hinted at a woman's hand. *Was she the only woman here?* From the size of the place, it looked like it. This woman certainly would have been expected to help with the backbreaking work, but how hard, how discouraging, it must have been for her to try to force civility into such a desolate, people-less place.

Did she fantasize about having another woman to talk to? Sam wondered. *Was she brought up in an ordinary, middle-class family, and maybe got caught up in an impulsive romance with some roughneck adventurer who promised her everything? One who knew of a place that was sure to be loaded with gold that no one else knew about? Just a little digging and they'd have all they'd ever need. Live in San Francisco, dress in the finest clothes, raise five children, go to the best places?*

But then the reality: perpetually sunburned, worn out, and broke. The closest town was thirty miles away. That didn't matter, since they probably had no money—all of it gone to provisions and tools and blasting powder that wouldn't last forever.

The curtains and wallpaper, Sam surmised, were not for appearance, but to keep the outside out. While her man, or men, kept themselves occupied thinking of the riches they would probably never realize, this woman likely thought of escape. Did she dull her senses by lying on the bed, looking at that one corner of the wall, perhaps seeing a framed picture and imagining herself somewhere else? *Anywhere* else? *Children?* Sam hoped not.

Then he thought that maybe she hadn't come from an easy life. *Maybe she didn't have high expectations because she grew up in a tough world.* If they had lived here during the Depression, her life may have been one of limitations. You just had to make the best of it. *We wouldn't tolerate such a life,* Sam thought. *But then again, we have choices.* For one, he liked to think that this woman was tough, that the day-to-day struggle had its compensations—that they protected her from the pain of thought.

Having exhausted his search of the shack, he turned to confront what had been nagging at him since he arrived: he wanted to check out the mine. He knew full well the dangers involved. The ranch where he had grown up claimed a mine far back in the hills that he and his brother used to investigate—at the price of punishment from their parents if discovered. Yes, it was dangerous, but at least they could count on each other in a jam. Now Sam was alone. Any call for help would go unanswered.

But Sam was always drawn to the mystery of how a single pickax strike in a hard rock mine could instantly produce paydirt, and with his natural curiosity overcoming his concerns about getting out, he grabbed his pack by one shoulder strap and hustled to the entrance. At first, he just wanted to go a few feet into the entrance, and he took out his flashlight, water, and knife. Then decided to just take the whole pack with him.

He went in feet first, quickly discovering that the hole went down at a forty-five-degree angle. He pulled the pack behind him while thinking of Alice descending into the rabbit hole, and hoped that he wouldn't come face-to-face with the Queen of Hearts.

Inside, the air was cool. He stood carefully, knowing that the most common injury in a cave or mine occurred at the meeting of jagged rock and head. But this ceiling (or "back") was high and the sides (or "ribs") were wide. This gave some clue to the mine's productiveness. He had been in some mines that were so low and narrow that he thought the miners must have been Hobbits. But those people were just in a hurry. It took twice the effort to excavate passageways large enough to walk and carry ore through than it did to dig short, narrow ones that forced you into a continuous stoop as you tried to dig and excavate. Stooping over took a lot of energy and provided a lot of back pain. It looked as though these people had been here for the long haul.

Sam directed his flashlight ahead into places no light had penetrated for decades. Every step he took caused his adrenaline to flow, from the dread of danger to the excitement of discovery. With each new step, he was thinking how incredibly stupid he was; that he should turn around and go right back out like he planned. But the pull of discovery overwhelmed his sensible judgment, and he pushed on.

After a few hundred feet, with the shaft taking a few turns left and right, he came unexpectedly to a large, cavernous area. The back suddenly disappeared as he glanced upward into the airy darkness. The cavern itself was about fifteen feet in diameter, with the main shaft continuing on the other side at a slight left turn.

There was a great deal of quartz glimmering through the rock, enough to sparkle up the cavern. *This must have been where most of the serious ore lay.* But the most arresting sight, when his beam caught hold of it, was an old wooden ladder. It went up a good eight feet to what looked like another tunnel (or "drift") overhead. *They must have found a vein and followed it up to the room above.* Sam, as was his nature, was tempted, but resisted climbing it. He could visualize himself crashing to the floor and breaking enough bones to prevent him from getting out.

He surveyed the rock, looking for any sign of valuable ore, but figured that if this exposed rock were any good, it would have been mined anyway. He continued through to another tunnel on the right side. This one was short and narrow, and came to a dead end only twenty feet ahead.

The end had been enlarged, but there was little evidence of it being worked. Miners would follow quartz veins wherever they led, yet there didn't seem to be any indication of that here. There was some debris lying about, probably just as the last people had left it. Wood planking, scraps of clothing, some scattered bones, no doubt from coyotes bringing in their prey.

Sam sat on a protruding rock at the far end and pulled out his water bottle. Oddly, he didn't see any dog-like tracks, or any signs of nesting or droppings.

Then he noticed footprints, quite a few, and not his own. They had been preserved because neither wind nor water could get at them. They were of two different sizes that seemed to circle around the untrammeled center of the room. Then Sam noticed a leather object protruding up from the earth; he leaned over and pulled, tearing part of it away.

After scraping off the dust and dirt from the remaining portion, he ran into a hard object. He picked up a bone and used it to scrape away the dirt. It was another bone. After digging further, Sam was able to dislodge it from its burial. It was over a foot long, and it looked like... well...like...

"Shit!"

He dropped his digging bone like the proverbial hot potato, tripped over the stone he was sitting on, and sprawled face-first into the dirt. He jumped up to the entrance side of the room, jerking his light this way and that, hoping there were no other surprises. He remembered his pack back on the rock and took one mighty step, grabbed it, and took one more leap back out of the room.

Now he was running—scrambling, really—mostly to avoid the rock protrusions jutting out of the walls and ceiling. He didn't care. He kept his head down. The darkness, the stale air...things were closing in on him and he had to get out. That rock on the floor had markings on it. Most tombstones did.

He reached the cavern portion and looked straight ahead for the continuation of the tunnel that wasn't there. *Wrong turn? Missed passage?* He knew he should calm down, but he couldn't.

He had never really felt claustrophobia before. He used to think that all you had to do was stop and think clearly and rationally. Nothing to get worked up about. But his mind had other ideas. Fundamental, primitive, irrational ideas.

He spun around in crazy circles, continually overlooking the main shaft. Third time around, he caught it and stormed through. Turns and more turns, and the notion of someone, or something, behind him—gaining. Two more turns and he spotted a pinhole of brilliant light ahead. The entrance.

As it grew larger, so did the unseen presence that forced him into higher states of panic. He pushed forward with fear feeding on itself. He was near frantic by the time he dropped his pack, scrambled through to the outside, and rolled down the incline.

Blinded as much by the glare as by the darkness behind him, he squinted and shielded his eyes. The air, the light—he was safe. The terror vanished as quickly as it had come, but he was shaken, now more so by his own irrational reaction.

His curiosity overfilled, he reached back in with his leg, and with not a little trepidation, hooked his foot through the pack's shoulder strap, pulled it up, and took off toward the dirt road with decidedly less interest in dark places.

He held his pack in one hand while walking so he could pull out some food. A couple of energy bars, some bread, but no water bottle. *Left it in the catacomb.* Well, he had brought enough anyway, but he didn't like his resources to diminish. He decided to sit under the shade of a nearby mesquite bush to have lunch and allow himself to calm down.

Once back on the dirt road, he had time to collect his thoughts— what was left of them. He still couldn't believe his reaction in the mine. He knew there was nothing in there but his imagination. It amazed him just how shallow that rational veil was compared to the incalculable depths of basic instinct.

Why was I so worked up? Just a shallow grave. But whoever heard of a mine being used for that purpose? Miners were practical people, not given to sentimentality. *And what was that whole side-tunnel business? Short as it was, was it excavated only for that purpose?* Most miners, Sam suspected, would not have gone to such trouble. That tunnel didn't seem ore-bearing, but who knew? They might have followed a hunch and dug through there before one of the miners died by accident, and they buried him where he was. With that, the other two probably left the site for good.

Sam began to climb up the far side of another wash, one of dozens so far, and it was tiring. He kept his nose to the ground and stayed on one side or the other of the parallel tracks. The sky was somewhat overcast, with high cirrus clouds and dust that veiled the sun. The wind was also getting lively. *Maybe a storm brewing.* In the desert, you could never predict. It put Sam further into a funk. Here he had just escaped from a closed-in mine shaft, only to be thrust into this wide-open space, and he didn't feel all that much better about it.

He finally hit upon a long, flat terrace between gullies. His confidence returning, he picked up his pace. Then he came to a fork in the road. The two paths darted away at a forty-five-degree angle from each other. It was next to impossible to tell which one he had come from. While driving from the opposite direction, it had been easy to miss this Y intersection, but from this direction, it was obvious.

"I don't have time for this," Sam said aloud. The heavy pit in his stomach reasserted itself.

He stared at the two roads for some time, trying to suppress his emotion-driven mind for a more rational one. *Which one looks the most used?* he wondered. *That would be the most obvious to take, since the one to the highway would be the most likely.* The left had the largest swing radius and did go closer to the hills. Unless it went over them, it would have to veer south from there and eventually lead to the highway.

On closer inspection, he found tracks in the dust. But what did his own tire tracks look like? He didn't know. These tracks weren't all that clear, anyway. The right road also had tracks, but fainter. Sam then realized that, by walking around, he was destroying the very signs he was trying to examine.

Well, if the clearest tracks were mine, and they continued through that curve, then that should lead to the main road. He followed the left track, all the while second-guessing himself, then trying to reestablish the rationale for his choice. *What a place to die in,* he thought.

Trudging onward was the only thing he could do. The road did begin turning south just as he had hoped, and it looked like it might stay that course.

It was four thirty. The sun was in its descent, but the weather had held. Sam was back to trudging up and down the washes, advancing at a slower pace than he wanted.

The lengthening shadows again began to expose the beauty of the desert. Everything stood clear and in sharp contrast. He appreciated none of it. He was on a mission—a survival mission as far as he was concerned. As with all the pioneers and their own survival concerns, an appreciation of natural beauty came only after all other needs were satisfied.

After another hour and a half of plodding along, staring mostly at his boots in a mesmerized state, his thoughts returned to the mine and the mystery it contained. Though a lot of mine cave-ins had their own never-to-be-dug-out graves, there was no indication of a cave-in with this one, and the grave seemed purposeful.

Then a thought popped into his head: *Maybe it wasn't a man who died, but the woman.* He realized that it would have taken at least two men to run that mine, as it would have been too much work for one. *Was she married to one and sister to the other?* Sam theorized that if she was the one who died, maybe neither of the men had the heart to go on and buried her in the most sacred place they could think of: a safe, everlasting burial chamber within and under tons of rock and stone, like a pyramid conceived to perpetuate a life no longer living. Then they just sealed it up and abandoned it.

Then another thought occurred to him: it wasn't the woman at the mine he was really thinking about. It was Helen. Was it that those miners found the quest for riches secondary to the caring they had for her? Had she been the heart and soul of their operation?

Why did Helen have to die first? It didn't seem natural. She had been a few years younger than Sam. On average, weren't women supposed to live longer than men? But then, who's average? Sam always felt that he was on one side or the other of that middle state. Of course, most people occupied one side or the other; the middle was typically just a mathematical center where few resided.

Everyone is an oddball in some way. For him and Helen, not having children was one major exclusion. There were others. But he always felt like an outsider, always thinking too much. *Maybe getting back into the real world would nudge me closer to that center.* If he continued to live in that now half-empty habitat he called home, he might start to become one of those recluses, waving his cane and yelling nonsense at anyone passing by his own personal park bench.

Physical exertion was causing his thoughts to ramble, but at least it was numbing the pain. Being conscious about his own survival made him think about how death was as natural as birth. Can't have one without the other. *Maybe the idea of death is the real reason behind this trip.* Charles, himself, even Sally, like all people, continued to act as though things could continue as they always had. *What happens when Charles gets to be seventy-five, and me right behind him? Then what?*

A cold wind kicked up in his face, knocking him out of his reverie. "Idiot," he said aloud. "Taking a side trip like I'm on some kind of adventure. Should have brought the sleeping bag. Got enough food for tonight if I don't get to the road. Can't wait too long to stop—it'll get dark soon. Could start a fire right here."

Then he remembered Vihaan echoing Sam's own warning about not going into the desert casually. *Can't even live by my own words.*

Sam tried to reassure himself that he had enough provisions and hoped he would be warm enough if he had to stop. The worry was a mental weight so heavy that it slowed him down physically. "Don't fill your mind with regrets," he countered again, aloud. "Shoulda, woulda, coulda. Well, what the hell? The highway has to be up ahead somewhere. Just keep moving, and you'll laugh about it later."

It was after seven now, but he couldn't see himself stopping just yet. Another rise, a steep one this time. "One more and that's it. "

Sam scrambled to the top. Asphalt. The highway. He started to laugh.

4
At the Ranch

The desert is a land of many contrasts, and none greater than the meeting of two irreconcilable cultures: the natives and the newcomers. For hundreds of generations, the native peoples of the area, the Paiutes, lived in balance with the land; that is, they took no more out of it than what they put in. Undisturbed, they would have continued that way for hundreds more. Their culture adapted to the surrounding landscape, and like primitive cultures the world over, it was all they knew. And it was sacred.

In the late 1850s, gold and silver were discovered a few miles northeast of Carson City on Mt. Davidson. This is where Virginia City rose. It was also when the troubles began.

Miners and settlers stormed into this El Dorado from the mostly played-out mines in California, and brought with them their own mechanically dependent culture that was at odds with the natives' way of life. The contrast was striking. For one, the natives lived in karnees, which were nothing more than conical huts constructed of curved wattles and covered with coyote and other animal hides. On the other hand, the white settlers felt the need to import their eastern civility with them, and this required a hundred times more resources. They devastated the surrounding piñon pine that the natives depended on for sustenance, and used the timber to shore up their mines and build their large-frame houses—houses that needed windows and doors and walls and floors, then even more wood to heat it all. They required a massive substructure of machines and tools and iron, as well as wheels and roads and trains to transport them, then weapons to protect what they had made for themselves.

It was all that *they* knew. The optimism of manifest destiny was endemic to their way of life, and their survival meant war with the land. They couldn't have assimilated to the natives' way of life any more than the natives could to the whites' notion of progress. The Indians were in a dying struggle for their race. They never had a chance.

Sam was about to enter this once-contested landscape. He was not yet aware that it would continue to be contested, but with a new and different set of combatants. Nor did he yet know that he would become a player himself.

~~~

After having his truck towed and repaired in Austin, Sam was on his way. Once he reached Carson City, he turned north and continued on through Reno to the final leg of his journey to Charles's ranch, which lay some twenty miles further on. After turning left from the main highway, he drove slowly up a long dirt road, then left again and into the ranch's entrance road itself, all the while his eyes darting among the familiar sagebrush-covered landscape.

The ranch was nestled in a valley surrounded by high, sloping hills. It was common in the mid to late 1800s to identify property with the names of its owners, and when Jacob Ellis and his family settled there, and plot plans drawn up and printed, the shortened term JE Valley stuck.

"Samuel Ellis!"

Sam could faintly hear his name being called outside his truck window. He recognized the distinctive, roughhewn voice of Charles's wife, Sally, and caught sight of her on horseback, waving from the hillside.

She pointed down the road toward the house, and he replied with a wave before continuing on.

Cresting the final hill, he could see the weather-beaten barn, battered toolshed, and a modern, one-story, cinderblock bunk and guesthouse—"modern" meaning anything constructed after the Truman administration. Sam slowed a bit, taking in the earthy smell of alfalfa as he rolled past the old, inactive windmill still perched atop its rusty tower, then past the various horse and cattle corrals and all manner of farm equipment replete with the requisite spare axles, tires, and whatnot lying about. The place looked just as he remembered.

He stopped alongside the barn next to a pickup with a long, double horse trailer attached, ready and waiting for the next round of four-legged passengers.

"Well, it's about time you showed," Sally said as she pulled her horse alongside his truck and dismounted, her short frame hitting the ground with a solid thump. "I thought you'd be here a couple of days ago." Her face, lined from decades of working in the wind and sun, creased with concern. "We got a little worried."

"I should have called you, I'm sorry. Trip took longer because I had a bit of car trouble," Sam said, smiling, as he climbed out of his dust-covered truck. "I'll tell you about it later."

"It's good to see you, Sam," Sally said as she pulled him into a big hug. "You look fit."

"Sure I do! A little more weight and a lot less hair," he said as he ran his hand over thinning scalp. "You, however, do look good."

"After all these years?" She pulled away with a smirk, then grabbed her horse's reins and tied them to a nearby post. "I can see we're going to get along just fine, as long as we keep lying to each other."

Sam went around his truck, opened the tailgate, and pulled out his daypack.

Sam felt that age hadn't dampened Sally's spirit one bit, and was relieved to be in her sphere of optimism after being pent up with his own troubled thoughts for five days. He hefted his gear into one hand and offered his free arm as they strolled toward the house.

Surrounded by several very old cottonwoods in the lea of the north-facing hillside, the great two-story gothic Victorian with its numerous gables and large wrap-around porch awaited. Built more as a show of substance than function in the late 1850s, the house's grandeur seemed out of place in its setting.

Sam stopped to look at it. "Even though I grew up here, I just now realize how odd this old house looks. I wonder why they put so much effort into it."

"I've wondered about that, too. I think your great-great—however many—grandparents were just determined to bring a bit of their eastern home out here. I don't think it was meant as a statement to others, but maybe as comfort to themselves. This dry land was so different from where they came from. I wonder if it was built as a buffer against it."

"Maybe it was part of their determination to bend the land to their will and force that eastern civilization into it."

Sally laughed. "Well, all this dust and dirt would certainly put an end to any pretension of living anywhere but in a wild setting. It was certainly harsher than back east. I think once they got things under control and the land became their full-time job, they needed this house more for respite than reassurance."

"Maybe it's because the tables turned on them. While they thought they'd succeeded in taming the land, the land subdued them to its own ways."

Sally smiled at that. They went up by way of a small path that ran through an untended garden bordered by rocks of different colors and sizes, all local curiosities picked up over the years.

"So, how's Chuck doing?"

"Better now. Gave us a scare with his heart problem. Thankfully it turned out to be fairly minor." Sally stopped at the foot of the stairs leading to the porch and turned to him. "I suppose I overreacted, asking you to come all the way out here."

"I was glad to come." Sam wasn't altogether sure he meant it, but he certainly wasn't about to display any doubts.

"It's just his age and general health I'm worried about," Sally said while shielding her eyes from the afternoon sun. "The doctor's got him on heart medication, so it's serious enough. He wants him to retire. Can you imagine? Retire to what? You know that's impossible here. He can't do what he could twenty years ago, not that he'd admit to it. The work is no easier now than it's ever been. Well, you know that, since you worked on it yourself long ago. But he certainly can't continue on like he has. So I don't know where that leaves him, or us."

"What about help? Could you get more?"

"Sure, I suppose. We do have Dave and his son Henry, but more would be costly and we're running pretty tight as it is. We do outsource some machinery for reaping, plowing, and planting, but no one is going to look after your own place as well as yourself. The point is that if you live here, things always need to get done. Just stepping outside, maybe just to sit or relax, you find yourself getting up and doing something because it needs to be done. I just don't want to see him die trying to pull out a fence post—or is that how it should be? We're supposed to die with our boots on? Well, sooner or later, I guess. I just don't want it to be sooner," she said and laughed. "I'm sorry, Sam. I'm going on about our problems before you even get out of the saddle. I've set up the downstairs guest room for you."

"Where's Chuck now?"

"He went with Dave to Sparks this morning to get his saddle repaired. He should be back before dark."

"That's twenty-five miles away. No horse can go that fast."

"Right. The buggy needed a new wheel rim, too. We do have a pickup, you know."

"It's good to see you're using modern transportation."

"Not to mention the indoor plumbing we put in last year," Sally teased. "Get yourself settled. I've got to feed the chickens. Food's in the kitchen—help yourself."

She turned and headed off in the direction of the chicken coop. Sam stood watching her, noticing the obvious purpose in her step. That positive attitude seemed reflected in her face as well. Though she did possess more than her share of age lines, those only seemed to improve her image.

Short, stocky even, but with no hint of excess weight, she had a rounded face with a small nose and smiling eyes that, Sam surmised, could turn on you in an instant if circumstances called for it. He thought that her positive attitude most likely enlivened everyone she encountered, which in turn reinforced her own self-worth. A work-type shirt and jeans set the rest of her off as the competent authority in charge.

Charles and Sally were married just before Sam headed east, and he remembered her then as being a bit shy and withdrawn, but the land, again, may have been the catalyst that changed all that.

Sam stepped onto the porch toward the back door and pulled open the screen. It had obviously seen better days, having had about four pairs of hinges all up and down the side—each newer one a replacement for an older pair, until there seemed more hardware than wood. The idea of just replacing the door itself did not seem a priority.

Walking in, he already felt the guilt associated with being inside when work was called for outside. The house itself was no place for lounging in midday. It never was. He was transported back to his old world, a work-ethic world, only now as a stranger. The effects were immediately palpable. *While I'm lying about,* he thought, *Sally's working and doing things for my comfort.*

But first, there was one item he wanted to revisit. He went into the parlor and stood in front of the still-working mechanism. The large "grandmother" clock had been hauled overland in the covered wagon of Sam and Charles's forebears, Jacob and Ruth Ellis, in the late 1850s. Back then, it was the pride of the house. It was called the grandmother clock because it was Ruth Ellis who persuaded her husband to bring it along with them. It was an unnecessary, heavy luxury item for any wagon, but amazingly, it survived the ordeal. At St. Joseph, the starting point, the innards had been disassembled and carefully packed, and the hollow box was used for the storage of clothes and other items for their travel west.

The overland trails were littered with other such heavy paraphernalia. The detritus started about midway through the Rockies and continued well into Nevada, when there was little left to throw overboard. Its wake left a conspicuous route for the trailing emigrants to follow. As their trek became more difficult and the travelers more hardened in mind and body, the naiveté for many of the once-tenderfoot pioneers had been discarded along with the residue of the no-longer-relevant society they had left behind.

But Ruth Ellis was not to be dissuaded. She was determined to take this clock the full distance, or as her children used to quote her, "They woulda had ta bury me in it." Their choice to remain on the eastern side of the Sierras did make things easier, since they didn't follow the rest of the party up the last and difficult Truckee or Carson River routes over the Sierras and into California.

Back in those days, the great clock was to become the centerpiece of the house, and the talk of the surrounding populace. It represented a civilized barrier between themselves and the rawness of the land.

Neighbors would sit at the foot of the contraption, tracing the arc of the great pendulum, and listen to its persistent ticking. At each quarter-hour, the magical chimes resounded throughout the house, and anyone listening could imagine themselves transported, if for one brief moment, back to a refined society for which they so longed. But in the middle of the night, when all the extraneous sounds of the house had finally played themselves out, the soft ticking could be heard all the way into the upstairs bedrooms. Especially for the women, such a precise rhythm was the comfort, however illusory, of an ordered life against the harsh land they found themselves in.

Sam stood staring at the contraption for some time, its pendulum swinging a wide arc toward its opposite side, only to be pulled back again. He wondered if it might be a metaphor for something deeper

He was tired—no, exhausted. He went to the spare bedroom, took off his shoes, lay on the bed, and was out in minutes. He awoke two hours later to the sound of a truck pulling up outside. He listened as doors opened and closed, then heard two voices. One was Chuck's. The other he figured must belong to the hired hand, Dave, whom he had met only a few times before. Helen met him only once. She used to play at trying to picture him fitting the stereotypical cowboy image. Wiry, weather-beaten, smokes rolled into his shirt sleeve, and a hat looking older than its wearer. She also had him rolling his own, and one-handed at that. Sam countered that only happened in Gary Cooper movies.

Charles's voice sounded strong the way Sam remembered, but he couldn't make out what they were saying. He found himself straining, concentrating on that far-off noise, alert like a wild animal. If his ears could move, they would have. Then came the sound of the truck door opening, closing, and moving off and re-parking at a distance—probably to the bunkhouse. Footsteps crunched on that gravel path, then up the wooden steps and through the door.

He heard Sally and Charles talking in the kitchen, but it wasn't the same voice he had heard outside. This one sounded weaker. It was the voice of a man in confidence with someone he had lived with for nearly thirty-five years. A lot of shorthand communication and knowing what the other one was thinking would do that. Then he could hear Charles's voice rise. Were they arguing over Sam's presence?

Sam felt uneasy about that, but for good or bad, he was going to face up to it. He got up and went to the kitchen.

Charles turned to him and smiled. "Sam! How have you been? Boy, it's been a long time. What? Six years? Too long. Sally said you drove here. You goofball, that's a long way."

"Chuck!" Sam replied while extending his hand. "Yeah, well, I wasn't in a hurry. I also wanted to camp out. Well, for one night anyway, since I hadn't done that in a long time. But you look good. You used to be six feet four as I remember. Have you grown even taller, or me shorter?"

"Just wider, but we all shrink over time. You look great yourself, except for that lack of hair. That's okay. I have enough for the both of us, even if it is white. Come and sit. Sally, is supper about ready?"

"Yep," Sally said, smiling as she placed salad plates on the table before sitting down herself. "I just can't believe you two are finally in the same room together."

The dinner conversation was a slightly stilted one full of pleasantries. It was clear that the three of them were feeling uncomfortable. Sam told them about his retirement and about the service clubs that had kept him busy since Helen's death. He led a tame life by any standard, which was why the conversation shifted to talking about Charles and Sally's life on the ranch.

"You haven't seen Dan or Robin for a long time, have you?" Sally asked as she reached behind her to the dish cabinet to retrieve recent photos of both children. "Robin was only a teenager when you last saw her. That's Danny. He's twenty-nine now, and Robin, as you may remember, came late—she's twenty-four."

The pictures shocked Sam into the realization of how long he had been out of touch. He expected to see maturity as the children grew, but not actual aging. There was Danny's slight hair loss, for one. Robin, he hardly recognized at all.

With her elbows on the table, chin in one palm, Sally stared up at Sam with slight unease. "I never said much to you about them after Helen passed. Dan and his wife, Laura, are wonderful, but busy. Don't get to see them much. Dan works for a real estate firm in Reno and is doing pretty well, especially with all the growth going on around here. But Robin...well, Robin is finally getting her life back together, as they say. She lives in Sacramento now, but comes by fairly often. She has her one-year-old daughter, Hazel. Did you know that? Of course, you did. You know she never married the father. He disappeared after Hazel was born, which is just as well." Sally's tone carried sadness. "Robin was our problem child. She was always in some kind of trouble."

"Now, Sally," Charles said while poking at his salad, "it wasn't all that bad."

"Charles tends to forget a lot that's happened." Sally was looking at Sam, though her remark was directed at Charles. "Isn't that right?"

With a wave, Charles dismissed the comment, in effect conceding it.

"She had a tough time of it." Tears welled in Sally's eyes as she stared into the middle distance. "High school was the worst. Drugs, alcohol, staying out and partying till who knows how late. We could never get a handle on her. Disobedient and defiant, and sullen. I know teenagers can get that way, but heavens, the yelling that went on! We—no, I—finally gave her an ultimatum, and she left." Sally sighed. "How can you love someone you hate, and hate someone you love so much?

"But only later, after she moved out, did I finally learn not to say anything, or give any advice that she would have countered anyway. It's so sad what being rebellious does to a person. I mean, it made her go against everything we stood for just for its own sake. I've always considered myself a decent person, so she had to be the opposite. It's not that we're snobs or anything, she just got involved with a bad crowd. Other kids with dead-end futures. I think they just pulled her down with them."

"There was nothing we could have done, Sally," Charles piped in. "After she left, she was just another rebel with her cause taken away."

"It was the only thing we could do," Sally added. "It's just that she was so young. She still needed direction. I guess today they would say that I had bad parenting skills."

"That's not true, Sally. You did the best that any parent could do. Robin was the cause of her own misfortune. Kicking her out forced her to be on her own, and yes, she was old enough." Charles looked over to his brother. "When Hazel was born, she stayed here for some time, then, on her own—not in a huff this time—she went to live with some friends in Sacramento. We helped her with her finances and for a few classes at the local community college. Now she's got a job at an insurance firm and is doing pretty well. Besides, Sally, look at Danny. He came out fine, so you can't blame yourself. These kids nowadays, they make their own lives."

Sally seemed somewhat mollified by that. Sam thought that this must have been a conversation they had played between themselves hundreds of times.

Sam said, "Remember, I was a high school teacher before teaching community college, and had to deal with teenage mental anguish constantly—boys *and* girls. So don't think you're alone, Sally."

"That's good to know. I think maybe that headstrong nature, in its own way, helped her pull through it. She has certainly matured a great deal, maybe realized her mistakes and that we still love her even after all we've gone through. We've gotten along better over time. Being a new mother will do that."

"That's wonderful," Sam said. "Maybe I can be thankful I missed all that. But Sally, if things are so much better, you still seem bothered by it."

"I think I still need—what's that word? Closure? Some meeting of minds so that we can forgive each other."

"So tell me more about Dan. I guess he never wanted to work here."

"No, he didn't," Sally said. "He's like you in some respects. For him, he likes the city life—real estate, dealing with people, that sort of thing. Not everyone is cut out for this rough life. His wife, Laura, is a real sweetie. I just love her—but no children yet."

"I know how they can get some," Sam teased.

After dinner, they moved their coffees outside to the covered porch behind the house. The sun had already descended below the far ridge and left a silhouette, an erratic line that gave the effect of some enormous graph of meaningless ups and downs. Charles commented that he thought it looked like his own EKG. Sam surmised that it looked like his stock holdings, only this looked way too positive. Sally laughed and said her boys had no imagination. She always saw the outline of a coyote chasing a rabbit.

"Now see there?" Sally pointed to the left. "To the right of that tree and just above, you can kind of see the coyote's ears and tail, and it's going after that rabbit in front of it—sort of."

"Well, if that's the ears you're talking about," Sam teased, "there's only one, and that tail looks more like a beaver's tail. And I don't see any nose on either of 'em."

"Nobody said it was perfect. And anyway, that's what we used to tell the kids. They bought it, filling in the rest with their own imaginations. You do the best you can with what you got."

"It's like people are always saying they can see a face in the moon," Charles said. "The man in the moon…I don't see any damn face."

"Well, our kids liked the animal story. They made their own stories up about them, where they came from, what they were like, probably like what the Indians used to do. Although I suppose they were more serious about it, inventing gods and things to fit their needs."

"Say, Sally," Sam said, changing the subject, "when I left here for good those many years ago, wasn't it just after you guys got married?"

"I should think so. You certainly didn't leave before. You *were* the best man! At least I think it was you," she said with a twinkle in her eye.

"I get confused on the timeline is all. Besides, I don't remember much about the wedding."

"I shouldn't think so, considering all the champagne you drank. Remember when you tried to get up to speak at the reception, but couldn't?"

"No!"

"Well, you didn't embarrass yourself too much, and I have the pictures to prove it."

"And she could sell them to you if you'd like." Charles laughed.

"That's okay. No one would recognize me now. Anyway, tell me again how you two met. It was on the Reno campus, wasn't it?"

"Well, yes. Charles was finishing up some credits at Ohio State, and I was a young, lowly freshman with no major. Just looking to land a rich man."

"And she thought she found one," Charles said. "Boy, did I fool her."

Sally smiled over at Charles with a look that, Sam mused, made Charles uncomfortable in public. "It was love at first sight. Well, you should remember, for heaven's sake; we were together almost all the time—made your mom and dad crazy, but I managed to endear myself to them. I think Charles and I both knew from the start that it would be for good. Over thirty-five years now."

"Humph, we'll give it another twenty to see if it sticks." Charles grunted as he struggled up from his chair, claiming old age and stiffness to no one in particular. "I'm going on in and do a little paperwork. See you two in the morning." Then, hesitating at the door before going inside, he turned back and said, "Sam, I'm glad you came."

This left Sam and Sally alone as daylight quietly turned toward twilight.

"This is the nicest hour in all the twenty-four. Quiet and peaceful, don't you think, Sam?"

"Yeah. Reminds me of when I camped out in the desert a few days ago. Being alone, I mean really alone, I felt things I haven't felt in a long time." Sam was hesitant to elaborate, but for some reason, his mouth seemed to work on its own. "When I settled on a campsite, I decided to take a stroll up a nearby hillock. It was incredibly quiet. Not a peep. A stillness, really. I still had all my wits about me, but as I looked out over the land, I had the distinct feeling of clarity, not just in the view, but about everything. For a minute there, I felt I could see and understand the interdependence of it all—the rocks, the vegetation, the wildlife, every molecule of water and air. It all seemed in balance, with nothing out of place and everything dependent on everything else. Including me. I never felt so alive."

"You had a spiritual revelation!"

"Well, maybe." Sam shrugged. "Though not a religious one, I don't think."

Sally leaned back, seemingly disappointed.

Sam knew, as his wife Helen had described it to him, that Sally (for the two would talk endlessly over the phone) was a woman of strong principles with a fairly solid set of Christian values. He appreciated Sally's religious devotion, or at least the general moral tenets that most religions had, but he didn't feel the need to counter with his own view, which was simply non-belief. Only until someone attempted to get in his face and proselytize did he feel them fair game for criticism.

"Mystics might call it a transcendental experience, or some such," Sam said. "Mostly, I just felt an awareness of being able to see how things really work, as of a great machine of cogs and wheels and whatnot, all in balance and in working order. I thought of myself as having been in real time."

"How do you mean?" Sally leaned forward with renewed interest, her confidence restored at having perhaps found a kindred spirit.

"Well, I think most of our daily lives are reactions. We see situations and react to them, so we always tend to be looking back. Maybe the key to life is experiencing the present moment...without all the filters we carry around..." Sam tapered off in a slow decrescendo, feeling slightly foolish.

"That's all very sensible sounding, Sam. But if you ask me, it was the Lord's way of getting your attention. Everything happens for a reason, and we just have to figure out what he wants for us. People just overthink things, that's all."

Sam turned his gaze from Sally to the mountains and beyond with a wistful look. Then, to avoid countering her, he smiled and said simply, "Yes, I do overthink things."

Sally got up. "Time for me to go in, too. And Sam," she whispered in a confiding manner, reaching back to touch him on the shoulder, "I'm glad you're here too." She then went into the house.

Helen used to say that Sally was the rock around which all others in her sphere could wander off, with only a little impunity, so that they could succeed in their own obligations; that because she shouldered the higher responsibility—the welfare of her family—she was the one critical element that allowed the separate parts to mesh into a balanced whole.

Sam felt bad that he couldn't be the like-minded soul she was looking for, but he sensed that her beliefs encompassed pretty much only those tenets that suited her nature: love, forgiveness, charity. Fortunately, she seemed to lack the fundamental teachings of guilt and shame so often hammered through dogmatic tenets. This probably gave her a malleability, and the confidence that, when you got right down to it, elevated her to that level of being so highly longed for by the most devout in the first place. But he figured that she would probably continue to feel isolated, as most people in authority do.

Sam decided to take a walk before going in, and in the darkening twilight, followed the path the led out behind the barn. For a second time, he was surrounded by total silence. Even when talking to Sally on the porch about the quietness of the place, he could still hear the refrigerator compressor or some such mechanical device, but now it was exceptionally quiet. Sam felt like he was enclosed in a soundproofed room, where you think your hearing has gone bad. Compounding that was the near darkness that engulfed the area. The only visible configuration was the pale, furrowed path ahead that led to a small rise above the stable. Finally, to his relief, a welcome breeze provided a three-dimensional quality to it all.

In the short time that he had been here, all the sounds, smells, and sights had triggered the slumbering recesses in his brain. This was no transcendental experience this time around, just vague feelings from the past that would suddenly arise and, just as suddenly, vanish. He was unable to grasp any of it in a meaningful way.

All he knew was that this place must have been hardwired into his brain years ago when he was growing up. But an absence of forty years hadn't lessened his feeling of belonging—the house, the barn, fences, and trees. Smells mostly. Hundreds of combinations, some probably only in this one little section of the world. And only he would know if it were the right smell.

Cattle droppings and elms, sage, and wildflowers, alfalfa grass, and maybe diesel oil to top it off. His mind was replaying bits and pieces of that old recording. But like trying to see an object in a darkened room, where you can only perceive it askance, he couldn't get a grip on any of it by concentrating.

His mind then reverted to the reason he had traveled here. He hoped that the unease he felt during his journey wasn't as dire as he had feared, but he wasn't sensing much relief. He felt he might be needed, and was concerned that his role might be more than an observer, or even advisor. Maybe he was more of an interloper, tipping the scales of a balancing act that Charles and Sally had been playing out all these years. He could sense that their smoothly run system was fragile, and now one going through change—age-induced change. Maybe glacially slow and undetectable, but change just the same. One small disturbance might suddenly cause a major upheaval that would throw their entire system out of whack. It seemed more obvious to Sally than to Charles, possibly because Charles was at its center.

Like most everyone else, Sam subconsciously ignored his own body's ultimate dissolution that forces us out of our mental lethargy at unexpected points along the way. He thought about how, as we grow older and death nearer, we find ourselves forced to take steps. But sometimes those steps become leaps in the attempt to preserve the status quo. Such leaps become more difficult each time around. Eventually it becomes a counter-leap that seems alien to all our preparatory conditioning.

Somewhere along the way, his thought continued, *we are no longer required to build on that which came before. We're no longer expected—or worse, needed—to do the things that require the agility of the young. No matter how hard we fight it, physical and mental stamina go into decline, ultimately forcing us into retreat. Despite all the warnings, we seem surprised at its emergence. It is humiliating. Living is all about respect, and the loss of responsibility leads to the loss of respect.*

He figured that Charles had no clue, that he probably thought he could have a heart issue and continue on just as he had. Of course, he could, for a while. Then would come the inevitable interposition of others telling him to slow down, relax, let someone else do the work for a change. Always expressed in placating ways, as if that was what he, or anyone for that matter, had always wanted. *It may be something we strive for, but not what we want.*

Sam was not only the younger, but smaller brother. He was always aware of his underling status. Being the first, Charles was the one sent off to college, perhaps against his own wishes. But meeting Sally at the University of Nevada was his big break. She was quite a few years younger and far more energetic than Charles. It was she who saw his true potential, and it wasn't sitting behind a desk. She encouraged him, as did his parents, to take over the ranch. Together, they both grew into the job that was to define their lives.

By that time, Sam had already graduated from high school, but his parents could no longer afford college for him. Although Sam knew that he was more sensitive and a bit less pragmatic than his brother, he too was determined. He worked his way through community college for two years with the idea of getting into a major university. At that time, he wanted to be a writer. He was perfectly capable of working the ranch, but thought he wasn't suited for such a lifelong commitment.

He migrated east all those years ago, only to be met with the inevitable reality check. He worked his way through the University of Wisconsin, where he got his teacher's degree. It was also where he met Helen. They married after his graduation, and he ended up accepting a middling teacher's salary at a small high school in upstate New York. He first taught English; then, when the school needed a part-time math instructor, he volunteered, and found he could do well in that. After a few years, with the need for cheaper lodgings and a higher salary, they moved to St. Louis, where his versatility in diverse subject matter got him into a good community college at which he taught for the next thirty years.

Sam turned and started back toward the house. He was thinking about the age-related changes happening within himself. A new thought occurred to him: *Maybe it isn't so much that they need me as it is that I need them; perhaps if I stayed longer, I too would adopt a more stereotypical toughness.*

~~~

Early the next morning, Sam rose before the rest of the house. Feeling rested, he decided to go out again and along the old mine road that snaked westward along the bottom portion of the valley. But this time, it was only to take in the atmosphere.

The sun was just peeking over the eastern hills. Its warm, electric radiation served as a contrast to the still chill of the air. *Another most beautiful time of day.* Sam laughed, mainly because he had it all to himself. The great outdoors was putting on a delicate show of light and smells, with the sounds of aspen leaves rustling at the smallest insistence of any gentle breeze that happened along.

The path running along the wash was the lowest and the wettest section of the valley. It served as the concentration point for most of the vegetation. Poplars, cottonwoods, and aspen clung to both sides of the road. Sam always liked this area. There were enough trees in spots to give the illusion of a small forest. Oddly, he felt comfort in the deception.

He found concentrated forests of tree after tree without any vista monotonous. Contrasts appealed to him—the yin and yang of opposites, where the presence of a small bit of yin within a large bit of yang demanded attention. A single tree in a city, an old windmill in the wilderness—both were treasured because they didn't seem to belong. Sam liked the specialness, the independence of things out of sync and struggling in their alien surroundings.

He could feel the new and renewal all about him. The ongoing struggle of the fittest was an ancient voice, he thought, one that modern humans seemed no longer a part of. Sam wondered if millions of years of essence had disappeared when consciousness arrived.

Then he caught himself overthinking things again, and attempted just to take in the atmosphere as he originally planned.

The road ahead continued to deteriorate, eventually winding up out of the trees and into the sagebrush hills. It ended miles further, at the mine. That mine had brought Sam's forebears to the valley in the first place. Although not on their property, the family had a claim on it, meaning they had to work it periodically in order to keep that claim active. However, there was never enough gold or silver to make much of a living, and they rekindled their efforts toward farming and ranching, as there was just enough water to sustain a small crop and a few head of cattle. This was enough reason to entice them to stay. It wasn't a rich area by any means, as it provided just enough to survive. The standing joke of the JE Ranch was that the first two initials stood for "just enough." Nonetheless, few ranches in the area had such a continuous history.

Sam retreated to the house to find Sally busy in the kitchen.

"Good morning, Sam. How was your walk?"

"Morning, Sally. Great. All the old sights and smells bring back a lot of memories. Don't know why I ever left."

"You left for all the same reasons a lot of offspring leave. If you hadn't, maybe you would have regretted it." She paused, probably thinking of her own daughter's rebellion.

Sally was in constant motion about the kitchen, washing errant dishes that happened to get caught astray, dirty or not, putting things away and taking others out—all the while seemingly at total peace in her own industries.

"So, you slept okay last night?"

"Oh, sure. I can't believe you still have that old bed."

"Yeah, we got a new mattress for it some time ago. It was your aunt Mae's four-poster, wasn't it?"

"I think so. This house is so full of the past. A lot of old stuff still around. Maybe that's one of the reasons I left. Too much of a past to live up to."

"That's how I feel sometimes," Sally said to him over her shoulder. "Sometimes it's more of a burden than anything else. If I can't use it, I want to get rid of it. Charles is the one who saves these old things, and I do respect his feelings, but to me, sometimes they feel like an anchor. I love this old house, but we seem to be haunted too much by those who were here before, like it's some kind of revered authority we have to live up to." Sally placed an unasked-for cup of coffee in front of Sam. "But you know, the truth is, I don't think they were any better at making the right choices than we are now. They flew by the seat of their pants just like us. The difference is they had no history to tie them down, and since they survived, they get credited with being right. They may have just been lucky. Who knows? Maybe they made the wrong decision by staying here and would have been better off if they had gone on to California. We'll never know."

"They were free to do what they wanted," Sam said, "because they didn't have that past you talked about, that anchor. Then they built their own past in the process and left the anchor to drag down the next generation."

Sally chuckled. "Exactly."

Sam lifted his mug and breathed in the coffee's aroma. "But thinking on the past can make you dependent on it. You get to thinking about what was, and then you begin thinking about what might have been or should have been in your own life, and that can lead to resentment."

Sam realized that he may have made too strong of a statement, but Sally seemed to ignore it and continued with her own thoughts.

"Our whole life here is centered around your brother's family. This house—this land." Sally brought over a plate of sliced cantaloupe, then pulled out a chair and sat down across from him. "It's your family, too, of course, but you and I are alike in some ways," she said as she reached over and patted his hand. "You're not as caught up in it because you distanced yourself years ago. And me, I'm not blood, so it's Charles who feels he has something to live up to. But even when I sit in one of those creaky old chairs, I can't help thinking of where it came from, or who sat in it long before."

Sam ran his hand along the tabletop, feeling the divots of age and wear. Attempts at updating the old house over the years had been haphazard at best—new carpeting here, new piece of furniture there. The kitchen, however, because of its functional needs, had received some modern upgrades. Since the old table was as functional now as when he was a boy crawling beneath it, it remained.

"Who knows?" Sally said as she continued her thought. "Maybe trying to live up to the past can be a good thing. Gives us reason to keep going. If we didn't have it, we would have been like Robin was in some ways, unstructured and at loose ends. Kids nowadays, they never seem to know what to do. They just don't seem to have that work ethic we had."

Sam nodded. "I don't mean to be blunt, but I'm not sure what I can do to help here, particularly in a short space of time."

After a pause, Sally gave a somewhat sheepish smile and said, "I suppose I did have an ulterior motive in urging you to come. I do wish you would consider staying on, at least for a while longer. You're part of this family, and what happens here affects you as well. You still have an interest in the spread, and I'd like you to be part of the decision-making. But we don't have to go over all that now. Besides, I made you both some lunches for your overnights."

"Overnights?"

"Oh, by the way, you and Charles are going out riding and camping for a couple of nights, you know, on horses? Lord knows it's time you get reacquainted."

"With the horses?"

"No, silly, with Charles. And don't think you can weasel out of it. It took me long enough to get him to go. There's no reason he has to work for a couple of days. He's just in the habit of thinking he has to. Besides, Dave's son…you know, Henry? He's a good kid. He's working here again and he can help his father take care of things while you and Charles are gone."

"Sounds like you have a plan," Sam said, trying to suppress a slight edge to his voice.

5
The Mine

"You remember Dave," Charles said to his brother.

It had been years since Sam had seen Dave, Charles's hired hand. Sam noticed that he was still wiry, but had grown a bit of a paunch to his midsection and had collected more sun-exposed age lines since they last met. But wearing the obligatory jeans and well-worn hat, he still looked the part. Sam was also aware of Dave's Paiute heritage, and that he had a hundredfold deeper history here than any descendant of the original settlers.

"Good to finally meet you again," Sam said. "The few times I've been here, you seem to have been off somewhere else. Helen only met you, what—once, maybe eight, ten years ago?"

"I remember Helen, and I'm sorry for your loss, Sam. She was a very nice lady."

"Thank you for that."

"But as far as work is concerned, I try to do as little as possible. Anyway, seems like you're starting to look more like your brother now, certainly not like you did in that picture—I mean you at Chuck's wedding with that glassy-eyed stare. We all get a kick over that one. I got your mount ready. I saddled Prunes for you, even used your old saddle since we still had it. He's a good horse."

"Why is he called Prunes?"

"Oh, you'll figure that one out. Came from the Ormand's ranch over near Fallon. Got a good deal on him, though he's a little old and kinda blind—and lame, too, for that matter. Just in the left foreleg, though. But that's okay 'cause he limps on the other, so it kind of evens out. I'll go wake him up for you."

He said this in such a deadpan manner that it took a few seconds for Sam to register his dry sense of humor. Dave gave a wink and glanced over to Charles as his way of showing his nonthreatening sense of fun.

"Chuck's got SOB. He's the only one that can ride him. Right, Chuck?"

"Right," Charles said, busy cinching up the last strap of his saddle. He went over to check on the pack mule, which had the biggest load, then returned to recheck his own halter.

"Take care of the ranch, Dave," Charles said as he, Sam, and the family dog, Scooter, set out along the same road Sam had walked earlier that morning. The plan was to journey miles further up the valley, where they planned to camp.

Once Charles and Sam had passed through the cool, overhanging branches of the cottonwoods and aspen and began ascending onto the exposed dry rock area so characteristic of the Great Basin mountain region, the sylvan atmosphere lessened. Now it was native greasewood, shade scale, and the ever-present desert sage releasing their pungent aromas; but being mid-April, few flowers had yet to show themselves.

The two riders, still being a little uncomfortable in each other's company, were silent for much of the way. For his part, Sam was ready to say something, but he didn't know how to begin or what to say. Was he supposed to be the problem-solver here, or just a friendly voice to convince Charles to slow his workload? He figured that maybe if he got the ball rolling, things would take their own course.

He didn't have to. Charles stopped at the top of a small knoll and turned his horse around to face Sam. It was the first time since Sam had arrived that they made full eye contact. "Sally must have given you some kind of sales pitch to finally get you to come back here. I hope she didn't paint too bleak a picture."

"Oh, no, it was a pretty soft pitch. I know I should have come back more often. Before Helen died, I was still working, and, well, we never found much time. After I retired, I just lost the incentive to do much of anything. But Sally's concerned about your health and all, and I figured it's about time I got off my fat butt."

"And do what? I appreciate your concern, but there's little you can do here that I haven't been doing myself all these years, or can continue doing for a bunch more."

"How much more? You're—what—sixty-eight now?" But Sam was reluctant to press the point further.

Charles, for his part, also did not want to pursue that line, and referred the conversation back to Sally. "For all her optimism, Sally's worried about a lot of things." Then, in a more subdued manner, he said, "I don't really blame her. She's worried about my health and what might happen here in the future—we don't have much of a plan. It's likely she'll outlive me, but even if I do hang on for a while, I may just become a burden. She's been pretty open about it, and I admire her for that."

"It sounds like she's more worried about *her* future than yours."

"Not at all. She just doesn't want us to sell out."

"Sell out what?"

"The ranch, of course. You must have noticed all the development when you drove up. A couple of the ranchers have already sold their properties to developers, and they made good money from it. The devil will most likely make a handsome offer on this place, too." He gave a derisive chuckle. "Real hucksters, they are. We ranchers are a pretty hard, stubborn lot, but those guys know how to say anything, tap into our sense of duty to community, to country, to all of mankind for that matter, all the while bolstering their justifications with offers we can't refuse. I don't want anything to do with them. They can offer everything except the only thing I would ever want, and that's this place. I couldn't see ever giving it up."

Sam was beginning to feel the force of the sun on the back of his neck. With an envious look at the full-brimmed hat Charles had on, he cursed the useless baseball cap he wore. Only function mattered in places like this.

"But you see the problem," Charles continued. "I want Sally to be secure when I'm gone, and selling it would give her that security. I don't know how she could make it without me here, as tough as she is. Since neither Robin nor Dan have shown any interest in working it, she would have to outsource more labor. 'Just enough' barely gets by as it is, and for her to try to keep it may not be realistic. But…" Here Charles trailed off, as one would when approaching a precipice. There was nowhere more for him to go. The face that had expressed such forcefulness moments ago changed subtly to one of doubt and uncertainty.

Sam couldn't help thinking back to his conversation with Sally that morning. Who was really the more sentimental one here? Was Sally just trying to act the tougher of the two? It seemed evident that both were more concerned about the other's needs than their own.

"It seems like you're putting the world on your shoulders right now. I'm sure something will work out." It was the only thing Sam could think of to say.

"I suppose you're right. Besides, we may have another plan. But we don't have to go into it now. Well, you ready to go on up to the lake?" Charles said with a grin.

Sam realized that such an about-face in temperament might have been the result of Charles divulging the worries he had kept bottled up inside. Sam thought he must have been the first person his brother had felt comfortable enough to confide in.

"The JE lake," Sam said with a laugh. "I forgot to bring my fishing pole."

Charles laughed back. "Okay—the pond."

"We used to swim in that thing, remember? Haven't been there since I left all those years ago. Bet it's even smaller than I remember."

"It can still supply a constant stream to the ranch. Don't know exactly when the original pond was dammed up to make it larger, maybe turn of the century. They probably needed a steady flow of water before the wells were bored. But we adjust the weirs several times a year to keep the trees down below healthy, and now that they've grown around the pond, it makes for a good camping spot. It's where we'll stay for the night, then tomorrow I thought we would go up to the mine."

"The family mine, sure. I had my own adventure with a mine recently—tell you about it later."

"Really? I'll look forward to it."

After two hours, the brothers reached their destination, a three-acre pond with a shady Eden-feel of trees and surrounding grass.

"Let's set things up. You like the picnic table we brought up?"

"Homey."

Charles unpacked the mule and removed the saddles from the horses. Since they weren't about to wander far from the water and grass, he let them roam free. Sam set the provisions on the bench, got out a couple of beers, and put the rest of the six-pack in the shallows of the pond.

Charles got out a bag of dry dog food, put a few handfuls in a bowl, and brought it over to Scooter. "Sally made us some sandwiches. They're in that sack."

Sam pulled them out. "What are they?"

"Don't ask. Mountain oysters, swingin' steak, don't know. Been in the freezer a long time. No one wanted to eat them."

"Well, it looks like the supermarket turkey slices I saw lying on the counter this morning. Remember, Chuck, I used to live here, too."

Charles handed Sam a beer.

"Say, I always wanted to clear this up. Why does everyone call you Charles now? Dad and Mom called you Charles, but I called you Chuck. Doesn't Charles kind of sound highfalutin' for here? We used to call it 'putting on airs.'"

"Mom was the one who named me," he said as he sat down. "Dad just went along with it. Probably thought it was highfalutin' too. You and your friends were the only ones that called me Chuck, which was fine by me, but once I got into high school, some of the teachers started to call me Charles. I was afraid some of the other kids, new kids I didn't know, would make fun of it, but since I was pretty big, nobody really messed with me. I found out pretty early that not only could I get away with it, but it had become an asset. The kids always looked up to me, and I think that formal-sounding name added a bit of class in a school full of kids with short, tough-sounding names—you know, Jack, Bill—Sam?"

Sam grinned.

"I gotta tell you though, it still works," Charles said. "People always seem to show me a little more respect. Maybe my name has something to do with it. I have to say, I felt I *was* putting on an act, like I didn't deserve that respect. Then I thought, hell, everyone else is, why should I be left out? I found out a long time ago that a little pretension can go a long way. Perception can sometimes be a great asset. Don't know if I deserved it, but I never felt guilty about it either."

"Oh, you deserved it, all right. You've always had that natural-born leader in you. We all think of ourselves as phonies anyway, manipulating our way through life, hoping no one will find us out. Maybe that's why we all try so hard to protect ourselves." He paused to take a bite of his sandwich. "Turkey's pretty good."

"Right. Well, Sam, you did pretty well for yourself, didn't you? You made your own choices. I just let life lead me where I thought it was heading. I got sent to college but ended up working the ranch. You worked on the ranch for a while, but ended up a teacher. I always admired your pluck."

"It wasn't pluck. I just didn't think ranching was right for me. After our father died, I was glad when Mom persuaded you to take it over. She knew what she was doing. It actually took a load off my mind by not having to worry about it. I couldn't have handled the ups and downs of this job as well as you. You have the ability to bend to your condition and not panic when obstacles come your way. And talk about pluck, you have it in spades."

"Well, we do have different temperaments. This job probably *wouldn't* have worked out for you," Charles said with a chuckle. Then, as if to mitigate that statement: "And if I had been as smart as you, I wouldn't have stayed either."

"I felt I could do better if I left, this ranching business being fraught with so much uncertainty and all."

"That's for sure. Will the cattle bring in enough money at market? Is the grain too expensive? Will the rains ruin the crops? Maybe there's a drought next time, or the machinery breaks down, and it's another three thousand bucks you don't have. Then the loans have to be paid. But then again," Charles mused, countering himself, "there's always hope, that old shock-absorber to thought. Maybe one year the costs aren't so high, or beef prices are up, or some such thing. Just enough to take the edge off and give us a sense of peace, however temporary."

"I had my own dreams...is it me, or is it getting cold?"

"It is, and it's going to get colder. Remember, we're at a high elevation now."

Sam went over to his pack, got out his coat, and put it on. "I see a fire pit, do we have any wood to start a fire?"

"Yeah, we can start one later. There's some fire wood behind the trees over there that we brought up some time ago, so don't think about cutting up our bench. But you were going to say something before you got off the track."

"Oh...well, the other reason I wanted to leave was that I wanted to be a writer. The problem was that several of my high school teachers thought I had potential. Back then, that kind of encouragement could go to a kid's head. In the real world, I would have only been good enough to fight my way up the ladder to mediocrity. Running with that crowd would have been as uncertain as running this ranch. So I did what everybody calls the cowardly act. I became a teacher. Of course, there's nothing cowardly about that."

"Life is tough no matter what you do, I guess," Charles said. "Remember that old myth about Sisyphus?"

"Sure. The Greek story about how Zeus forced this guy to roll this rock up a hill, then when he gets near the top, it takes a turn on him and rolls back down, and he has to go down and roll it back up—for eternity."

"Probably laid his wife or something," Charles said.

"Never heard that version." Sam laughed. "But it makes for a better story. I do remember, though, the aggravation our parents went through just to make ends meet. You're not saying running this ranch is as hopeless as all that, are you?"

"Of course, not. But I read one writer who had a unique take on that myth, Camus, I think, that no matter how hard it was to roll that boulder up the mountain, his most agonizing moments came when he had to march back down the hill. That's when he had time to think and ponder his suffering. Trudging down the hill only brought on regrets over his hopeless situation." Charles issued an audible sigh. "So, selling the property would lead to that Easy Street, but it's a downhill road full of those regrets. There's nothing to replace it."

"You read Camus?"

"Only in my college days. I wouldn't bother now."

"I get it. So, no tent for tonight?"

Charles looked upward. "No rain forecast. Thought we would rough it and sleep under the stars—sleeping bags should be warm enough."

The brothers arose and traipsed up a small mound to have a look around and check the outlying Bureau of Land Management area that Charles's cattle were allowed to forage on. When they returned to the pond, Charles pulled out two fishing poles from the mule's pack.

"I was kidding about fishing here! There's never been fish in that watering hole."

"There are now. Don't know how they got here, but they are. Let's go to the other side, I've been lucky there."

The two sat on a downed log, near enough to each other to have a conversation.

"Use the salmon eggs," Charles said as he handed him a jar. "Whatever we get we'll have for dinner."

"The eternal optimist!" Sam said. "I guess we're different that way. I think too much, always worrying, always trying to make sense of things."

"Well, 'We do no end of feeling and mistake it for thinking,' don't we?" Charles cracked.

"Don't tell me…"

"Twain. Save you the trouble. Still know my literature. I'm not the bumpkin my role plays, you know. We both graduated college, and back then I did a lot of pondering too. But, you know, when I took over the ranch, it seemed like all that other stuff was pointless. When you focus on trying to survive, everything else takes a back seat. Things always need to get done, and they don't get done by thinking about them. Oh, I still read at times: histories, biographies, some fiction maybe, nothing too challenging."

"But you were the smart one," Sam said. "We both know it. You were a thinker, too, and could write. I remember some essay you wrote in high school that Mom showed me. Better than I could have done. I wanted to be like you, I followed the writing path you let go of. In any event, you could have gone anywhere with your degree."

"I suppose, but that's all atrophied out of me. The practical world took over, and I never looked back."

"But you're not like these hard-ass people you're surrounded by, are you?"

"I wouldn't stereotype them that way. There're no more hard-asses in this field than anywhere else. It's just a role some feel they have to play. I play it myself when I need to. Look, we all play roles. I have mine and you have yours. And maybe it goes against what you were born with, but we all try to fit in out of necessity. If you go against it, you pay the price. Nobody likes a deviant." He paused, thinking. "You know, Sally is a good example of someone forced to fit a role. You remember her before we got married—a sweet, young girl you would have never thought could don the mantle of toughness. But she did because she had to… strike!" Charles yelled as he pulled his rod back.

"Probably an old shoe. Always the optimist."

"You're wrong—a sunken branch." Charles laughed as he pulled it above the water.

"At least it's well-marinated. But I hear what you're saying," Sam said, continuing the conversation. "I don't think we ever lose our basic natures. We may lose the craft of it, but not the core of it. I mean, you used the word yourself when you called it a role. That means it's an act. And everyone around you does it because everybody else does it. For us men, I guess it becomes a cycle of cowboy posturing that we all get locked into, where any sign of real contemplation is a sign of weakness."

"Then after a while, it's no longer a role," Charles added, "and you become what you need to be. That writer you talked about, Sam? He isn't there anymore. You were in the same position, weren't you? You worked the ranch for a while before you went back east. Back then, you probably would have affected the attitude I have now if you stayed, and I may have been like you if I had left. We don't just play it, we be it."

"I suppose. Circumstance. We're all chained to circumstance."

The two fished for the next few hours, each catching one eight-inch trout.

"I didn't say they were very big."

Sam went over and got out the ice chest, and to the surprise of Charles, pulled out a couple of big steaks for dinner.

"Damn, I haven't had steak since my attack."

"Filets. Sally doesn't know about them. When Dave told me to grab a six pack from his refrigerator, I found these, and after a bit of pleading, he said we could have them. I'll wrap the fish up and we'll cook them for supper tomorrow."

~ ~ ~

Late the next morning, Charles and Sam adjusted the weir to let a bit more water out and allow to flow down to his fields below, perhaps helping replenish the wells in the process.

"Is that our work for today?" Sam asked.

"Yep, see how easy it is?"

After they had Sam's favorite breakfast of bacon and eggs, they saddled up and pressed on toward the mine.

"I don't remember how far away it is."

"Not far," Charles answered, "but on horses, and with all the switchbacks ahead, it's going to take a few hours."

As they ambled along, both seemed to run out of talk, and they continued on in silence—at least outward silence. After having distanced themselves from each other for so long, there was a lot to process.

For Sam, the importance of his presence resurfaced. He thought back to the life he had made in St. Louis with all its ties and acquaintances. Funny he didn't think of them so much as friends. Who would notice, or even care, if he didn't return? To Sally at least, Sam would be a welcome disturbance. Like a wind finally surfacing in the doldrums: you didn't care where it led, so long as it got you the hell out of the place you were stuck in. But he knew that he could be an asset, even if only to help restore and stabilize what seemed to him a potentially unbalanced situation.

After turning north into a V-shaped canyon, then later into another side valley, they ascended onto steeper and rockier terrain of mostly loose scree and large, angular rock slabs. The pack mule with its burden had a hard time of it, constantly slipping, dislodging rocks, and making the road worse with each passing. Sam noticed one partially washed-out portion that would need some widening. It was obvious that it hadn't been worked on for some time.

Sam had seen how roads on steep hillsides would inevitably collapse if not attended to. The tendency of earth was to always seek its angle of repose, where rocks and dirt settled to the point where gravity could no longer level them further. Because dirt roads are an unnatural element in a natural landscape and defied that concept, they needed constant attention. The soil up here, being consistently blown and washed away, did not last long between the exposed rocks, but over

73

the years of sporadic use, the roadside itself provided an impacted and flattened area where dirt could settle and plants could survive along the sides. It was a rare occurrence when the hand of man assisted in the promotion of life, however unintentional.

Coming upon more level terrain, the going was easier and the brothers were able to ride side by side.

"I gotta get this road fixed someday," Charles said.

"Looks like it's been a while."

"Haven't had time. Only think about it when I'm up here. Then it's too late. A Jeep might be able to make it, but a few areas need to be worked on. For now, it's just been too much to bother with."

The party continued along in a state of apparent semi-slumber, except for Scooter, Charles's thirty-pound, scruffy ranch dog of who-knows-what-breed making his own nimble way underfoot.

Sam wondered why he seemed agitated, running ahead before returning and barking as if to egg them on. "I've seen a couple of marmots running around. Has he found a scent, or is he just impatient to get to the mine?"

"He's just dumb," Charles said. "Next dog I get is going to be a lot smarter than this good-for-nothing."

Scooter may have had similar thoughts about his owner.

A chilly gust of wind from behind caused Charles to turn up his collar. Except for the dog, neither had a clue what was pursuing them, and not until Sam turned around did he understand the enormity of it all. "Holy shit! Where did that come from?!"

Charles turned as well, then looked back to Sam for confirmation. The full confluence of a vast and volatile black storm wall was bearing down on them from the south. No more than several hundred yards away, its darkness entombed everything beyond it. It had caught both men completely off guard, and their astonishment at its appearance froze them in place until a searing lightning flash struck a nearby hill followed by a thunderclap a second later. That shook them out of their reverie.

"We gotta get outta here!" Charles said.

"Maybe we can outrun it to the mine," Sam said.

"We're not going to outrun it, but we have no choice. We're sitting ducks out here." They began pushing their horses, who needed little prompting, upward.

Another flash, this closer than the first. Now they were moving at a good clip. They both knew how exposed they were, and that they were the most conspicuous lightning targets among the low terrain.

Sam, moving as hard as he could, heard Charles behind him, laughing.

"We make good lightning rods, huh, Sam? But I have to say you move pretty good for an old fart."

"You're older," Sam yelled. "Giddy up, Prunes!"

"Giddy up? Well shit! Hi-ho, Sonofabitch!" Charles yelled at his own horse.

Sam and Charles, energized by the danger, rushed hard up the road. The final portion of it to the mine was again rocky and steep, with several more switchbacks ahead. The horses and mule had a hard time in places, slipping on the loose scree and being generally spooked by the thunder and lightning.

Soon they came to the tailings of the old mine. It was situated at the end of Stubborn Canyon, framed against the deceptively clear blue sky to the north. Behind, the oncoming storm was overtaking them. Directly above was the line of demarcation between empty sky and the black mass with its great cloud curtain unfurling earthward. Like an out-of-focus photograph, the hills and valleys were turning white from the hail, as if in answer to the darkness behind.

Then the rain came as expected, sparsely at first in huge drops, then all at once. The downpour gave way to more hail that pounded the far hills. The incessant noise was eclipsed by another flash and thunderclap almost simultaneously—a hundred yards away, Sam estimated. The wind must have felt it appropriate to accelerate its presence at this time, apparently just for the hell of it, and blew Sam's cap off, far enough away to kill any thought of retrieval. Their attention needing no more prodding, they continued up and into the mine.

Sam and Charles dismounted and led their horses into the entrance, which, though shallow, had originally been excavated high and large enough to act as a storage facility. It involved a clever set of wooden beams and posts, and while expensive to construct, it saved labor and material costs of having to build an additional stand-alone structure outside. It also made for a great shelter in cases like this.

"Get your saddle off and tie him up to the post over there."

Charles took off his hat, slapped the water across his duster, and began unloading the pack mule. Scooter shook and sprayed water over everything before retreating to a back corner and lying down on a bare rock, his duty for the day complete.

Charles got out the dog food bowl, filled it, and set it by the dog, who gladly accepted the offering, probably considering it Charles's way of making amends.

Sam was soaked. He had no boot-length duster like Charles, and now no cap, whatever good that would have done.

"You look like Scooter—a wet dog," Charles said sarcastically. "And where's your hat?"

"It blew off. Yeah, never mind," Sam said as he pulled out some dry clothes from his pack from the mule. "I thought you said it wasn't going to rain."

"That was yesterday. Not responsible for today." Charles stood at the entrance and leaned his forearm against an overhead beam. "Look at that storm. Isn't that great! It should blow over in a little while."

This was no winter storm, but more of an early summer storm, the type that tended toward high drama but with little lasting effect. Safe within the mine entrance, they settled down to watch the passing spectacle.

Charles brought out his Primus stove and set out to make coffee. Sam laid his saddle on the ground against a side timber and stretched out with the contentment of one in a totally secure and comfortable environment only a few feet from chaos.

The rain stopped as predicted, and the sun began to peek around the fast-moving clouds. At a 6,800-foot elevation, the air was thin, and Sam could feel the difference. The shaft was situated below Stubborn Hill, the highest in the area. It had a commanding view of the surrounding landscape—all similar, endless, and but for the drama of this storm, barren. If ever an accurate description of "desolation" existed, this would have been it. Treeless, with only the occasional low-scrub brush to break the rocky monotony. The romance of the desert, with its endless expanses, shadowy corners, untrod peaks, and mystical canyons, was a fickle one. In a twinkling, it could feel hard and uncompromising—ugly even. Enchanting and scary all at once. Sam thought it was a perfect example of how natural surroundings and situations could affect a person's psychic nature, like when his own truck broke down.

Soon the sun was completely exposed, and it was warm again. The damp ground made the air humid, which in turn released the imprisoned scents of sage and other plants.

The brothers emerged from the mine. On the level section in front of the opening, a small oasis of greenery, including a seven-foot-tall mesquite bush, offered a bit of contrast to the surrounding terrain. When the original mine was dug, the tunnel became an easy conduit for an underground spring. This was a critical factor that allowed the mine to be worked in the first place. Without it, mining would have been impossible, as precious water would have had to be transported in.

The spring could be traced trickling from a trench inside the mine, and in turn, flowed outside. From there, an old iron pipe had been jerry-rigged to allow water to run to a nearby cistern for human use, then to a trough further down for horses and mules, then to disappear into the surrounding rocks to resurface at the pond.

There were remnants of wooden buildings about the entrance. Built well over a hundred years ago, most had long since collapsed. All that was left were a loose jumble of weathered, nail-protruding boards and twisted corrugated steel that had once been siding and roofing. It was much like the mine Sam had encountered a few days earlier, only more of it, and with obvious signs of a larger operation.

The original shacks looked to have been hastily built, not for comfort but for work. They were meant for storing explosives, tools, and other items. The remains of a bunkhouse, with its cast-iron stove half-buried beneath broken floorboards, indicated that little looting had occurred. A one-stamp mill leaned precariously on the level portion of one section—actually the tailings—along with a monster steel pulley wheel from a long-since disassembled and removed steam engine used to power it. This and other various mining articles indicated that this operation, though small, was at one time considered important enough to haul all this material to.

As for the mine itself, since the rock was structurally sound, little interior framework was needed. But the unusually large entrance did require some complex bracing to keep the overhanging hill from collapsing. The overhead entrance still had faded lettering gouged into the lintel: the initials NE. It was another play on the JE initials, this time for "not enough."

"Come on," Charles said. "Let's go back in."

"I need to tell you something, Chuck," Sam said as they started walking back through the entrance.

"Sure," Charles said, wary of Sam's tone, and went back to the far side of the room. He shooed Scooter off his perch, sat, and allowed time for Sam to speak.

"Well, it's not that big a deal. But you know that I decided to camp out for one night, and that I had car trouble. But it was more dramatic than that. I told you that a rock or something had put a gash in the oil pan. What I didn't tell you was that I was camped far off the main road at the time, about eight miles off the highway, ten or so miles out of Austin. It was an adventure, to be sure; it's why I was a couple days late getting here."

Charles said nothing, sensing that Sam needed to get something off his chest.

"Anyway, I had to hoof it to the main road. That was midmorning. I packed up what I needed: water, food, clothing, and started back toward the highway. Well, I came across this mine that was off another side path, and like an idiot, I went into it. You know me, chicken explorer extraordinaire. Well, it was spooky in there by myself, and then I found this grave . . ."

"Grave? Inside a mine? That's not legal."

"Yeah. Well, I don't think they worried about that. I know some mines become graves just from cave-ins, but this seemed on purpose. After going in a ways, I found a passageway that seemed too short and narrow for mining. I followed it to a circular room, then sat on a rock at the end of it and noticed some peculiar stuff, like footprints around the center, then bones sticking out of the ground. One bone I dug out looked human. Then I caught a glimpse of the stone as I hurried out. It had an inscription on it. That's when I realized it had to be a grave, and that's when I flipped out.

"I panicked and shot out of there, thinking that there was someone, or something, chasing me. I got out, but I was pretty freaked. Then, when I continued my walk, I ran into this fork in the road and, Chuck, I was never so scared in my life. I had to decide which one to take. The wrong one could have been bad. I made the right one, of course, but I felt sick to my stomach, all that time thinking I had made a wrong turn, until I finally hit the highway. My anxiety almost stopped me in my tracks. I couldn't think like a rational human being. I was all fear. Have you ever felt that? I mean that you couldn't think clearly just because your mind wants to screw with you? I don't know. My sense of judgment isn't so good sometimes."

"Well, don't be so hard on yourself," Charles said as he got up and pretended to inspect the rock wall. "You and I have done some pretty stupid things that could have turned out badly, and we survived. But I know what you mean. Frankly, I don't like being in here myself. Does this mine scare you?"

"Oh, no. It wasn't so much the mine that got to me. Mostly, as I think about it now, it was being alone. About as alone as anyone could ever be, in a far-off portion of an obscure mine no one's been to in seventy years. No one would have found me. I should have called ahead of time to tell you where I would be. Dumb. But, well, this mine I'm familiar with. Mostly it's just that I'm not alone. Family and familiarity, all the comforts of home."

"Hmm. I see what you mean about the 'being alone' part. How'd you get back and all?"

"Once I hit the road, I knew everything would be all right. Had to wait about an hour for a truck going to Austin. Got a room, showered, and shaved. Ate at a restaurant, watched TV. Next morning, I got a tow truck. Apparently, the driver was used to situations like this. City slickers getting stuck out where they had no business being. Took all morning to get it towed back, but fortunately, they found the right oil pan and skid plate from a wrecker's yard. Wasn't cheap, of course, but I didn't care. It could have been worse—much worse."

"Maybe I should show you something that might cheer you up. Let's go a little farther in. Come on, Scooter."

Once beyond the entrance, the narrow main shaft began. It was cool, dark, and quiet but for their own muted and slightly echoing footsteps. They walked hunched over for several hundred feet. The opening behind them closed like the iris of a camera, leaving the walls and any distinctive features impossible to make out. Their jerky flashlight movements sending light and shadows skipping along the walls only added to the schizophrenic feeling.

"It's changed a little since you and I used to play here," Charles said.

"Against our parents' strict rules, by the way."

"Well, isn't that what made it all the more fun? It's a dangerous place, no lie. We could have died several times in here."

They came to the main Y that led at equal angles left and right from the main route. The right was the shortest, Sam remembered. It was the section dug first, the original miners believing it to have the best possibilities. But the scant leads turned out to be false, and the section was eventually abandoned. The left branch led to more branches and shafts. These were the sections that yielded what little profit the mine doled out.

"Let's go this way," Charles said.

Sam was surprised when he veered right. They went a good hundred feet more before they came to a side tunnel Sam didn't remember. Nailed to one of the timbers was a faded playing card, possibly the ace of clubs. More hardship humor. Further on, they came to a large room, this one big enough to require a few timbers. Another side passage led off in a different direction.

"I don't remember this at all," Sam said.

"You shouldn't. What you're seeing has been excavated in the last twenty-five years. You know that to keep our claim on the mine, we have to show that it's being worked a couple weeks every year. You and I worked a little on it when we were young. Dave, Henry, and I have been at it off and on since. We only do it when we can afford the time. Mining is a big gamble with the stakes against us, so we don't take it seriously. We made an agreement that it would only be worked as much as we had time for. We did find some decent ore, but certainly not enough to pay for the labor we put into it. I could have made more flipping burgers. That's the kind of reality we keep ourselves tuned to. Henry'd hand me a shiny quartz rock and say, 'Want fries with that?' It kept us grounded. But there's always that hope of finding that payoff ledge."

"But I haven't seen any evidence of any recent work, and the road's nearly washed out."

"It's been a couple years since we moved any rock. We phony'd up a nonexistent work party last year. Have to do the same again, but we can't keep that up. Anyway, the small amount of ore that assays well is taken to the big mining operation at Sulfur, and they do the processing. We almost broke even a couple of years ago. But who knows? All we need is to find a decent lode, then lease the rights to someone else and let them do the work."

"Really? You think that could happen?"

"No, not really," Charles said with a snicker. "I know the odds are against us, but mostly, I think it provides a needed break from ranch work."

Sam heard a sound, a low moan emanating from the last tunnel on the left. His imagination impulsively attributed it to Scooter, who was continually underfoot, but then he realized it was merely the air differential flowing between the shafts. Eerie and unsettling, it renewed that sense of uncertainty, and for Sam, a bit of irrational fear. His uneasiness seemed to infect Charles the same way.

"I think that last mine you were in carried over to this one," Charles said. "Now you got me spooked. I never felt comfortable in here anyway. I let the others do the hard rock mining. I worked mostly outside."

"What do you suppose it is that makes us fear things we know don't exist?" Sam asked over his shoulder as the two started on their way back toward the entrance.

"Don't rightly know. I don't try to figure those things out. I just take it as it comes. It doesn't do me any good to sit and ponder such stuff. I figure I'll never find out, anyway."

Sam went over and sat down on some drilling machinery. Charles followed, crouching near a jackhammer and some piping.

"Talk about perceptions—despite our fears about being in here, this mine is actually safer than being in a house. We may be under tons of rock, but then again, it has been this way for, what, over a hundred years? Why would it decide to collapse now? Because we're here? Seems like a lot of our fears come from things that don't exist."

"You're right. I guess we are safe in here."

Sam rose to leave, momentarily shining the light away from where Charles had gotten up. A second later, he heard a dull snap behind him and a sound like a heavy sack hitting the ground. Then a moan. Then the words,

"Ah. Shit. Shit! Ankle!"

Charles was down, in pain and quivering. His left foot was stuck under a horizontal pipe running only inches off the ground. The foot was not going to give, so Charles's ankle did, and badly. Lodged under the pipe at an awkward angle, it would not allow his foot to get free.

"Okay, okay, let me check," Sam said, rushing over. "Now look. I'm going to have to get you twisted back so I can pull your foot out. All right?"

Sam wasn't sure his brother had heard him through the pain. All he could do was to try to lift and twist to pull Charles free. At over two hundred pounds, it was going to be a problem, but Sam didn't have time to think it out. He lifted and twisted as best he could. Charles screamed, but Sam was able to free him.

"Damn! Man, oh, man, oh, man, I think it's broken!"

There was no doubt about that, twisted as it was into an unnatural position. Sam didn't want to touch anything, but he had to check it out. After getting Charles on his back, he pulled at Charles's pant leg and sock as gently as he could. The foot was crooked, all right, and he screamed when Sam lifted it. No bones were protruding, but Sam knew that it might be more than a fractured ankle—maybe a torn ligament or internal bleeding.

He had to figure out what to do to help him. The quickest would be for Charles to somehow ride his horse down, which he claimed he could do, but Sam knew he was in no condition for it, that the jarring would throw Charles into fits, and he certainly couldn't set his bones for a trip like that. All Sam could think of was to ride down and get help. Sally had assumed that they would spend one more night out, so Sam was going to have to leave.

"All right, but take SOB. He's the faster horse. Just leave me the water and stuff."

"I thought only you could ride that spirited steed," Sam said.

"Bullshit. Of course, you can. He won't be a problem."

"It's three o'clock now. It's going to take some hours to get down, then someone has to come back up for you. It may be a while."

"I know how far it is. Just get moving."

Sam set him up as best he could. It was cool in the mine, but it would remain constant throughout the night, so that with his coat, blanket, food, water, an ice pack for his ankle, and other provisions Sam brought back from the entrance, Charles would survive well enough. Sam set out some bedding for the dog, hoping Scooter would stay with his brother and serve as something Charles could swear at. Sam left him both flashlights, so he had to feel his way out.

"So much for being in a safe place," Charles said as Sam was leaving. "I think we should have listened to our parents."

With only three or four hours of light left, Sam would have to hurry, but not so fast that the rocks and ruts would put the horse, or him, in danger.

Horse and rider pushed their way down the hill. Sam began making mental notes about how a vehicle coming up the road could get over the narrow sections, and thought that most could be traversed without much trouble.

After a while, his anxiety subsided. He had it pretty well worked out in his mind. First, call an ambulance and get it as close to the mine as possible. Get as many men as possible in the shortest amount of time. One, maybe two good four-wheelers. Get shovels, picks, flashlights, water, whatever; drive up ahead and backfill any low spot and move on.

It was going to be a long night.

It was dusk by the time Sam passed over the last ridge and caught sight of lights at the ranch, and he let Charles's horse move at his own fast clip down the last section of road.

He could see movement at the back door. It had to be Sally. He saw her pause for an instant, then race back inside. She came out again holding what looked like a remote phone. She looked one more time, then started dialing. She must have figured one lone rider coming back this fast was bad news, and she didn't waste any time.

~ ~ ~

Sam's plan worked well enough. With Dave and Henry and one other neighboring rancher in one Jeep, they were able to clear much of the road for the ambulance, which was able to get to within a quarter mile from the mine. Charles was looked over, given pain meds, and his ankle restrained. They carried him by stretcher to the waiting ambulance and got him to the hospital that morning.

Broken ankle and a pulled tendon. After three days, Charles was allowed home, but more surgeries and physical therapies would be needed for quite a while, meaning that Charles would be on his back, then in a wheelchair, then on crutches for some time.

Sam's prognostication about being needed at the ranch, at least for the time being, had come true. The ranch was going to need another willing hand, and it wasn't hard to imagine all eyes leveled at him. He knew the ropes here, and he was still fairly fit. Ever since he arrived, he had felt the ranch's gravitational force. Now with Charles out of circulation, he was getting in even deeper. He wasn't without resolve and could stand up for himself and say no if he needed to. Then he thought: *Maybe I made my decision before I left St. Louis.*

6
The Gathering Storm

It had been over three months since the accident, and the diagnosis was not as devastating as first thought. The bones would fuse and heal, but the tendon would take longer and would probably always give Charles problems. The good news was that he could use crutches at times instead of being in a wheelchair. That proved a great relief to Charles's pride.

Sam, Sally, and Charles were sitting on the back porch, soaking in the morning sun.

"I thought you said this ranching business was hard," Sam joked before leaning back in his Adirondack chair, sipping coffee.

Charles's and Sally's dagger stares caused him to modify that a bit.

"Okay, maybe sitting here makes me forget the work I've planned for today."

"That's better," Charles said.

"While you guys are planning your weekend workload," Sally said, "I'm going to Audrey's for our monthly quilting bee."

"Are you wives still using that excuse for your wild parties?" Charles asked. "Still haven't seen any sign of a quilt." He turned to Sam. "Us menfolk have always had our doubts about this quilting business. None of us have seen any sign of it, not that they don't give us plenty of excuses for its absence. Depending on who you ask, you'll get a different story each time. It's either really big or very small. It's in bright colors or plain hues. Then they claim that it was misplaced or at someone else's home when they get together. But it never seems a reason to abandon their meetings, or keeps them from having a good time. Isn't that right, Sally?"

"You boys just have no faith." Sally snickered as she got up and started to walk away. "I'll try to get back before Robin arrives."

"Robin's coming by? Good, haven't seen her for a while," Charles said.

"I just found out myself this morning," Sally said over her shoulder. "We'll have her stay the weekend. Certainly wouldn't want her to drive all the way back to Sacramento tonight."

Sam had seen Robin and Dan several times when they came to see Charles in the hospital, and then when they helped him get settled at the ranch. But he didn't have much of a chance to talk with either of them other than about his brother's condition. Then they had to go right back to their own lives.

"When the dust settles a bit, I would like to get to know them better," Sam said to Charles.

"Don't know if the dust ever settles in the lives of young people. Robin has her own busy workload, and Dan is always absorbed with his real estate business. But you'll get your chance." Charles sighed as he adjusted his position in his chair.

For a while, both sat in silence, then Sam got up. "Time to do some work."

"Don't go too far," Charles said. "I'm expecting some people to come by. Developers' agents, as a matter of fact. They called me yesterday, and I told them they could come by. Actually, they've been hounding me for a meeting for some time, and now that you're here, I want your take on it. It's just a preliminary meeting, and I want to see how interested they really are."

"You're not really thinking of selling out, are you? Don't you think you should have told me about this earlier?"

"Sorry. I'm so used to Sally and me making all the decisions around here. No, I wouldn't ever want to sell, but information is always a good thing. Mostly I want to get a gauge on how serious they are. Even if we keep the spread, development will affect us as well. Water concerns, encroachment issues, what have you. But there may be another option that I won't go into now, and now with you here, I thought this would be the right place and time."

"Shouldn't Sally be here when they come?"

"She knew about it, but left it up to me, and you for that matter, to hear what they have to say."

"Sometimes I forget myself and my interest as a very silent partner. You think our parents gave me one-third interest for a reason?"

"Who knows? Maybe it was a way to entice you to return."

After completing a few morning tasks—feeding the horses, general cleanup of the stalls, and discussing some things with Dave—Sam took a break and went back to the porch.

Charles seemed distracted as he stared down the road. "Here they come!"

Sam could see a car coming up the road, trailing a line of dust that engulfed a second following close behind. Obviously not used to traveling on dirt roads, they were approaching the ranch at a pretty good clip.

Dave had come over when he saw the cars coming and cracked, "That car behind ought to turn its lights on so he can see ahead and not run into the first one."

"That wouldn't do any good." Charles laughed. "Maybe turn on the wipers. Now if we're patient enough, maybe one of them will run into the ditch."

"They're going fast enough. They look like pretty fancy SUVs. At least the first one does. Can't tell about the second one. It's got enough of our dirt to plow a corn row. I'm going back to check the horses. See you later." With that, Dave trotted back up to the stable, most likely knowing—and not wanting to know—what was coming.

The cars pulled up to the back of the house. A man from the first car got out and waited for the second to arrive. Sam saw a set of golf clubs in the back seat. Apparently they had more important things on their minds. When the second car pulled in behind the first, Charles had to turn around to avoid revealing his smirk.

88

In what must have been an attempt to get fresh air, the second driver had opened the air vent. He and his passenger were coated with dust. Just opening their doors caused a flume of brown fog to exit the vehicle. It was everywhere, inside and out, the occupants dusting themselves off and coughing. Dave, visible up at the barn behind them, pointed and laughed. That didn't help Sam try to keep a straight face.

"Now, Sam," Charles whispered before they got within earshot, "let me do the talking. I just want to find out what they want."

"Charlie Ellis!" the first man said with a little too much familiarity. "How have you been? Heard you broke your leg."

Charles pulled himself out of his chair and onto his crutches. "Just my ankle, McLaughlin. It's no big deal. Hey, that car on fire?"

"Just a little dust, I suppose," McLaughlin said as he looked sheepishly behind him. "I hope I didn't catch you at a bad time."

By design, in order to keep these people at arm's length, Charles did not introduce Sam to them.

"Hi," the visitor said uneasily as he turned toward Sam and extended his hand. "You must be Charlie's brother. Reginald McLaughlin here— Rege—and that's Bill and Leland from the other car."

"I'm Sam, I am," Sam said with a straight face.

"Yes, uh, well, ha! I like that, yeah…" Rege didn't seem sure about whether Sam was kidding, or whether he should laugh or risk feeling foolish, so he took a fumbling middle course.

Sam could already see through his casual banter, and sensed Charles could as well.

"Come up on the porch and sit," Charles said, sitting back down himself.

The others found and sat in various chairs that lay about. Sam sat a little behind Charles, intending to be the observer. He already had an inkling of what was to come, and he had no intention of giving himself away. *Let them wonder.* Would he help or hinder their efforts? They must know that his name was on the deed, but as to how much influence he could have, *Let them worry. None of their damn business.* Already he was taking sides. Already he didn't like them, even if they put on a good show.

They were dressed neatly but casually, sweaters over buttoned-down shirts. Talk began casually, too. If Sam hadn't been so suspicious, he might have been taken in by their good humor and easy manner. They possessed none of the outward attributes of the cunning salesmen. Of course, that made for a good one. By quashing a prejudice, by making your mark think that you're not the stereotype like all the others, it tended to loosen others up and put them at a disadvantage. They had already seen part of Charles's hand just by his willingness to listen. Somewhere in Charles's stubborn facade was a crack, ready to be exploited. A good salesman would know where to look and how to pry.

Some would call it unethical, but this buy-and-sell game was the nature of the beast. They were all about to engage in a bob-and-weave business with offensive and defensive maneuvering, and all to gain an advantage. But then again, even if Charles despised its methods, he was about to do it himself.

The initial bantering over, Rege eased into the purpose of the visit: determining how much the property would be worth if Charles was interested in selling it. No hard numbers yet, of course. Just talking. But if he did sell, he could buy property anywhere and never have to work again. Swimming pool if he liked, sit on the porch all day if he wanted.

Charles let them know that he was already sitting on the porch. Good laugh. Okay. The occasional glance in Sam's direction, looking for some sign so they could get their bearings and set a course. Sam gave them none.

Sam, having had some experience with realtors when he and Helen bought and sold their own homes back east, and having been burned one time, was not unfamiliar with the give-and-take game.

The salesmen, also not new at the game, kept adjusting and probing, being careful not to display any sense of eagerness or greediness. Only once, just once, did Sam see the indignation born of frustration, but they pulled back the reins in time.

Professionals, Sam thought.

"A rancher over in Story County sold his property for a lot of money, and this place is far superior. Just thought we'd let you know."

Now the push. (*Hurry, sale ends Saturday.*) It was a ruse designed to raise the adrenaline and cause a slight panic with the turn of the screw. Would Charles falter?

"Recession may be right around the corner," Rege said before turning to his colleague. "What about these new restrictions coming up, Bill?" He then turned back to Charles. "Bill knows all about them. Communities are starting to clamp down on unlimited development. May not be able to sell later on, especially when you might need to. But who knows, huh? None of us has a crystal ball, do we? Great view you have here, right, Leland? I'd probably buy the place myself—if I could afford it—ha-ha."

Rege then lowered his head and voice, leaned toward Charles, and adopted a serious tone. It was to be a confidential conversation meant only for the privileged few, and Rege had singled Charles out to accompany him into that rarefied atmosphere.

"But even in today's market, one farmer took a big hit last year," he said, again looking over to his partners, "and had to sell off everything just to pay his debts. Got next to nothing for the land because they knew he had to sell. How's your water rights? May not have an aquifer in a few years. Reno's just sucking it up, sucking up its whole future till there won't be any more water, period. Then what? This whole place goes to hell." Finally, he turned to Sam. "What do you think, Sam?"

Sam shrugged. "I'm just visiting."

The wall held against the baiting. Sam could act like a professional, too. The salesmen, just by being here, were out of their element. Like a wild animal displaced from its territory, they were disarmed and uncomfortable and could not function effectively in these surroundings. To Sam, they looked almost pathetic in their vulnerability.

"Well, we gotta be going," Rege offered abruptly, beginning to rise. "Certainly appreciate being able to talk things over. Think about it. I know it's a big decision. I'd have trouble making it myself. But we all have to think about the future, and the future of our loved ones."

The best-aimed volley saved for last. At that, a chink appeared, but only slightly, in Charles's face. It was a weakness Rege sensed at once. He was ready to pounce. Sam pounced first.

"Is that Jeep Cherokee new? I hear they have suspension problems. How's yours running?"

"Huh? Oh, yeah, no, it's all right. Bought it last year."

"Well, take it easy going back down. You might have a tendency to skid on that road." Sam walked them over to their cars, not letting them back in the game. And so they left.

"You should have offered them something to drink, Sam," Charles said as they watched the two cars speed down the road.

"I suppose," Sam said dryly. "I could have offered to hose them down. It would have been more entertaining."

Charles looked over at Sam with a smirk. They had survived the test. With a common adversary, each felt just a bit closer to the other.

"I don't think they'll be too pushy for a while," Charles said. "But I think they found their target with that last statement. My God, throw a guilt trip, why don't they?"

"I think you did give a little bit away there."

"Did I? Maybe so. They can smell fear." Charles shrugged. "Well, I can't hide it all that well. That's the stick they'll use from now on, but they certainly offer an attractive carrot. Sometimes that's better than a stick. But they're just city people; they sit inside their air-conditioned offices and are as contemptuous of those of us who work with our hands as we are of them for being soft and incapable of dealing with the real world. There's a big difference there, but it's harmless enough. It just provides a certain amount of self-importance we all look for."

"That's pretty deep, but I get what you're saying. We see them as dishonest and conniving, and may dislike their methods, but it's inherent to their job. But you know, we're using the same tactics ourselves in countering them. Maybe the best course is to just be aware of it and not let it get personal."

"Maybe I think about all this because Dan's a realtor—and a salesman himself. But he's mostly residential and not as pushy as big-time developers."

"Is he doing okay? Does he talk to you about his work?"

"Not much, but I do worry about him. He doesn't seem to have the gift for gab. He showed no interest in ranching, and I wonder if he chose his profession just to get away from this one."

"What does he think about this?"

"We don't talk about that either. I don't bring it up because I don't think it would be good for him to be involved." As Charles said this, a slight furrow in his brow appeared, as though he had just thought of something.

"Well, you're doing okay here, aren't you?" Sam said. "I mean, you don't have too much debt or anything?"

"No, we get by. We can continue well enough. Hell, this place has been through all kinds of hardships: depressions, recessions, and inflations that should have wiped us out, but didn't. But like I said, my ticker ain't going to last forever. Then what? Who takes over?" Looking off in the distance, Charles added, "I wish there were no choices. Then we could let life just go on the way it's supposed to. Now I'm forced into making a decision. And just doing nothing is making a decision. If we were forced out by one thing or another, that's different. No doubt or guilt. You just do what you have to. In this case, I'm hounded by choices, neither of which would let me sleep thinking about the other. I'm not usually affected this way, but this does bother me. Those guys are definitely serious, but you know, like I said before, we might have another alternative."

Sam raised his eyebrows. "You hinted at that before; think you might let me in on it?"

"I will, but I don't want to get into it until I have more information. And by the way, Sally and I have always appreciated that you never tried to interfere with our operation, even with your interest..."

Just then, Dave came over, waving his hand in front of his face with an alarmed look. "I thought we unloaded all the stuff from your outing months ago, but I just found a daypack over in the corner, and when I opened it, I just about fell over. It reeked!"

Charles looked at Sam. "Good God, those fish we caught!"

7
Reunion

At four thirty, another car came up the drive. An older Mazda this time. Charles stared, then after gesturing to Sam, hobbled over to him.

"Robin. Wasn't expecting her for a while."

Sam had seen Robin for the first time at the hospital, then many times after when she came by to help her mother during Charles's recovery. It was an attractive, brightly clothed woman he saw exiting the car, one who had a smile for her dad and uncle.

"How's your foot, Dad?" she said while walking up onto the porch. "You okay?"

"Yeah, I'm fine, honey. Hey! You got your hair cut. Did you dye it?" he said as he feigned an alarmed expression.

"It's called a perm, Dad. And you never ask a woman if she dyes her hair," she said as she patted her short, reddish curls.

Sam rolled his eyes at the two of them.

"Hi again, Uncle Sam!" she grinned. "I love saying that. Mom said you might be staying a little longer."

"Hi, Robin. Have to get your dad back on his feet, don't I?"

"Wait a minute. I have to get Hazel out." After an unsure back-and-forth check between the car and Sam, she decided first on a quick hug to Sam, then back to the car to retrieve her one-and-a-half-year-old daughter.

"I didn't know you were planning to move back here," Charles said as he eyed all the paraphernalia Robin was removing from the car.

"Most of that is just Hazel's stuff, Dad. She needs more things than any three people, I tell you," she said, walking up to the screen door with her daughter on one arm.

To Sam, it was obvious that Charles was delighted to see her. Sam hoisted Robin's small luggage and Hazel's equipment, and the two followed her into the kitchen. She got out the high chair and put her daughter in. "I've got to feed Hazel, then get her upstairs for her nap—where's Mom?"

"Your mom's with her drinking friends."

"What? Oh, Dad, you mean her quilting group. Boy, what a drive! I got off work early, and would've been here even sooner but there was an accident outside Truckee. Had to wait an hour to get through." She reached into one of the many bags she brought and pulled out a cracker. "Here, honey, have this," she said to her daughter. "This will hold her till I get her meal started—now don't start with that. It's good." She turned to Sam. "She's tired and cranky. Didn't nap at all in the car. She gets so impossible sometimes."

"You're your mom's daughter, that's for sure," Charles said.

~ ~ ~

When Sally came home, it was obvious that she, too, was glad to see her daughter. They chatted a bit together as they prepared Hazel's snack of crackers, cheese, and apples. When Sam went to grab one of the cheese slices, Sally playfully swatted his hand away. "Now you wait Sam, we adults will eat soon enough." Then relenting a bit, she nodded to a pitcher on the counter. "Go pour all of us a glass of iced tea, would you?" Sam happily obliged just as Charles shuffled in from outside and noisily made his way to a seat at the kitchen table.

From observing the interplay between Robin and Sally, Sam would never have guessed their contentious history. But while Robin had obviously come into her maturity, Sally went right into the questions.

"So how is your job with the insurance company? You doing okay there?"

Sally asked this in a seemingly casual way, but to Sam, it felt like she was trying to suppress a nagging tone in her voice. He surmised that behind that simple question lay deeper meddlesome messages, such as: "You don't get paid enough," "They're taking advantage of you," and, "Maybe you should quit and find a better job."

She was still Robin's mother, after all.

Robin seemed aware of it too. "Yes, Mom," she answered, sounding a bit exasperated as they had a chance to sit down at the kitchen table. "I'm doing fine." And in answer to another unasked question, she said, "The other couple and single mother I'm renting the house with are all responsible people, Mom." She then turned to Sam. "Because the rents are so high, we all live together. Even then, it's hard to make ends meet." Then, turning back to her mother, she added, "We're all working, and we take care of each other when we have to. No more parties. I'm too tired after work, anyway. Plus, I have to take care of Hazel after daycare. And no more men," she emphasized. "At least for now."

"Maybe you should take some computer classes so you can get ahead."

Sam hadn't thought of that one.

Robin smiled a little. "Computers are all I work with, Mom. I could teach a class myself."

Verbal communication within families could be aggravating, especially when arguments over words were really arguments beyond words. Sam sensed that tension was brewing, so after taking a sip of his iced tea, he intervened.

"So, Sally, I didn't get a chance to ask you: how's the quilt coming?"

"Oh! Well, bigger and better every time, Sam." This was her standard answer.

"There's some talk that this quilt doesn't even exist, that it's used only as an excuse for your wild parties."

"Oh, now Sam, of course it exists. Just because it gets misplaced once in a while doesn't mean we're making it up out of whole cloth. Hey! That's funny. Now of course for you, since you haven't seen it, it exists only in your mind, so it's quite reasonable to expect you to have doubts about it. After all, the mind is a complicated thing. I mean, imagining a quilt and then doubting whether it exists at all. Heavens! Quite puzzling when you think about it. But I quite understand, I really do, so it isn't something you should be ashamed about. Just because your mind plays tricks on you doesn't mean you're crazy. I certainly don't—think you're crazy, that is. So we'll just keep it between ourselves."

"She's got you there, Sam," Charles cracked, not bothering to peek over his paper.

Just then, Dan and his wife, Laura, pulled up.

"Jeez, I guess the whole family's here," Charles declared.

"I forgot to tell you they were coming. Laura was able to get off early, and Dan freed himself from afternoon meetings so they could both be here. I asked them to come because there's something us girls want to go over with you guys," Sally said as all of them started to go outside to greet them.

Having come straight from their jobs, Dan and Laura were neatly dressed; Dan was clad in a business jacket and tie, while Laura sported a stylish outfit from her bank job.

The group assembled back in the kitchen, and multiple conversations started at once. "Why don't you guys go outside while we plan the meal?" Sally said.

"I need to go out and talk to Dave anyway," Charles said as he started for the door.

This left Sam and Dan free to talk. Ready to swap out his iced tea for something stronger, Sam opened the fridge, pulled out a couple of beers, and handed one to Dan. "Let's get away from this noise."

They walked outside and sat on the porch.

Dan was a handsome lad, and to Sam, seemed self-assured. Of course, that was a necessity in his profession.

"You're almost as tall as your father, Dan, just not as thick."

"I do watch my weight, but not so much my height," Dan joked. "I'm sorry we didn't have much time to talk at the hospital. Sally said that you might be staying longer."

"For a while, at least until your father recovers."

Sam then shifted course to talk about what was on his mind. "It's been a long time since I was here. I can't believe all the development going on. Used to drive straight through Pyramid without a single stoplight. Now there's a dozen of them."

"Even I'm shocked by it sometimes. One year, there's a wide-open field, the next, a full housing development."

"Well, you're certainly in the right business now. You doing all right?"

"I don't get involved with the big developments. I work mostly in residential home sales in some of the older areas. But, yeah, we're doing well enough. It keeps me busy."

Given what Charles had said about how rarely they talked to each other about the wholesale development in the area, Sam assumed that Charles wouldn't want Dan to know about the representatives who had come by that morning. Because it might only complicate things, Sam decided to just keep the conversation of development general, and hoped that Dan might reveal his own thoughts on the subject.

"Do you think developers would ever be interested in going much further north?" Sam asked.

"I really don't know how far they can go. It's possible, I suppose."

Sam was perplexed. *He must know more than he's letting on.* Maybe he was just being cautious. Sam sensed that he wasn't going to get much more from him and decided to drop the issue.

The awkward conversation lull was interrupted when they saw Charles hobbling toward them on his crutches. "Be nice to be rid of these damn things," he said as he ambled onto the porch.

"You may need them for a while, Dad."

"What are you guys doing out here? Oh, the women are in there! Well, we can't put it off any longer. Let's go in."

The brothers went and sat at the table and Dan stood next to Laura.

"So here's the plan, guys," Sally said. "I called the Hess's, and they said that weekend after next we could have the use of their Tahoe cabins at Zephyr Cove, and Laura, Robin, and I have agreed that we should take advantage of it." Looking over at Laura, she added, "I think the whole family should go since we are seldom able to get everyone together at the same time."

Laura nodded.

The family had been going to the same two Tahoe cabins for as long as anyone could remember. There were photos of Charles and Sam there from when they were mere babes on the beach. The cabins had been built in the early 1900s by a couple who had become friends with Sam and Charles's parents. After boating around the lake, the Hess's had had their choice of almost any spot to build a summer home. Constructed from the surrounding boulders and local timber, the main cabin (they had also built a small log cabin behind it) would become the smallest and yet the most attractive of all the houses on the beach. Surrounded now by million-dollar palaces, this place still shamed them all with its simplicity and homey-ness. It seemed to be the only structure people would bother to stop for and photograph.

Sally knew that despite her cheerful, optimistic proposal, the one person who would balk at the plan was Charles, who would probably groan and find excuses not to go—anything to avoid disturbing his secure position as sole proprietor of his personal recliner.

Sally was prepared to argue the point, but with as much enthusiasm as Charles could muster, he looked up and grunted in the affirmative.

Sally looked a little taken aback. Primed to counter his objections, she was a fully loaded weapon with nothing to aim at.

"Well…I guess that's settled," she said, sounding unprepared to use her energies in organizing the trip itself. "Robin, do you think David's son Henry would like to come along if his father's willing to stay here?"

"I don't see why not," Robin said, "but I think he felt out of place the last time he went with us."

"That's true. I would like him to feel less guarded around us. Could you ask him, Robin? Maybe he would feel more at ease if you had something for him to do. That way he would feel more a part of the process."

"Good idea. I'll think of something."

The mention of the ranch hand's son prompted Sam to say, "Henry seems like a real nice kid—wasn't he involved in a big accident some time ago, Sally? I remember Helen saying something about it."

"He sure was," Sally remarked with concern in her voice. "Some drunk kids, three of them, went over the divider on South Virginia and hit Henry head-on. One of them died, a girl, and the others were hurt pretty bad. Henry was alone. He smashed his head on the wheel and broke his arm, but the sheer mass of his pickup kept him from being killed—I think it's affected him ever since. I helped nurse him because he had no mother to care for him, and I got to know just how sensitive a boy he was."

"Remember the time his mother dumped him off on Dave when he was twelve?" Charles said. Then, turning to Sam, he continued, "She told Dave in no uncertain terms that it was his turn to shoulder the load. So Henry lived here and helped his father while he went to high school."

"And after he graduated," Sally went on, "he shared an apartment with a couple of friends in Reno while he went to community college. But after he got his AA degree, he spent most of his time working here. I think the accident affected him, and this place, this ranch, is where he probably felt the most comfortable—and safe."

"He seems quiet and responsible," Sam said. "I notice he works well with everyone, including his father."

"They do work well together, though no one would guess their relationship," Sally said. "While they seem on friendly terms, their talk is limited to mundane matters like sports and such. I doubt if they've ever carried on a meaningful conversation."

"Maybe they don't need to," Sam said. "A person doesn't voluntarily stay in close contact with someone they don't want to."

"Maybe it's just that show of stubbornness so typical of *you men*." Sally laughed. "But I do wonder what he thinks concerning his own future. He never lets on about doing anything other than working here. I would never bring it up, and I certainly have no aversion to paying him whatever hours he wants to work. He's become a real asset."

Sam pondered a bit. "I wonder if *you women* really understand the process by which *we men* learn to protect ourselves, like, early on. Shame is always a great fear for boys, and that closed shell they—I guess I should say *we*—all envelop is a way of getting through years of humiliation. Early on, at least in our generation, boys were judged against certain masculine standards—good and bad—and the wall of toughness we build up stays with us the rest of our lives. Right, Charles?"

Charles looked up in annoyance. "Speak for yourself."

~ ~ ~

The next weekend, the Ellis family took two cars: Sam, Dan, Charles, and Henry squeezed into the Toyota, with the rest following. After descending Kingsbury Grade, they turned right onto the main road encircling the lake, then onto a narrow dirt road that led toward the shore and cabins.

Sam stepped out and exchanged smiles with Sally. Every sensory organ seemed to come alive as he acknowledged another resurrection of forgotten memories. Large pines towered over a carpet of fallen cones and needles, with the interplay of light and shadow giving depth to it all. A gentle, soft, cool breeze, more heard than felt, provided a backdrop of white noise as it moved through the overhead branches. Then there were the verdant aromas of pitch and dirt and plants, along with the smoke from the wood stoves wafting through it all.

While everyone was still gathered around the cars, Sally said, "We girls have decided that Charles and I, and Laura and Dan, will sleep in the two bedrooms of the main house, and Robin and Henry in the two rooms of the cabin out back. And Sam—I'm delighted to say that you've been chosen to sleep on the couch there."

"Delighted?" Sam laughed. "I'm thrilled!"

"Say, Henry," Robin said, "would you mind rustling up some needles and cones to start a fire in both cabins? Logs are in a crib behind the second cabin."

"Sure, Robin. I know where it is."

"I'll help you," Dan said to Henry.

While the others were unpacking and opening the cabins, Sam descended a hundred feet to the lake's edge. It was another world. Gentle sounds could be heard of pebbles washing over themselves from the chaotic waves lapping onto the shore. All was enhanced by the sharp, iridescent expanse of lake and the far-off, snow-covered mountains that seemed almost touchable in this elevated sanctuary.

Because of its great depth and coldness, these waters had at one time been some of the clearest in the world. But over the years, development and climate change had caused an imbalance in the lake's ecosystem, causing its clarity to diminish. Still, it retained most of its outward grandeur.

Sam decided to walk out on one of the wooden docks that jutted out from the lakeshore. These docks had been here ever since he was a child. At the end, Sam came to several boats tied to the pilings. Small waves caused the aluminum ones to bounce against the dock, producing low, booming sounds from their cavernous interiors. The effect was a chaotic pattern of noise, like a percussion ensemble in disorder. It was a good sound, and Sam sat down and leaned against a pier post, legs dangling over the water.

The warm sun and cool air was comforting. Looking down, the rippling water shimmered, creating a mesmerizing effect that made it hard to look away. He thought about how challenging it must have been for impressionists to capture the detached dancing of such ephemeral light and make it look real.

In the spring and fall, the weather around Tahoe was disarmingly gentle. Summers could be hot. Winters could also be gentle, though at other times, harsh. The Sierras had played home to some of the hardest winters ever recorded in the lower forty-eight states. Snowstorms could develop suddenly and unexpectedly and continue for days, immobilizing everything and everyone, like it did in 1846 when the Donner party made the fateful decision to try to make a late run over the high passes just west of Tahoe. But for Sam, just sitting here in comfort, the remnants of last year's own harsh winter seemed a distant reality, surrounded as he was by this drop-dead beauty displayed in every conceivable manner and form. It seemed unimaginable that it could ever be anything but thus.

Then a memory came to Sam—a disturbing one. It was to be the last time he and his brother went out on the waters together. It was as vivid to him as if it had been yesterday.

~~~

When Charles and Sam were young, daring adventurers (Sam being eleven or so and Charles in his mid-teens), they would sneak out in the early mornings and commandeer one of the small rowboats that some unwary owner had left unguarded at the pier. They rowed out and away from the shoreline and around the point, just in case its owner had an inkling to check on his possession, though at six in the morning, unlikely.

That was when the lake was at its quietest. Its glassy sheen gave the illusion that you could just step out and walk around. Rowing out, Sam liked looking into the depths at the boulders strewn below. It was like some giant had just thrown them about like a handful of marbles, a chaotic mass of rocks that continued up the shore and into the hills. Some were as big as houses, and floating over them, he could feel like he was flying. For the first ten feet of depth, the terrain below was as clear as the air above, every pebble and boulder so distinct that Sam felt as if he could just reach down and touch them.

Farther out on the lake, in the deeper waters, the hue on the surface was a darker blue-green, where objects below became indistinct and mysterious. Finally came the ledge—the jump beyond the middle depths where no bottom could be seen. That was where the lake began its plunge to its great and horrible abyss. There, the waters were an inky-blue, where its palpable coldness would penetrate the mind and shiver the body. Even the surface looked angry.

"Trout!" he said to Charles, looking down into the water. "Big one!"

"Where?"

"There! Must be two feet long."

Those ghostlike monsters would materialize out of seemingly nowhere and evaporate just as quickly. Sam always thought the big ones came from the deepest parts of the lake. No one knew what it was really like down there, which only made the lake all the more mysterious.

On that fateful day, Charles was rowing farther and farther out onto the lake, and Sam begged him to row back closer to shore. For some reason, Charles felt none of the fear Sam did. He felt freer. Away from shore, away from those who told him what to do, and away from the demands and responsibility that older children were expected to shoulder, he became more daring. In truth, he felt that it was an escape into danger with little risk, but because his little brother was scared, he took advantage of it. Out on this lake, if you made one slip-up, the danger was anything but trivial. At only a few degrees above freezing, these waters could send a person into deadly hypothermia in just a few minutes. Falling overboard was no joke.

Out a good quarter-mile, the early morning lengthened and a cold breeze came up, chopping the waters into little waves that caused the boat to rock wildly. The slapping noise of the water against the aluminum hull made it even more foreboding. Sam felt surrounded by danger, and this precarious contraption of a boat was the only thing keeping them alive. Sam used his oar to start rowing inward. Charles countered him by rowing out, forcing them to go in circles, and him laughing all the while.

"Cut it out!" Sam said as Charles slapped water on him with his oar.

"Don't be a sissy. Come on, let's see how far out we can go."

This panicked Sam, and he threatened to throw his oar over the side.

"I dare you," Charles said, laughing. Knowing that it was an empty threat, he stood up and started rocking the boat back and forth, mocking Sam by swinging his oar over his head. The more panic Sam showed, the more brazen Charles became.

"Hey, look, I'm going to throw my oar overboard!" Just then, it slipped out of his hands and went sailing over Sam's head and into the water. Sam instinctively jumped up in an attempt to grab it, causing the boat to lurch and Charles to go over the side.

They had been told stories of how people had drowned in these freezing waters. When Charles surfaced, his eyes were wide with shock. Sam knew there was no time to waste. Charles had to get out—fast. Neither of them had life preservers, but that wouldn't have mattered in any event.

Charles swam to the boat and clung to the side. At first, he tried to swing his leg over, but that just tipped the boat more precariously.

"Get over to the, oth...other side!" he stammered. The chill was getting to him.

Sam moved back as instructed. He was terrified. This boat was too small, and it tilted as Charles pulled on his side. As much as he tried, he couldn't swing his body over.

Sam tried pulling at his arm, but that only made it worse.

"Go to the back end of the boat," Sam said. He didn't think he could tip it as easily from that end. Charles, now blue and shivering, labored his way to the back. Sam had no choice but to get him out of the water. He couldn't just hang on while Sam tried to row to shore. It was too far.

The back end was now low in the water, but Charles still couldn't pull himself up. He was swallowing water and clearly losing strength. The look on Charles's face at his last effort would be forever etched in Sam's mind. At first, it was puzzled, then incredulous, and finally, one of pure vulnerability. It was the look, Sam thought later, of one seeing his own death. It was a pleading for Sam, his younger, inconsequential brother—his last hope—to do something.

Sam inched slowly toward him, trying not to destabilize the boat any more than it already was. Every movement was awkward with arms and legs trying to navigate across the bench seats with everything in the way. The waves seemed to be getting bigger, and Sam was getting shocked by the cold spray coming over the side. The front end of the boat was tipping too far up, but Sam figured he had to get Charles out no matter what.

With his arms over the side, Sam tugged on the back of Charles's shirt, which only brought up the shirt. With both his feet against the gunwale, he gripped his hands under his brother's arms, but that was only pulling Charles's chest harder against the back of the boat instead of up and over.

Sam looked around for something—anything that could help. There was a piece of plywood on the floor of the boat about two feet long that must have been used as some sort of worktable. Sam got it and put it down the front of Charles's chest. This time, Sam was able to get him up beyond his chest until Charles could wiggle himself up past his hips. From there, it was an easy slide inside.

Sam fell backward as Charles collapsed in a shivering heap.

The sun was well enough up by then that he was out of danger. Cold but safe, he would thaw. It took Sam a while, but he used one oar to retrieve the other that had drifted beyond reach. They didn't need any more problems. Sam got them back in the oarlocks, and headed toward shore.

It was still early enough that no one was up yet. Charles stripped outside the cabin while Sam snuck in and got him some dry clothes. They were somehow able to get his wet clothes dried without their parents knowing about their little adventure.

Neither brother talked about it afterward. After the initial shock, they both wanted to pretend that it hadn't been the potential disaster it could have been. Instinctively, they both knew better. Charles never admitted it, and Sam couldn't say for sure that he saw any difference, but he believed the event had an effect on Charles. Maybe subtle, but perhaps it led to larger consequences down the line. The open and unfettered personality that Charles lay bare that day just before he fell in the water was never observed again. Had he become more cautious just from that one incident? It was only lately that Sam had made the connection.

~~~

Sam was knocked out of his reverie by the sound of paws padding up the dock. A young puppy, whose enthusiasm exceeded his adroitness, came charging toward him. Whether Sam seemed to be the potential carrier of food or just another of those big beings willing to smother him with attention didn't seem to matter to the dog. Scrambling and stumbling, he was all legs, tail, hair, and flopping ears compressed into one mass of unmitigated joy. He took up most of the pier in his effort to reach Sam. Sam was afraid he might continue right over the end and into the water, but he stopped short. The lab or retriever, or most likely a mix, came bounding into Sam's face with tongue and paws all going at once.

His owner was running behind him, a young woman. She was a little heavyset, and moved in a similarly awkward fashion. She first apologized profusely for the puppy's behavior, then gave the dog a rather long and unrealistic set of commands. "Spot, get away from the man," along with "sit," "down," and "here." The fact that they were all conflicting commands did not seem problematic since the pup paid no attention to any of them. "He's friendly!" she said in defeat. She reached for her dog and pulled him back by his collar. "Sorry about that. He got loose."

"Spot? Why not Fido?"

"That was taken," she laughed. "Besides, the kids picked it from a cartoon or something. But I seem to have to explain that every time we go out."

"Well, it's a good solid dog name, anyway. You'll never confuse him with a cat."

After finally catching her breath, the woman had the luxury to look around. She seemed about Dan's age. Her short blonde hair was a little tangled from the wind and the run. Looking out over the lake, she said, "Isn't it beautiful? My parents own that two-story house behind those trees. It's still their weekend retreat, but I don't get up here as much as I would like to. I just love it here. Do you have a place nearby?"

"We're staying at the Hess's cabin, right over there," Sam said, pointing.

"I remember a girl named Robin and her brother Dan who stayed there. We used to play together years ago."

"Well, you still can—they're my niece and nephew, and they're in there now with their parents, my brother Charles and his wife. I'm Sam, by the way."

"I'm Jennifer," she said as she reached her hand toward his. "I don't remember you, though."

"I haven't been here myself for years. I've lived back east for the last forty or so. I can't believe how much I've missed it. Come on by when you get the chance. They'll be thrilled to see you."

"I would like to see Dan again. Had a crush on him a mile long. Tall and cute and everything…of course that seems ages ago. We actually dated for a little bit, though no one suspected it. Summer fling sort of thing. I broke up with him at the end of the summer for something he said. I thought it was pretty serious at the time, but now I can't remember what it was. Isn't that silly?"

"Well, his wife Laura is here with him, so you two can talk about it."

"Right," Jennifer said as she and Spot turned to head back. "I'm sure she would appreciate that! See you later."

With that, Sam staggered to his feet and followed her to the shore, to the picture-postcard rock cabin that had become just one more resurrected recollection. The eggbeater that was fomenting those slumbering portions in his mind went to work every time he looked, smelled, or heard anything.

Sam concluded that all this thinking wasn't making him any wiser, and that the passing of time hadn't settled anything. *I thought I would've had it figured out by this time. Things are happening here. Life is happening here.*

Sam ascended the stone steps and came upon Charles sitting next to the door, looking as though he was waiting for him.

"Sam, grab a couple of beach chairs and let's go sit by the lake."

When they had settled in, Charles piped up, "We haven't talked about it, and only hinted at it after my accident, but what are your plans, Sam? You planning on going back to St. Louis?"

Charles's bluntness caught Sam off guard, but then Sam figured that it would have to be talked out sometime.

"I have to be honest: I was thinking about the possibility of staying, even before I left St. Louis. I was certainly needed after your accident. But if I did, I wouldn't want to step on any toes, or be an interloper to a system you and Sally have built up all these years. Otherwise, yes, I'm open to making the move, but I want to know how you feel about it."

"When I heard that you were coming, I wasn't all that thrilled, to tell you the truth. I knew Sally had a hand in it right off, and knew she would want you to stay. At first, I thought it *would* be an imposition, but now I'm getting used to it. I'm even getting used to you." Charles smiled over at him. "Now with this bum leg, I'm actually beginning to feel mortal and may have to accept some changes. I'm not as stubborn as some people think."

"I'm glad you brought this up. It's good to clear the air."

"So, what about your own home? You must have a lot of ties there."

"Not so much after Helen died. Because we never had children, we were left out of a lot of social interactions, and now with her gone, a lot of the remaining connections are gone, too. Then...being alone in that empty house...well, being here has taken my mind off Helen, for the most part. Only when there are things I want to share with her do old longings come up. But distance provides clarity as they say, and I'm realizing the unhealthy pattern I had settled myself into back there. Being away from that and getting involved here in this new and busy one has helped.

"And frankly, I'm beginning to enjoy the work. Well, maybe not so much *enjoy* as be engrossed in it. I find myself continuously thinking about projects that need doing. I get up early, which I never did back home, and rehearse in my mind what I want to do and how I want to do it. It forces me to concentrate, and that excludes most everything else I would habitually think about. Maybe that Sisyphus legend has some relevance for me, too." Sam laughed. Then, he continued in a lighter tone, "Plus, it's helping me lose weight. Amazing what a healthy sense of direction can do. I'm surprised my hair isn't growing back. But if I were to return to St. Louis, it would be heavy with momentum, and near impossible to reverse. After your accident, I was thinking of renting out the house, but I could sell it, no problem.

After a pause, Sam added, "Yes, I would like to move back permanently, and just between you and me, we could work out some sort of arrangement with the finances. I can bring in money from the sale of my house, my small pension, and eventual social security as compensation for you having another mouth to feed. I just didn't want to get Sally too excited by saying anything, you know?"

"That would be good. That would be real good."

Thus ended a critical conversation that needed little continuation.

"Why don't you go on in. We'll discuss this with everyone when we get back home. I'm going to hobble over to the pier myself," Charles said.

Sam was tempted to say something about their little boating venture so long ago, then thought better of it and decided to let that sleeping dog lie.

As Sam turned and walked to the cabin, he had to admit, laughing to himself, that all this had gotten his juices going. He continued through the door alive with noise and the bustle of people caught in a web of their own making.

"Family," Sam said aloud.

Overhearing, Sally sneaked a peek over at him, and smiled.

8
Sally and Robin

"Don't feed her too fast, honey," Sally said from across the kitchen. "She'll get colicky."

"Don't worry, Mom. She does fine with food. She's tough—like you."

Hazel was glad to be able to sit in a booster seat at the grown-up table. But now into her terrible twos, she was reluctant to eat her steamed carrots. While able to eat on her own, Robin, impatient, opted to feed her.

"I don't like it!" Hazel said. Robin, miming her own eating, took a rather large spoonful and aimed it toward its destination, which at the time was shaking left and right evasively. The more Hazel moved, the wider Robin's mouth got, until something had to give. In this case, it was the tot's hand, which rose up just as the spoon was nearing its target, sending its contents in a rather graceful arc up and over Robin's head.

"I give up," Robin said, even though she thought she shouldn't. "You've had enough for now. Besides," she added, shifting the blame, "Grandma says so."

Sally just smiled as she cleaned up the spill on the table. "She's got a little on her face, dear."

Robin found the spot and scrubbed it like she was removing a stubborn stain from a sink, distorting the cherub's face in the process.

Sally leaned down and said to Hazel, "You're a sweetie, that's what you are. Yes, you are."

"Don't encourage her, Mom."

While grandmas are typically nicer to their granddaughters than their own daughters are, they are often pushovers as well. But Hazel settled down and started to eat on her own.

"So how was Dad's latest checkup?"

"You mean his heart or his leg?"

"His heart, Mom. He goes in every month, doesn't he?"

"He goes every week for physical therapy and sees his cardiologist every month, and you wouldn't believe it. The doctor said his angina is actually improving. He sticks to his diet pretty well, although I know he still smokes those damn cigars. But I think breaking his leg has actually helped him because he can't do any heavy lifting; and he doesn't get stressed out like he used to. And Sam! That's the other thing. I think a lot of it has to do with Sam being here—a lot of the responsibility Charles has shouldered has lifted because of him. And they get along so well now! They're really getting to be good friends."

Robin rose and lifted up Hazel and gave her a smooch on the cheek. "Crib time!" She went over to the kitchen crib with all its colorful toys and put her in.

"She's so cute. Looks a little more like Sam than Charlie, don't you think?"

"She looks a little too much like her father, which I'd just as soon forget."

"Well, we can't change the facts, honey, so we might as well live with them. Besides, Hazel really does have Sam's mouth, don't you think?"

"Maybe if Hazel's mouth could say, 'I don't know what to do. Should I stay here or not? I just can't make up my mind.'" Robin chuckled at her mimicry of a whiney Sam.

"Now Robin…"

"I'm just teasing, Mom. I really like Uncle Sam. I heard that he might be moving back."

"I thought Dad told you that. Yes, he certainly will. After we came back from Tahoe last week, your dad and uncle and I had a talk, and

Sam said that he had wanted to make the move, but only if we agreed to it, which of course we did. Remember, it was a big decision for him. It's harder to change as we get older, you know. I think he just thinks too much. But he will definitely be selling his house. Why he waited for so long, I don't know. I just had to keep my mouth shut and not say anything that might bring up more doubts. He comes around on his own eventually, but if you push him, he gets stubborn."

"So how would you work it? I know he owns one-third of the property, but do you have any plans?"

"Well, we should have been more open about the arrangement here. Why we haven't, I'll never know. Because Sam owns a third, and your dad and I, two-thirds, we make all the decisions, pay the bills, and reap any benefits. Sam is fine with that. And since he is part owner and will be living here, he'll be putting in most of his money from his house and pension. And just so you know, because Sam has no children, he has agreed that you and Dan will inherit his holdings when he passes.

"You might say we're putting the family back together again," Sally added wistfully. "Sometimes it seems life is like one big cycle, like we'll eventually return from where we started. Like that big old pendulum in the clock, it starts at one side, swings away, and comes back again. The harder you push it away, the faster it comes back." Sally was looking out the window as she said this. "I wonder if Charles's parents planned it that way. I mean, by giving Sam a third, it might eventually get him to return."

"That's one way to pull the family back—part of it, anyhow. But this putting the family back together, do you mean us? Hazel and me?"

"Now that you mention it, well—no."

"No? I didn't expect that."

"Sure, I would love it if you and Hazel would move back. It would be great for your dad and me to have a child here. But you coming back may not be up to me, and maybe not even up to you, for that matter. Remember all those horrific battles we all went through? I couldn't do it again. But I know you're responsible now, and I couldn't be more proud of you." She leaned over to touch Robin's arm. "Would you want to?"

"I've never really thought about my life in the long term. I guess I was so busy trying to distance myself, I never thought of you and Dad passing on." Robin then looked straight at her mother. "Maybe it's time I made some changes…" She paused for a moment. "It wasn't easy for me either, you know. But moving back home? That's a big step. I've done pretty well in Sacramento. I have friends there now—I don't know…" Robin trailed off, her eyes focusing on her young daughter's face, as if searching it for some answer. Robin bit her nails, and added in a more subdued tone, "Have to find a job in Reno, of course."

To Sally, it seemed a real eye-opener for her daughter. Maybe a chance at redemption—a starting over.

"Who knows?" Sally said calmly. But she wasn't calm. This unexpected meeting of the minds was an eye-opener for her as well. "Maybe a trial period, live here a few days a week and see how we get along. That would be the real test."

"That's an idea," Robin said with a little more vigor. "For starters, I can find a place to live, no problem. You know, the insurance company I work for has an office in Reno. No reason I can't transfer there. I'm tired of Sacramento, anyway."

Could it be that easy? Sally thought. *That simple? Could years of anguish dissolve in such a simple conversation? No falling all over each other in emotional apologies and forgivenesses?*

"But we still have to work some things out," Sally said. "One thing that's always bothered me was the disrespect you showed my faith. I want to know what you think now. One of the tenets I believe in is forgiveness, but I have to say that it went against what I felt at the time, and I've been battling it all these years, wanting—no, forcing myself—to forgive, then blaming myself because I couldn't."

"Oh, Mom, I only did that because I was rebellious. It had nothing to do with what you believed in. Actually, later, I did feel the need to find some guidance, but in my own way. That's why I got into, as you might say, the trendier stuff: Buddhism, meditation. But instead of it fulfilling some sort of, I don't know...payback? I found that they were full of wisdom. For one, it allowed me to let go of that rebellious streak."

"Maybe I should look into that myself," Sally said with a smile.

The discussion gave them a lot to process. Sally felt tired, and at least for now, thinking was something she wanted to avoid. So, to change the subject, she did the only thing she could think of: gossip. There was Sally's friend Constance, whose daughter Sara and son-in-law Rob just had a baby.

"First-time parents and they're talking about a divorce!" Sally said before remembering her own daughter's similar situation. "Maybe they'll get back together—at least that's what Constance is hoping for. But I don't really believe it."

"I went to high school with Rob. You remember him, Mom? A year ahead of me, I think. I thought he was kind of a nerd, but now nerds are making all the money. Shows how smart I was."

"You had to have some smarts. At least you didn't end up with him. He may have had an eye for making money, but also a roving eye. She caught him by going through his computer. Nice long list of phone numbers. She only had to call a few to find out. Of course, she did this when she was four months pregnant. Not the best timing."

"What's the matter with men, anyway? Promises don't mean squat to 'em. They're all a bunch of manipulative jerks."

"The little dears," Sally said with a smirk.

"Hah, that's funny. Wasn't that from some old movie? I forget the name."

"Yeah, what was it? Had Katherine Hepburn in it. I forget who else. I'll think of it—can't when I try."

"It seems to me that men were more trustworthy in your day."

"Oh, I don't know. There were plenty of shenanigans going on back then too. But then again, I think men were more, I don't know, controlled—or guided, I guess you'd say. They were expected to behave a certain way and not to be so free and easy with their selfish wants. Responsibility, that's what I mean. They were more responsible. Not like today's kids." Sally realized that she might be treading on slippery ground, so she stopped. "I think it's time for Hazel's nap, don't you?"

"Okay. Let's get her upstairs."

The two of them went into put-the-child-down-for-a-nap mode. Robin picked up a now-heavy, ready-to-be-cranky Hazel while Sally got her stuffed animals. Hazel, rubbing her eyes out of exhaustion, was beginning to start in on her whine.

"Now don't you start," Robin whispered as she adroitly shifted her daughter from one arm to the other. "You're cranky because you're tired, so the sooner we get you to bed, the better. Cranky butt, cranky butt, can't wait for that warm crib where it's nice and dark and snugly. And you have Peter Rabbit waiting for you. That's right, he's been asking where you've been because he's lonely."

Hazel pushed her face into Robin's shoulder, impervious to her mother's chipper tone, but too tired to even be a cranky butt, and mother and daughter put her down for a nap.

"Well, I was pretty irresponsible myself," Robin said as they descended back to the kitchen, referring to what Sally had said in their conversation earlier.

"You're mature now. Don't forget, I was young once too, and I rebelled a bit against my parents."

"You never told me that."

"There are a lot of things I haven't told you—maybe shameful things that I would never admit to anyone. Would you tell Hazel everything about your past?"

"No, not everything, that's for sure."

Sally was about to add something, but fortunately for both, the outside kitchen door opened and Henry walked in.

"Henry!" both women shouted in relieved unison.

"Hi, Mrs. Ellis," Henry said. "Hi, Robin."

"Henry, okay, what was the name of that old movie that had Katherine Hepburn and—oh—and James Stewart in it?" Sally asked. "About high-society people."

"I don't know, Mrs. Ellis. I don't watch too many movies."

"Well, this is an old one, but fairly popular. It's on the cable channels once in a while."

"Who's James Stewart?" Henry asked with a shy smile.

"Uh, never mind, Henry," Sally said as she and Robin laughed.

"Sam and Mr. Ellis should be back pretty quick, and I have to get a receipt off Mr. Ellis's desk, if that's all right."

"Sure, go right ahead."

Henry went into Charles's office, got the papers he needed, and left.

"What a nice boy he is," Sally said. "He does such a good job around here. I don't know what we would do without him."

"Can I ask you something, Mom? I've been wondering about it for a while. Do you and Dad think of Henry like a son, maybe like what you would have wanted Dan to be?"

"Oh, heavens no. Where would you get that idea?"

"Well, because Dan never had any interest here, and Henry just seems more...I don't know."

"No, we would never consider him like a son. But your dad and I both knew that Dan wasn't suited to this life, and we never pressured him into it. It would have been the perfect scenario if he had wanted to work here, but life doesn't always work out the way you want. I'm just sad that we kind of lost him after high school. He just distanced himself—not in a rebellious way, but maybe in a more hurtful way. You never felt close to him either, did you?"

"I had my own problems. But no, we were never close at all. He was just part of the family I was trying to get away from."

"Dan never really confided in us how he was feeling," Sally said with sadness. "I just don't think he ever had a very high opinion of himself, which is too bad. On the other hand," Sally continued in a more upbeat manner, "he's done pretty well for himself with his real estate work. But I think his lucky break came when he met Laura; she's stable and tolerant, and accepts him for who he is. And the way she interacts with Hazel, I have no doubt she wants to have children. I wonder if she is waiting because she may be worried that Dan might feel overwhelmed."

"Well, she can't wait too long. They're both pushing thirty."

"You're right there," Sally said with a grin.

"But back to Henry, I can't believe he calls you Mr. and Mrs. Ellis, especially after all these years."

"It's just his way of showing respect, dear. I could ask him to call me Sally, but he wouldn't be comfortable with it—and frankly, neither would I. Maybe it's our way of keeping non-family people at arm's length. It's nice to feel respected, though." Then, realizing an opening, she said, "But I wouldn't blame Dan if he were a bit jealous. Blood relations are like that. Possessive and contentious. I guess it's always been that way. You and Dan are the only ones that call me Mom, you know. Even when Dan distanced himself and you had green hair to match, I loved both of you then just as I do now."

There was a long pause before she continued.

"It's just that everyone nowadays wants to be independent. I think that just separates us from each other even more. Why people think they have to make it in this world alone, I'll never know. Family is the only thing that counts, dear, and you'll be finding that out with Hazel. You won't ever want to let her go, and she'll probably break your heart. But then, later…"

Here, Sally trailed off, as Robin was staring directly at her with a strained look Sally had not seen before.

"I'm sorry we were a disappointment to you," Robin began as she put her head in her hands and assumed a resigned attitude. "No, that's not it. It's me. I treated you and Dad terribly. I'm not the daughter I should have been. I'm so sorry, Mom."

"I know you are, dear. I'm sorry, too. Instead of fighting you, maybe I should have let you be the one to find your own place in the world."

She and Robin were searching, exhausted, *ready*—not with fanfare, but with a falling away to forgetfulness, time being the healer of most wounds.

"Are we having that meeting of minds?" Sally said.

"I guess so," Robin replied with a slight smile.

"If you can work in Reno and stay here, maybe a couple of days during the work week, I'd love to take care of Hazel. I know Charles would also."

"That would be wonderful. My insurance company likes my work, and if there's an opening in Reno...I'll start working on it right away."

Sally got up from the table, as did Robin, and went over and gave her daughter a big hug. Then pulling lightly away, Sally said, "*Philadelphia Story*," and hugged her again.

9
The Meeting

"We're having a ranchers' meeting at the hall Tuesday night," Charles said to Sam as they were inspecting one of the ranch's troublesome well pumps. "I want you to come. You know we have these meetings every few months or so, but it's time we talk over all the development going on, and how it's affecting all the ranches in the area." Then, getting no response, he added, "Two ranchers have already sold out, and that's putting pressure on the rest of us."

Sam could only affect a grunt as he closed up the electrical box and began putting his tools away.

"You've been here, what, eight months now? Since you're going to hang around, it's time you got to know these people and get more involved," Charles said as they both started back toward the pickup.

"I know, but I've just never been one to join a group. Never got involved in political situations, you know?"

"No one likes political situations, at least if they have any principles. But there's no other way to fight for something except through it. This development push is the biggest threat to ever come our way, and even if we hang on, it will affect us too. Once someone sells out, there is no going back."

"Sure, but what can we do?" Sam said as he opened the passenger door and helped his brother climb into the truck. He got behind the wheel and started the engine, but before they started moving, he turned to Charles. "It's not like you can just band together to stop this thing. They don't come after you en masse where you could put up a fight. They come at you one-on-one. Divide and conquer. That's their strength."

"Not if they can be persuaded that it isn't in their best interests," Charles said.

"How?"

"Well, the upside is pride and stubbornness in their heritage and history. No one wants to leave their home, the place where they grew up. That's a huge factor. Second, no one wants to sell out and lose face to those still working their asses off. Go talk to someone who sold out and see how they're doing. I bet not so well. No question they would pine for their old homesteads."

"I wouldn't count on that, Chuck. They would probably like living in comfort."

"Only at first. What kind of luxury is it to just sit around? That's a death sentence if I ever heard one."

He's exaggerating, Sam thought, *but there's truth to it.*

"Okay, but they only find that out after it's too late. You can't tell someone that just sitting around doing nothing is worse than the stress and strain of this work. I mean, we know it is, but we don't really think like that in the long run. We think that we'll keep ourselves busy, but then we get lazy. Sorry, Chuck, I think we bail out at the slightest opportunity. Maybe not you because you're proud, but most need only the right excuses."

"I'm counting on that pride, Sam," Charles said with emotion in his voice. Then toning it down a bit, he continued, "Dan will be there. Since he's in the business, you can talk with him. Because he lives in Reno, he's been to a few of these meetings. I'll tell him to come."

"I tried to get his ideas on this issue the other day," Sam said as he put the truck in gear and started to drive up to the barn. "But he wasn't very open about discussing it. He says he's not involved with the big developers, so why would he bother?"

"He has to have some connections, but it's one way for us to get together since he doesn't have time to come out to the ranch much. In any case, I'm wondering if you might talk to him, prod a bit more and find out what he thinks about all this, because he might be more open to you than to me.

"Also, I have something that just might cause a stir at this meeting, and I want you and Dan to hear it. Remember when I said there might be a way out?"

"I remember you said something like that to me after those developer agents came by. All right, if it's the only way I'll find out what you have in mind."

~ ~ ~

The brothers stood in front of the Farmer's Exchange Hall. Built in the late 1880s, it once served as the heart of downtown Reno, but no longer. The city had migrated away, literally if not figuratively, from the building and its inhabitants, as if it were embarrassed by the anachronistic ranching descendants it no longer had use for.

Having distanced itself from the very organization that helped the city develop, the building was left to the seedier elements—a vacuum invaded by trash, graffiti, darkness, and the homeless.

"Let's go in, Sam. You haven't been here since you were a kid."

With Charles now able to use a cane, and Sam assisting at his brother's elbow when few were watching, they walked up the wide marble steps, past the huge Greek columns, through the ornately decorated foyer, and into the main ballroom.

The hall was older and had more history than most any building in the city. Traversed with ancient-looking rafters, the twenty-foot-high ceiling was obscured by several large florescent lights that gave the place anything but a warm feel.

Sam noted that its rundown look also mirrored many of its aging inhabitants. Folding chairs were scattered aimlessly, and the tables around the side walls were either old and dilapidated, or newer Formica and aluminum that looked worse than the battered furniture they probably replaced. But the lack of people was what gave the scene a sense of despair. Missing was the noise and commotion of the past that would have let you know that something notable, driven by people of importance, was going on.

Many decades ago, the ranchers were a united force to be reckoned with. All the politicos from the nearby counties would assemble here on a rotating basis, schmoozing, drinking, making deals, breaking deals, and playing the politics that would ultimately determine the fate of the surrounding land and the people in it. Little did these ranchers suspect that, in essence, their own fate was being sealed.

Excepting for the echoes of the ranchers who no longer existed, there were no more than twenty-five members assembled—or perhaps more accurately, survivors. Their organization wouldn't exist at all if it hadn't been for the city charter that allowed them, and the meeting hall itself, to endure in perpetuity, free of taxes, fees, and other annoyances. It was all thanks to their predecessors who had once wielded the power to install the right political people. Now most of them were either gone or old, but that didn't keep them from acting as if they still had influence. There would have been even fewer in attendance this night, except that it was slated to be an important meeting.

"Sam," Charles said, introducing him to one of the members, "you remember Howard? Frank Howard? Has a ranch near Reno. Still call him Howard Frank just to piss him off. Serves him right for havin' two first names."

"So you're Sam," Frank said, ignoring Charles. "Remember you from a long time ago. Better lookin' than your brother. How ya doin'?"

After this short introduction, Charles winked and went over to grab Dan, who was in the middle of talking to some men at the bar. This left Sam, who knew of Frank's reputation, to contend with his insufferable bluster. Sam could see him welling up, ready to pounce. His eyes grew large, his face invading well into Sam's comfort zone.

"Place looks as big as I remember it," Sam jumped in, cutting off Frank before he had a chance to start. "Been a long time since I was here...last." But Sam had nowhere to go with that, and so lost the initiative. *Amateur.*

Unfazed, Frank was more than willing to pick up the slack. He grabbed the opportunity as a thirsty man would the last beer behind the bar. "We used to have a lot more people here—you know, in the good old days. Take these kids now. Wouldn't give ten cents for the lot of 'em. They don't give a crap, except for Charles's kid, of course. Head on *his* shoulders. My boys, they wouldn't stay around when they grow'd. Wouldn't listen to me. Don't know why, 'cause I told 'em everything I knew—and more. Just got their own ideas. Now, when I was't their age...." He paused as someone else got his attention. "Hey, Reese—still abusing your cows, ha! Your Mormon friends frown on that kinda thing you know." He turned back to Sam. "Hey, go on over to the bar and get yourself something. Gotta talk to Reese here. Good to see ya again."

With a bit of relief, but annoyed at his brother for deserting him and forcing him to deal with Howard, Sam strode over to the bar, hearing Frank yammering all the way.

When Sam and Charles were young, their father had brought them here a few times. They and the other kids would climb around the backstage area, playing blind man's bluff or some such thing while the meetings were going on.

Sam, suddenly growing weary of these little reminders, longed for a good, cold beer, which, he noted, was not in short supply.

As Sam approached, he could see Charles pointing Bill Thornton out to Dan's attention; another old rancher talking to someone even older-looking. Sam remembered Thornton from years ago. Back then, he was a big, strong man with a booming voice. Now hunched over, the booming voice was still there, but, Sam surmised, he probably thought that yelling would compensate for his hearing loss.

"Call to the colors," came the command from somewhere.

Two vets from the Vietnam War emerged from a side door, one carrying the American flag, the other the state flag of Nevada. One wore a full navy uniform, the other, army. They marched forward, turned a sharp ninety degrees to face the front, and halted.

Hats were doffed, silence ensued, and the Pledge of Allegiance began in earnest. The once-boisterous group now effected a sober tone, at least as much as possible considering the general absence of sobriety, as they recited the Pledge. Afterward, a few sat down in folding chairs that were laid out in rows.

Charles turned toward Sam. "Have a nice talk with Howard?" Charles snickered.

"I'll get you for that!"

"Look, I have to go prepare what I'm going to bring up before I start the meeting; go find a seat and settle in."

Sam went over to one of the chairs toward the back and sat. Soon after, Dan came and sat in a chair behind and to the right of him.

"Not a whole lot of people anymore," Dan said lightheartedly.

"Oh, hi, Dan," Sam said, half turning around. "Yeah, pretty low turnout compared to what this place used to be like. I notice that there's only a few young people in attendance, all ranchers' sons, I suppose. Probably have their own friends to party with. Here they would get bombarded with reminders of how inexperienced they were, how easy their life is compared to how things were back in the good old days. Who needs that? It's a wonder any come at all. I can see why they distance themselves."

"Well, we distanced ourselves, didn't we?" Dan said with a laugh.

"Yes we did! But I think many would still follow their parents' ways of life. Their absorption in the ranching environment probably overwhelms most other considerations. I'm sure the land does have some sort of hold on them." Sam adjusted his chair in order to face Dan directly. "Your father told me that a couple of ranchers have already sold out to developers, and that he was going to bring that subject up tonight. So what do you think? As a group, do they have any influence anymore?"

"Each rancher does have their land to bargain with," Dan said, "and that's influence of a sort. But as a group, I don't know."

Other than Dan's six-foot-two height, few saw much resemblance to his father. Sam, however, could see the younger Charles. Mostly,

Dan lacked his father's commanding presence. He just seemed to be an easygoing person with little interest in the ranch, or land management in general.

Sam remembered their previous talk at the ranch some months ago, and sensed that, for whatever reason, Dan didn't want to open up to him. *Maybe he's just intimidated by his father. That would explain a lot.* But being here now, and having seen him in open conversations with other ranchers, Dan certainly looked self-assured. Although he had said that he was not involved with wholesale development, Sam wondered what he and the ranchers would have to talk about.

Sam kept prodding.

"Yes, they do have a bargaining chip, but it's an all-or-nothing deal. The land isn't much good as it is, is it? I mean, especially now with all the rising costs to run things. But their advantage is also their weakness. It's what makes them vulnerable. Once sold, they lose their power." Sam sighed. "Maybe that's what keeps them hanging on. They're the center of attention for as long as they can hold out. Sell, and they become nobody."

"I don't think they'd become nobody, Sam. I think they might be surprised how good things could turn out." Dan scrutinized his uncle's face as if looking for a reaction. Getting none, he shifted. "But you may have a point."

"I never thought to ask you, Dan," Sam said, deciding to finally broach the subject. "If developers were interested in your father's spread, what would you want him to do?"

Dan thought for a moment, looking unprepared for the directness, then answered with equivocating conviction. "I want what he and Mother want. I want them to be happy, and if that means keeping the ranch, then so be it. But I'm concerned about how they could afford to stay there. Costs are going up, and they can't work any harder than they are now, even with the help. Who's going to take care of the place? Or them when they need taking care of? If they sold, and sold now, all that would be behind them."

Sam nodded. "But then you take the place out of them, it's like removing a vital organ or something. I don't know. Maybe they would be okay if they sold it. The experience of others is no guide. Some make the transition, some don't."

"Well, something's got to happen. That's inevitable," Dan said.

"I don't really believe in that inevitability stuff," Sam returned. "We don't know what will be; we can only guess. And we're usually wrong because we extrapolate from some current trend. But who knows? Things can come right out of the blue when you least expect it."

Only Sam didn't really believe that himself. People had been on the one-way road of trading open land for "progress" for, well, most of modern human history. That trend didn't seem likely to reverse itself anytime soon.

"Well, I'm going to head back to the bar," Sam said. "Want to come along?"

"I have a couple people I want to talk to first. I may come by a little later."

Having another beer at the no-host bar, Sam again wondered what he would have to talk about with anyone here. Then it hit him. *Of course, why didn't I think of this before? If Dan's parents sold the spread now, he and Robin would be in line for a big inheritance.*

Then it occurred to him that they would eventually inherit the land anyway, so why the rush? *Dan seemed to have emphasized the word "now" when he talked about the selling of the property. Did he think it important to sell early before the others did, or before the inevitable land restrictions kicked in and land values plummeted? Get a high price now and avoid the panic? Dan is in the business, after all.*

Sam wondered if he should talk to his brother concerning what Dan had said, and what his own suspicions were. He then decided to wait to see what that "other option" was that Charles told him he was going to bring up.

~ ~ ~

Charles, as president of the organization, got up and called for the formalities. The rest of the standing members moved away from the bar and sat.

First came the roll call. "If you're not here," Charles said, "and didn't check your name off the list when you didn't come in, make sure you do going out." Looking over the assemblage, he spotted George Thompson. "Hey, Thompson!" he yelled. "I can hear you in the back there. Are you here or not?"

Laughter.

"Then put a cork in it. Treasurer's report. We got any money?"

More laughter.

"Okay. Fred says there's enough for the barbecue. I'm sure you'll all vote for having it at my place again. Secretary's report?"

"Same old shit as last time," came a comment from somewhere.

"Then on to new business. Okay. I have a motion here to ban all alcohol from future meetings. Anyone opposed?" Charles said this in such a deadpan manner that it sounded legitimate.

Walter Merton thought it was, and got up to protest, spilling his drink in the process. The others started to laugh.

"Well, I'm glad someone's paying attention. Thank you, Walter. You're an example to others."

Walter looked around, somewhat confused about what had happened.

"We'll just table the matter for now. All in favor say…"

"Aye!" came the loud response.

After looking sheepishly about, Walter sat back down.

"We all know why we're here tonight," Charles said. "Big Bob Whitney, as you know, looks like he may sell his spread to developers."

There was an uncomfortable shifting of bodies in chairs.

"And I'm sure a few of us may be tempted. We need to do a little serious business here—sorry about that—and discuss the land-grab that's going on."

Sam could see that this was not going to be an easy night.

"We've all been talking about it, but among each other, not as a group. I know most of us want to keep our spreads, and if we do, we need to act together. After all, our forefathers started this organization so we could act as a single force."

To Sam, it looked like Charles wasn't sure he was getting through. He was. Most of the members were either staring at the floor or up to the side—anywhere their eyes could go without meeting another's. Sitting in seats laid out in rows helped in that matter, but still, Charles had acknowledged the elephant in the room, and suddenly, the place had sobered. Sobered by the potential shame of fortune, and the ensuing guilt about betraying their friends if they sold out.

These men hadn't been raised to think indulgently. Life was a struggle where rewards were hard-fought and rare. If they took the bait, they would have a life they never could have dreamed of. Without lifting a finger, they could become rich. Yet it was contrary to the very precepts they professed to live by.

The weight of past authority, with all the hardships, obligations, and sense of duty, lay on them. Their forefathers might be long gone, but past traditions held greater power and influence over present conduct. Such was the rancher's burden.

Truth be told, the ranchers' forebears might have been given credit beyond their due. It wasn't a commitment to high-minded principles that had brought them here. Some had come to these lands because of the mining game and other get-rich schemes. Failing that, many were forced to fall back on what they knew best. The venerable, strong-willed concepts of sacrifice and struggle didn't emerge until long after the pattern was laid before them. Chances were that they, too, would have sold out had they been given the chance. But since they had made the commitment to long-term hardship and perseverance, out of necessity, principles had to be fabricated as a justification for those struggles.

Charles had told Sam on their way over that the two who had sold out in the last few years no longer came by to see their old friends. They had tried, pretending that nothing had changed, but things had changed.

From his early years working the ranch, Sam understood the mindset of this group, and that there was now a distinct split between those who remained and those who hadn't.

But how do you condemn an old friend who did what you are tempted to do yourself? Sam thought. *Friends who went through tough times with you, who stood by you, and for whom you stood by? Friends who were on the same side as you back when you swore that nothing could ever pull you apart. So you don't condemn, you keep quiet because you have your own doubts you think no one else has.*

But time and prejudice have a way of twisting conditions to suit one's needs. It would take some fancy footwork of rationalizing to justify a selfish act, but then again, it may just have been a matter of opportunity. "All things come to those who wait," they say. They didn't have to wait long.

"I have an idea where we might be able to live on our land and not have to work so hard keeping it." Charles paused to allow for the reaction.

He got it. The effect was electric. Like a platoon coming to attention, passive stares turned to an absolute focus on Charles as his audience waited for the second boot to drop.

"Politics makes strange bedfellows," Charles continued, waiting for the snickers that didn't come. Making quick eye contact over to his brother, Charles added, "We can have an ally if we want. But it's one that till now we've always assumed was an adversary, and if you'll listen a minute, I'll try to make this simple. Now there's always two sides to any problem. If there is a third side, one of 'em will eventually move to one side or the other. The enemy of my enemy is my friend. That's just the way it is. So when I say we might have an ally that we always thought was against us, I mean they despise the other side more than they despise ours. You get my drift?"

There were a few mumbles, but the crowd was still waiting for the other boot.

"Okay, so I've been in touch with this organization—a preservation group. They're interested in preserving open space like what we own.

They've been active mostly in certain areas of California, but now that development has been ramped up considerably in our own over the last few years, and with a couple of ranch lands being bought up, they are suddenly interested."

Bill Wadkins, who owned a ranch just to the south of Charles's, spoke up.

"Jesus! Sorry, Charles, but those prissy-assed Sierra Club dickheads have been on my ass for years with all their stupid rules and regulations. They even brought a health inspector from Carson to back them up on some bullshit thing about my cattle shitting in my own creek, like I'm polluting the water for those candy-assed yuppies building their houses downstream. I know they did it just to screw with me, I mean…" Just then, Bill spotted Alice Webber and her habitually disapproving eye. "Pardon my French," he muttered, and sat down, still fuming.

Alice, the group's secretary, was the accepted scold in the organization. A rancher's widow some twenty years ago, she had no compunction, as most wives did, about breaking into this good-old-boys drinking fraternity. Hardboiled to the core, she could out-drink, out-smoke, and out-cuss any of them. At least that was the legend. Nobody really tested her because they liked the legend as it was. But because she was a woman—in the strictest sense of the word, of course—the men would defer to her, mostly just to credit themselves with some sense of propriety.

"Now, Bill," Charles said, "we don't need all this cussing. Look, I hate these prissy-assed dickheads as much as you do. But that's not what this organization is about. For one thing, it's different from environmental agencies that want to return the land to its original, wild state. Remember, I said that there's only two sides to a problem, and this organization sees that it's going to be development or us, and they'd rather side with us just as much as we might need to side with them. Neither may like it, but that's the way it is, and I think it's worth looking into. I'm not going to go into much detail. I don't know yet myself what we can work out, but these guys have clout, and money— mostly private, and a little in federal grants—and like it or not, this environmental thing isn't going away. There's a lot of people with money willing to donate to them and vote their people in."

Sam could see that the men had the greatest respect for Charles and weren't about to challenge him. He was one of them, and if he had an idea that might allow them to save their ranches without having to go broke—and save face while they were at it—then, by God, they were going to listen.

"It all has to do with this outside interest, not a developer to change things, but one that would invest in our land so that it could continue to be worked as it is now. Unlike strict environmentalists who want to clamp down on everything, they'll allow the ranches to stay." Charles shrugged. "It's leverage they use against full-scale development. It means giving up some, but not all, of our rights, but we continue on as property owners. They buy easements to the property so as to protect the land's resources. They put it into a sort of public trust, and pay us a stipend so we can keep working. The arrangement also provides for large tax incentives, meaning less cost to us.

"So you see, they don't pay as much as developers would, but we can continue working for as long as we live. We get paid for the easement, and our kids can inherit it as well, but only if they continue working it, or they can still sell it if they want, but those easements go along with it, meaning its sale price would be less.

"On the other hand, with more people here, profits might take a turn for the better. Then our kids, or even *their* kids, could reap a decent profit. But that's all in the future. All that can be worked out. Every ranch has its own situation.

"Well, look, I said I don't know all the details. I don't know if they would want everyone's ranch, or just a few—stuff like that—but I think it's something we should consider. But we need to be together on this and show support for the idea."

The group sat transfixed. Just as Charles drew a breath to approach his pitch from another angle, Ray Wheeler stood up and asked, "Can we meet with these people?"

"Of course, Ray," Charles responded.

Once in a great while, more often through just plain luck than intent, an innocent comment can be a catalyst that alters the course of an ongoing order. Ray was a quiet man and seldom in the mix of things, but to Sam, it looked like he had blurted aloud what most of the members were thinking, that this may be a possible solution many had been waiting for. While it could have been seen as a show of weakness in this closed-minded group, Sam could see that it had the opposite effect: Charles couldn't have gotten better support.

Charles looked questioningly at Sam, and Sam responded by nodding vigorously in the affirmative.

A buzz of conversation quickly began in the room. "I'll be at the bar for those of you who have any questions," Charles said, with the implication that the short meeting was over.

Getting up from the table and removing himself from the center of action was Charles's way of allowing the conversation to develop on its own, and allow the members to turn their attention elsewhere, mostly to the man in the next seat.

Sam could see that this was pretty much what Charles had wanted: to get the ball rolling—to get them thinking.

Charles came over to where Sam was, now standing at the bar. "What?" he asked, smiling in mock answer to Sam's surprised look and unasked question.

"You know what. How long have you been holding out on this? And when did you ever meet those people you're talking about? I never had a clue."

"Well, I guess there's some things you just weren't meant to know," Charles joked. "Actually, I made some calls and met them a couple times when I went in for my physical therapy sessions."

"Now I know what you've been up to all this time you were supposed to be recuperating. Working on a way to reconfigure the entire ranch lands in the basin. I suppose you made designs for leveling Reno while you were at it. And Sally?"

"She knew. Well, no. She actually instigated it, to tell the truth, but we didn't want it to get around—raise expectations, you know. But these guys do seem interested now. I wasn't sure myself about bringing this up now until a few weeks ago; sometimes you have to wait for the right time. Too early and it might get shot down, and you'd never be able to resurrect it. But the preservation people I've talked to may be getting more serious, just as these boys seem to be."

Just then, Bill Wadkins, the one who had carped about the idea, and one of the men Dan was talking to, came over to Charles. "Sorry, Charles. I don't like it. I should be able do whatever I want with my land, whether sell or keep it. My grandfather would have never approved a compromise like this."

"That's okay, Bob. No one is under any obligation here. Not everyone will go for it."

Since Charles wasn't about to disagree with him, all Bill could say was, "Well, okay." Then he walked away.

"Each rancher has their circumstance," Charles said to Sam. "By the way, have you seen Dan? Saw him talking to you a while ago."

"He was just here. Maybe he left." Sam decided not to divulge to Charles his suspicions concerning Dan.

Charles looked quizzical for a moment.

Just then, four or five members began to surround Charles with a bevy of eager questions.

For the most part, Charles answered them with, "I really don't know yet," and "We'll have to see what gives." He wanted them to mull this stuff over before overwhelming them with details. No sense in spilling the beans right away, because he didn't know them all himself.

But Sam understood his brother's tactic. With the ranchers seeing him in conversation with those interested, it would compel others to get interested themselves, and the word would spread to the other ranchers not in attendance. In a way, it was somewhat like the gold fever that had driven many of their ancestors to this place. They didn't call it a fever for nothing. It was a contagion that only needed time to infest itself in the pondering mind. If you took the offer away at the crucial moment, all doubt would dissolve into the fear of being left out, turning a once-suspected scheme into a can't-miss opportunity.

"It's a wonder," Charles said to Sam, "that someone hasn't brought this up before now. While the preservation group is just now getting active in the southern, more fertile area, I didn't think they would be interested in our more desolate, dryer northern section. But they're aware of the development happening at our end, and when I told them there would be support from the ranchers from this side, they were more than interested. Of course, I took a gamble telling them that, as I wasn't sure it would go over, but it looks like it has. But, no more secrets—you and I can work on this."

"I like your plan. I'll help, you shouldn't have to do this on your own anymore."

Charles was beginning to feel confident that, once begun, dialogue would snowball into an us-versus-them condition. He understood that while both environmentalists and developers were a pain, at least one wanted to preserve the land, and that the once-scornful ranchers would slowly edge their thinking toward the side that would keep things as they were rather than handing them over to those who would destroy it.

Sam, for his part, was amazed at how quickly opinion could adjust in these men, then realized that opinion was merely wearing a different Sunday suit, one that would allow them to change their minds without having to admit it. Rationalizations would leave them secure in the notion that their consciences were clear and that no principles had been damaged in the process.

Charles broke away from the group to get a well-deserved scotch on the rocks, and sipped in peace while looking out over the attendees. Sam could see that his brother, not much of a drinker, was enjoying its comfortable, numbing effect.

"A good start," Charles said. After putting his glass down, he walked over to his chair, grabbed his coat off the back, and motioned to Sam. Both headed for the door.

"Definitely a good start," Charles repeated.

10

T. Bob

The road to power can be full of detours, often taking the traveler on a convoluted journey through unpredictable routes—and for the unwise, toward destructive ends. Power is the manipulation of authority over resources and people. It is also theater.

The objective among the wannabe powerful is to acquire authority without actually having to fight for it. Aggression is a last desperate act that wastes valuable resources, and once begun, irreversible. Just as in the animal kingdom, challenges to leadership are mostly show, and for the clever strategist, bluster and intimidation can be the most expedient recipe for success.

It can also backfire.

~ ~ ~

The imposing four-story Sharpenal office building was nestled in the Sparks commercial-industrial district. Situated among buildings of no more than three stories, it looked uncommonly impressive. The second, and a majority of the third floor, were leased offices to a variety of firms. The other third-floor portion housed the workings of the Sharpenal Development Corporation with its various managerial, accounting, legal, and administrative departments. Theodore Robert Sharpenal was its president and CEO, and he was not afraid to take risks.

Back when Robert was in line to inherit his father's (originally his great-grandfather's) century-old, and quite entrenched, Sharpenal Development Firm in Chicago, the family's alleged financial improprieties and creative tax-code interpretations compelled them to send thirty-five-year-old Robert west to Reno to begin anew with his own division of the company, under the assumption that, like Chicago, it too was not unfamiliar with questionable practices. Because of the gold rush in nearby Virginia City in the 1860s, Reno had inherited a history of boom-and-bust volatility. Only later did it acquire the stamp as a city of vices: gambling, quickie divorces and marriages, as well as an attractive tax haven. "A boss-ridden population" was how one writer framed it.

Whether inherited or learned, T. Robert Sharpenal (he thought parting his name on the side would give it a certain flare—"Teddy" would never do) had an aggressive business sense. In just a few short years, with his opportunistic attitude and a horse-choking family bankroll to match, T. Bob had set himself on a par with some of the area's more established firms.

T. Bob was a tall, imposing figure, but a lumbering in his movements and a crudeness in his speech would dispel any idea of cultural refinement.

Upon entering the building, visitors found themselves in a large atrium of high-vaulted windows. Scattered about the floor stood several towering abstract steel sculptures, and on the walls, equally imposing abstract paintings.

The sparseness of the atrium was designed to convey strength and power. More precisely, much like the early European cathedrals, it was designed to intimidate. Open space that could have been better served for generating income was meant to demonstrate that frugality wasn't necessary. Extravagance implied wealth; that was the point. Like the peacock attracting the hen, its colorful plumage may have used up valuable energy, but its show of extravagance implied a strong genetic trait. Apparently, peahens like that. For T. Bob, though, there was more theater than resource, more pomp than his circumstances would have led others to believe.

The entire top, or fourth floor, contained the penthouse suite—still more tinsel and sparkle meant to impress. All of the rooms ran along the perimeter: T. Bob's office, another office for his administrative assistant, a conference room, and two fully furnished apartments—each containing their own ample-sized kitchens, teak-paneled bedrooms, large living areas, and an assortment of furniture and paintings one wouldn't normally find in your average home-shopping warehouse. The master apartment contained a bathroom fully equipped with gold fixtures and a floor-to-ceiling tinted picture window overlooking most of downtown Reno. That was in the shower.

It was all for the personal use of special guests, clients, people of influence, and occasionally, T. Bob himself.

The first thing one encountered upon exiting the elevator was the receptionist's desk. It was unnecessarily large, considering the sparse assortment of paraphernalia: a phone, calendar, writing implements, some paper, a computer with headphones at the ready, and a romance novel tucked under some loose files. Behind it sat a middle-aged woman—on guard to prevent any unauthorized snoop from publicizing the luxury meant for only a select few. An engraved sign on the desk declared her name to be Mildred.

But the most outrageous spectacle of all was behind her—a waterfall. It was a ten-foot-high rock, glass, and steel contraption of modern design that towered above a pool of freshwater carp. Water was pumped continuously to the top to tumble down a series of stone outcroppings, ledges, and side-chutes before plunging into the pool itself. It was a noisy affair, which Mildred most likely turned off when no one else was around.

~~~

"Mr. Sharpenal," Mildred said as she poked her head into T. Bob's office. "Mr. Banks is here now—want me to show him in?"

"In a minute. Tell Jim to come, too."

T. Bob's assistant was a tall, thin, bespectacled man, and Fred Banks rather short and portly. This caused Mildred to smile as she led them both into T. Bob's office.

Completing the picture, T. Bob was dressed in his usual attire: a loosely fitted gray suit with a coat too large for his frame, and a maroon tie—poorly tied.

"Jim, I want you to hang around while I talk to Fred." He turned to Banks. "So, Fred! Can I offer you anything? No? Well, have a seat. So, how's the family?" Then, taking a quick peek at a note on his desk: "And Abbie?"

"Abigail's doing fine, thanks for asking."

Fred Banks was head of an investment firm that worked occasionally with developers. His company had done well with T. Bob's last project, and he was eager to know what new venture T. Bob had in mind.

"Just so you know," Banks said, "our oldest boy, Archie, has just been accepted at Stanford, and my two daughters will be graduating high school soon, so my company is definitely ready to hear what you have to say," Banks said in a kidding tone.

"Well then, I'll get right to the point. I think it's time we go big time, Fred, and I'll need you and a few others to help. I want to buy up and develop most of the ranch lands in the far northern section. This will take a bit more financing than we needed in the past, but I'm willing to foot most of the bill to show the others how serious I am."

"Sounds like a big project, Bob. I doubt you could get enough financing right off the bat."

"I intend to start small. After our last venture just north of Reno a few years ago, I wasn't interested in going further. At the time, I didn't think it would be profitable to develop that far north from the city. Anyway, I may have been right, because the Hammond development project is just finishing up near there, and I heard that they're having trouble selling off housing, and may begin to redirect their efforts elsewhere.

"That's where we come in. I think there's real potential out there for full-scale development. Not just housing, but businesses, a shopping district, the whole works. I've been studying the situation, and think we should jump in now while the others are backing off. But like I said, I want to start small. There's one ranch I want to buy up and begin developing right away."

"Which one?"

"The most attractive one in the area. The Ellis place."

"Charles Ellis's spread?" Banks exclaimed with dismay. "His family has one of the longest histories here. You'll have a hard time getting him to sell."

"I'm aware of that, but I may have a connection that no one else does. Because he's highly respected in the ranching community, by getting his place first, the others will feel compelled to follow and have to sell on the cheap."

"You sure about that? That's a big gamble. What if they won't?"

"The Ellis place is center to most of those ranches I want to develop. When they see what's going on, they won't want to be left out. Of course, right now, we keep this quiet."

"I hear you, but the development of that spread will have to be profitable on its own. You might not get support if the numbers don't look right."

"Don't think that will be a problem considering its location, but we'll work on preliminary sketches and come up with cost estimates."

"I'll talk to a few in my firm that I can trust, and see what they think, but you'll have to let me in on this so-called connection you have."

"Maybe," T. Bob said with a wink.

~ ~ ~

Later that day, another meeting was scheduled in the conference room. Reginald McLaughlin and Leland Boyd—two of the men who had visited Charles and Sam at JE Ranch—had arranged with T. Bob to talk over a serious matter that had just come up.

140

They sat on a large couch flanking one of the paneled walls. T. Bob stood behind his desk, and James, his assistant, sat off to the side taking notes.

Reginald informed T. Bob that a rancher he knew, Bill Wadkins, told him about the ranchers' meeting, and about what Charles Ellis was working on—that he was looking into getting support from a preservation group that would pay ranchers, including himself, stipends that could allow him and the others to continue to work on and keep their land.

T. Bob pondered this, but the more he thought about it, the angrier he became. "I thought you said you were making progress." His finger pointed skyward in accusation. "Now you come at me with this?"

"We didn't know about it till a couple of days ago," McLaughlin said. "I mean, we thought we were making progress, too. You can't blame us. No one saw this coming."

Indeed, no one saw this coming, but T. Bob was on a roll. "Maybe you should have. You kept saying all along that all we needed was a little more time, that he was going to come around eventually. You should have known what he was up to. All we need is the Ellis place. It would have sealed it. All the others would have followed Charles Ellis. Now it turns out that he's the one instigating this. You sat on this too long, gentlemen."

The two sat and looked at each other. When that came to be too much, they cast their eyes to the floor. They weren't used to being talked down to like this.

"Look, the reason I'm getting your firm to do the work is that I don't want Ellis to know I'm involved. I got you into the big leagues, and you take orders from me. If you can't cut it, you're out."

Sitting in his office was intimidating for Reginald and Leland, which was just what T. Bob wanted. From the way they avoided eye contact with the man looming over them, it was clear they felt in over their heads. Here they were, sitting in this extravagant suite with a bigshot from back east, getting chewed out.

It was here in his penthouse that T. Bob depended on the lavishness of his surroundings to sanctify his authority. This was his temple, built not to God and power, but to money and power. Power being the end, God and money only the means.

But T. Bob needed these subordinates, so he toned it down and began his good-cop speech.

"So far, everything is still aboveboard, just a little dealing with your firm, and the politicals, of course. No one can make a big fuss over that, especially when we're doing the city a big service. Hell, we'll be looked on as pioneers in this new building boom. The second round of pioneers! I know you can work this out. I didn't hire you because you're stupid." With that, he smiled to let them know that they had a second chance at redemption. Like all religions, if you kicked out all the sinners, you'd have no one left to preach to.

But T. Bob still had a problem that those two wouldn't be able to solve. This was the connection he hinted at to Banks. The one possible solution was sitting in the corner on the other couch, taking it all in. When walking a tightrope, diplomacy is called for—not always an easy thing for one who depended on bluster and bombast to get his way. T. Bob would need to tone it down with this man.

Dan Ellis looked up. "It may not be illegal, but it's improper not to divulge your involvement. There could be some consequences here. You're on shaky ground, and you know it."

Dan wasn't about to be pushed around like the others. He knew he held most of the cards—at least his father did. But he was a key to this venture. "And you could be the biggest loser, T. Bob," he continued. "All that goodwill you've been trying to build up will come crashing down in an instant if others learn of our relationship. This ain't Chicago."

T. Bob backed off somewhat, knowing the difficulty of Dan's mission in attempting to get his father to sell. Dan didn't like T. Bob, and T. Bob returned the sentiment. Only their mutual goal kept them on the same track.

"I'm sorry for talking about your father that way. But let's hear it, Dan. You tell me what went on the other night."

"You heard it straight enough. A preservation organization might be interested in the land you want to buy. They want to leave it as open ranch and farmland. You know the story. They can't pay as much, of course, but the ranchers get to stay on their homesteads as long as it is never developed."

"And when they're dead and gone," T. Bob interrupted in his own blunt way, "the inheritors must either continue to work it or get lost, knowing that the only future they have is status quo? Not something you would want to think about. Right, Dan?"

Dan wouldn't let himself get pulled into T. Bob's personal affront. "My interest is in what's best for my parents. I'm willing to persuade them to sell. Despite the preservation's interests, its involvement would take some time that my father may not have. So don't think I'm in this only for myself."

"Well, Dan," T. Bob said, trying to find common ground, "we both know selling it now, and not later, is the right thing to do, especially when he can get a high price before the others. So it looks like we're both in the same boat."

T. Bob realized that he needed another persuasive speech, a for-the-good-of-all-mankind speech. He needed to rationalize the whole thing for Dan. Right then, he sensed that Dan was feeling guilty, and that wasn't good if he needed him to convince his father.

"I know the realty firm you work for doesn't deal with large developments, but you're in this business, and I know you have the ability to convince your father that selling the property is the only logical course. Look, who's going to take it over? You're not. Your sister? Don't think so, from what I hear about her."

Dan looked up in affront, but T. Bob blundered on, unconscious of the gaffe.

"Look, the land has always had its uses. When the Indians lived here, they hunted on it, foraged for nuts on it, and hell, I don't know." In fact, he didn't know. He was making this up as he went along. "But then the pioneers came along, and guess what? They made better use of it. Planting crops and feed for their stock. And why? Because there were more people to feed. The gold rush kept bringing them in, and they demanded more. The ranchers gave it to them, and they made good money at it. They helped make the place civilized in the process. Now there's houses—not your flimsy wigwams, mind you, but real, going-to-stay-for-good buildings. And hell! Schools and churches, and the railroad, for God's sake. And pretty soon, a town becomes a city. Just look at it out there," T. Bob said as he turned to gaze out the window. "All because those people—people like your ancestors—weren't afraid to take risks. They were willing to move ahead, progress, leave the old ways behind and build something new. Think how exciting it must have been to have the whole world ahead of you and not be tied down to the old. I almost wish I could have been part of it. Think of it. No one told them what they could or couldn't do. No one said, 'Stop growing. We have too many people.' No one said, 'We have to protect the environment.' Why? Because they were making something better than what was there before, that's why. No one sat on their asses trying to keep things the same. If any did, they would've been run over by others with drive and ambition."

"Like you, I suppose," Dan shot back.

"Well, yeah. Hell yeah. Like me. But that was then, this is now. Your father and all those other ranchers, they're like the Indians who refused to change. They became useless in a progressive world. These ranchers can barely make ends meet now, and they're getting pushed out whether they like it or not. Progress doesn't ask if you want it; it just…progresses, you know? I don't know how to put it, but if the land can't support the ranches, then let it do some good. Let it support some houses and roads and people.

"I know you understand all this, Dan," T. Bob continued patronizingly. "But you have to convince him to do the right thing. He and your mother will get compensated big time. No more work, no more worries. He'll have it made. You know that." T. Bob didn't want to include Dan in this fall of riches, but he didn't need to. He figured Dan had enough to justify his betrayal.

Dan sat quietly. "I'll talk to him," he said finally. "But we've never been that close. We can talk, but I don't have your gift of gab. But if you were to talk to him…"

"No way. Your dad's a smart dude. Just knowing I'm involved would kill it. It's up to you. I know you can do it."

Dan grunted in what sounded like the affirmative. Then, he got up, pushed out of the room, entered the elevator, and descended.

T. Bob then gave Reginald and Leland a noncommittal sendoff. It was a show, after all.

"Hang on a minute, Jim."

After everyone else had left, T. Bob asked him what he thought.

Jim got up and started pacing the floor. "This could be a game-changer, Bob. If Dan can convince his father, well, you're back in business, but I can tell he has little respect for you. You need to back off him a bit."

Jim had been T. Bob's right-hand man since the beginning, and he depended on Jim's tactfulness. To T. Bob's credit, he was aware of his own deficiency in that regard.

"Dan feels conflicted," Jim continued. "You may not be able to depend on him, especially considering how easily you alienate people."

"Thanks for the insult. Why the hell did I ever hire you?"

"Because you need me—you need me to tone down your blustering ways. Didn't you tell Dan that you didn't want his father to know you're involved? That says a lot about your reputation. You are what you are; you just don't see what others think of you. You do have the ability to be charismatic at times, but other times, like today, not much when you get yourself worked up. As far as Dan's involvement, we'll have to see. By the way, from the way you talked to Banks, it sounded more like you want to develop a whole town instead of the usual suburban homes and small businesses."

"Why not? The Ellis place is far from Reno, and with new housing developments, those people will want to work and shop and do business closer to home. Yes, eventually I could see a new city growing there."

"Don't bite off more than you can chew. See you tomorrow." Then, while walking out of the room, he mumbled, "Think it's time I got a raise."

T. Bob strode over to one of the large-paned windows overlooking the business section of the city. It was getting to be dusk now. All the lights, especially those coming from the casinos, were beginning to overtake the fading sunlight.

Mildred poked her head through the door. "Do you need anything else, Mr. Sharpenal?"

"No, that will be all," he said coldly.

"Your wife called. Wants you to call her. Well…good night then," she said, and closed the door.

T. Bob liked looking out at this pre-night spectacle, with the artificial world overtaking the natural and the oncoming brilliance of glaring lights flaunting man's superiority.

Time to make a few calls to some political acquaintances, he thought. But he wasn't sure what they could do. Impede the preservation group, get them to raise taxes on farmland, maybe mess with their water rights. He was sure his lawyers could think of something.

He knew he could find a sympathetic political ear. Coming from where he did, his family's intimidating tactics got most of the right people elected. If there was one thing T. Bob understood, it was politicians. He knew that having to go through the grist mill of a campaign, they came out the other end quite different from how they went in—that they weren't there to do something, but to get away with something, and he felt at home among them.

Dan, however, didn't possess the politician's vulnerability. He had principles. *That could be a problem,* T. Bob thought. Receding from the windows and back toward the shadows, a small doubt crept into his mind. Having always been coddled, he had not been brought up to question his own superiority. Since he had seldom felt doubt, he didn't know what it was, and dismissed it as something he ate.

II

Unease

The predawn January emerged as it usually did, with an all-consuming gloominess that not even the glimpse of morning's early glow could alleviate. The moment in Earth's rotation most somber, and most alien to man. Grim and quiet…not tranquil quiet—graveyard quiet. The kind of quiet that foreshadows terror borne of a primal imagination disturbed from its slumber.

Charles awoke at this dead hour heavy-hearted and burdened with a shapeless dread. His thoughts flew to places of isolation, places he knew of from his travels. Real places, whole mountain ranges devoid of human presence: the Hot Creek Range, the Monitor, the Excelsior Mountains, the Snake and Black Rock—some so remote they go nameless. Alien and foreboding, and now more so cloaked in their frozen whiteness, an ominous whiteness capable of penetrating the depths of primitive fears.

Charles could imagine those inhospitable places at such an hour as this, under a waning moon, where haunting shadows outnumbered form, where light was unreflective and dead, and where modern man was now but a helpless alien incapable of surviving on his own. But ages ago, before he distanced himself from Earth, man endured, and when darkness fell, protected himself with his charms and magic potions as a barrier to his imaginings.

Modern man knows those fanciful images aren't real. But he only knows that; he does not feel that. Ghosts are stronger than thought, and now no longer protected by his superstitions, man's apprehensions leave him defenseless and afraid.

Charles struggled out of bed, and as quietly as he could so as to not wake Sally, limped over to the window. He sat in a chair by the sill and laid his roughhewn hands over his face, trying, futilely, to rub the demons away. He wanted no part of this sentiment-driven mind that had only recently asserted itself, where the once wordless was trying to take on the form of words. Words could both define and obscure thought, and thought only raised doubts.

He had been there before, when he was green and at his studies, trying to define the indefinites by categorizing them into manageable bits. A vain effort, he knew, since reasoning only becomes ever more entangled in the attempt to get at the nitty gritty, or "truth," as popular expression would have it. Like peeling an onion to find the core—there is no core. Nothing there but a labyrinthine journey that raises unanswerable questions and removing the traveler ever more from his impossible goal.

But there it was, his old life, when he was young, intruding into the one he had made for himself. Thought provoking thought, trying to make sense of things, and making a holy mess of it all.

It's all those words again. A word can mean any of a thousand things, distorting instinct and perverting reason in the process. But unlike some who had seen that elephant for the first time, and retreat to ignorance, Charles knew there must be some reason for his unease.

He put on his heavy robe, pulled his cane out from behind the bedroom door, and descended to the kitchen. The few lights—LED indicators, microwave timer, coffeemaker, and so on—gave some comfort with the illusion of human mastery. But he knew it was only show. Too early to rise, too late to sleep, he pulled his mud boots over bare feet and went out—just to get out, and maybe discover why he was feeling such dread.

As he sloshed through the mud and snow up toward the barn, his mind began to relax and clear a bit, his fears slowly dissipating along with the wisps of condensing fog. Then the sun's rays found the western mountaintops and began a waterfall flow down toward the pastures below.

He was thinking about how all the animals around him, both large and small, were waiting in stillness for a new and undefiled beginning, for such was their nature that all previous beginnings were unremembered and meaningless.

Not so for the man, his thoughts continued. Cursed with memory, he felt no new beginnings, but only reminders of his defects, and for that, there was no salvation.

Finally coming out of his stupor, it came to him. "Sam, that's why."

Sam was the outsider one could count on to analyze, question, and awaken in Charles an awareness of perspective. The rigid posturing of Charles's close-knit society, for instance, or pointing out the art in nature. Things too close for Charles to see. Sam could define and compartmentalize things, label and put a grid over them. Charles knew there was truth to what Sam said, but words meant to liberate could also constrain.

Charles mused about his own past. He had walked the fine line between the free thinker he was educated to be, and the not-so-free thinker demanded by his vocation and his contemporaries. He went to college at his mother's insistence, not his father's. She had helped get him into Ohio State, thinking, perhaps naively, that the Midwest experience would offer a balance between the realistic and the academic. The only problem was, she sent the wrong son.

But his educated background did allow for some sympathy for the youthful rebellion of his time. He knew how to think, and to think critically. He read, and so he knew there were different versions of reality. This life he was living now was only one of them. He did what he had to when he took over the ranch, which was to block out the past and come to grips with the practical present. *Look where it's gotten us,* he thought. *Rules that suppress can also enrich. But then that premium on toughness and the stifling of independent thought for the commonality of thought. And for what? Punishments of shame or pat-on-the-back praise? Hell, may as well try to move a mountain as fight it. Arbitrary or not, rules are necessary.*

Charles's route along the pathway led to an open area above the barn, one he didn't normally take. He paused to look about the ranch from a less-familiar perspective. Just as unfamiliar were the thoughts working themselves out in his head. He was tired, but his mind seemed to continue on its own whether he wished it or not. It was about to reveal to his conscious mind what a younger and a not-so-exhausted Charles would have never allowed.

It first led him to think back to when, out of necessity when his father died, he was forced to take over the ranch. Back then, it didn't take him long to abandon book-learning for a life of hard knocks. He found out that nature's uncertainties can often defeat men of more sensitive natures. So he became less sensitive.

He had entered a climate that allowed for few errors, so he looked for stability. Opinions are black and white, not contemplated. There was only one right way, one right answer, and one right God. He had to admit that suppressing uncertainty did make life easier to handle.

But now his mind steered him in the direction of his domestic life and his culture's need for a strict family structure, where families were expected to expand from a secure foundation through a continuing cycle of marriages, births, and deaths for ages on end. Charles knew that such a pattern so devoutly wished for was most often thwarted. Fate did tend to steer its own unasked-for course.

Robin and Dan. They hadn't become what Charles and Sally had expected or hoped for. *But what did we expect?* he thought. He and Sally hadn't always followed the dictates set down by their own parents, so why should their own children's independence have come as a surprise? They certainly weren't the first to deviate from the script handed down to them.

But a strong, rebellious child? He hadn't been prepared for those knock-down, drag-outs with Robin. There they were, having to defend a way of life that had taken generations to build; then came that day when she just stood there, mocking them for everything they stood for, all of them yelling things they never should have. Then her moving out in a huff.

It had left him and Sally with the sting of frustration and the opening of doubt. Not a "maybe we were bad parents" doubt, but a doubt that colored their entire world. Doubt, that child of thought, was there again, just as it had come to him from atop Sentinel Hill, witnessing the transfiguration of all that he depended on.

Well, at least Dan wasn't a problem. Not so much rebellious as independent. There must be some comfort in that.

His meditation was interrupted by a rustling in the shrubbery to his left. *Rabbit,* he thought. He stopped to listen more intently. Now it was a continuous rustling among the fallen leaves. *No, a snake. A rattler—always assume it's a rattler.*

Charles sidestepped to the right. The snake didn't worry him. In all his numerous encounters with them, he had never been attacked. Threatened maybe, but only when they inadvertently crossed paths, and then it was always the snake who was the first to move away, followed by himself in the other direction.

The unexpected—always be prepared for the unexpected. I could have stepped wrong, then everything would have changed. Life out here is always full of surprises, so why shouldn't our so-called well-thought-out plans be full of surprises?

First came Robin's rebellion to shake his confidence, then the developers to threaten his land. Then Sam, who came to interpret and comment on it all.

Well, Robin has certainly grown up. Really a responsible adult now. Becoming a mother will do that. So, then, what was the problem?

Then it came to him. That unencumbered thought process finally broke through his subconscious denial and made the connection. It wasn't Robin, and it wasn't Sam. It was Dan.

Dan? The son who was the least amount of trouble, the nice kid who never made waves. *Is this the cause of my unease?*

Charles started backtracking, making connections between the forces he was dealing with and Dan's recent behavior. Nothing that would mean anything by itself, of course, but things started to add up to a disquieting picture. Dan's lack of enthusiasm or unwillingness to talk about any plans for the ranch, for instance.

When the potential deal with the preservationists was announced at that meeting, Dan had said nothing in support. Then Charles had seen him in what looked like private discussions with other ranchers he suspected were not supportive of the idea. Then his leaving the meeting early. Other instances were coming to him.

Now that he thought about it, if the issue of the ranch came up at all, Dan only seemed interested in the investment aspect—how much it was worth in dollars, not in personal attachment. Did Dan want him to sell out, lining himself up for the big payout? More importantly, was he involved with others to make it happen? Why couldn't Dan just be man enough and be straight with him?

Charles tried to find justification for Dan's actions, but couldn't. He had always dismissed his son's attitude as just part of the realtor's banter, thinking of property in only buy-and-sell terms. He was a salesman. Get people to sell their homes because prices would never be so high, then get them to buy because they would never be so low. Charles liked people to be straightforward, not calculating, and there were few professions more calculating than sales, except perhaps politics.

Charles and Dan lived in different worlds of different values, with little common ground between them. The old saying about not being able to keep 'em down on the farm certainly applied to Dan. From the get-go, he never showed any interest in the spread, spending most of his time with friends of families with urban jobs and interests.

While they were never at loggerheads, they were also never close enough to be so. The lack of intimacy would also explain the lack of enmity. Charles had assumed that Dan held very few opinions of importance. Of course, Dan might have sensed that. He might have felt inadequate, disrespected in a world of tough-guy posturing. Who knew? In any event, he clearly felt no roots to the ranch, and had always done what he could not to be a part of it. Charles thought that, to his own credit, at least, he never tried to force it on him. On the other hand, it occurred to him that he also showed little respect for Dan. Dan had made it on his own, hadn't he? Had he ever been praised for that, or was there always the implication of failure because he didn't follow in his father's footsteps? Another guilt trip. Was the wall of apathy about to become one of animosity?

Charles's stomach felt heavy and his legs weak as he turned to head back to the house. The top of the sun had just begun to peek over the distant mountains in an explosion of brilliance, and he was unsure of his footing on the icy slush. Worse than slipping and falling is slipping and almost falling, so he walked with caution.

He felt more cautious about a lot of things: first his heart problem, and now the bum leg. Cautious not just for his physical well-being, but in other ways, too. He was less sure of himself and not prone to think in his usual dynamic way. Worse, he was aware of it. He could feel himself becoming fearful, pulling back, getting old.

Charles stopped in his tracks at that thought. *So this is what it's like. Age doesn't creep up like a fog on little cat feet. It comes with a thud. I'm not getting old; I am old.*

He limped, hunched over his support on a leg more painful than he let on, toward the house with thoughts of age and frailty and Dan and guilt. Then he ran into Sam bounding out the kitchen door, ready to do the work he used to do.

"What are you doing up?" Sam asked.

Charles looked up in surprise. He was absolutely not ready for this. All he could do was stammer as he looked directly at Sam with tired eyes and a mind not of this world. He wanted to buck himself up, but couldn't find the sarcastic answer Sam deserved—something on the order of the "I've been getting up this early for forty years, and I've got a good forty more before I quit" kind of banter.

"Couldn't sleep," was all Charles could dredge up.

"Well, you shouldn't have any problem staying awake now. It's freezing out here."

Charles forced himself to reconnect some dislocated synapses and pulled himself together somewhat. "What are you doing out here?"

"Dave and I are going to check the western section for some strays beyond the property line. Care if I use SOB again?"

"Use him as much as you want. You know I haven't ridden him since the accident," Charles said, not looking directly at his brother.

"He's your horse. I don't want it to seem like I'm taking over here."

"Don't worry about it," Charles said, still looking down.

"Yeah, well, listen," Sam added, "when do you want to have another meeting with the preservation people? I'd like to find out your plan of attack. If you have one."

"I don't know," Charles answered. "I'm not thinking about that now."

"Okay," Sam said cautiously. "We can work it out later. You get into the house and warm up. Get back to bed and relax."

"Yeah," Charles said as he passed by Sam toward the house, toward a comfort that was no comfort, but a suffocating closeness. He wanted to fight it, but for the first time in his life, Charles felt like giving up. Along with age and frailty and guilt could now be added the disgrace of being inconsequential.

Sam continued in the opposite direction. To the hills. To being needed. To life.

12

Riding Herd

It was midday out on the southwest end of the ranch, where the foothills rose to ever-increasing heights leading onto Bureau of Land Management land. No fence was needed because of the terrain, but cattle would occasionally stray onto the steeper portions and need to be redirected downhill. The combination of government land and the JE Ranch provided a sense of endlessness to the whole scene, as it must have looked hundreds of years before.

Sam and Dave were looking for a few strays around the low shrubs and sporadically spaced boulders. The work was tiring for both horse and rider, but there was no other way to do it other than on horseback. Sam quickly learned that Charles's horse, SOB, was anything but the fearsome force to be reckoned with that his name implied. Sam joked that he was the most somnolent creature he had ever run across.

"What the hell is slombolent?" Dave asked sarcastically.

"Uh…sleepy," Sam said, realizing that he should be a little more careful in his choice of highfalutin words.

Once the cattle were located, they began herding them down, but going downhill was harder than going up. The difficulty of the horses' braking to avoid the protruding rocks caused a lot of slipping and jarring. It made Sam's innards feel as if they were being rearranged, not to mention the hint of saddle sores he felt developing. There was nothing to do about that but suffer the consequences later.

Sam let Dave give directions, and with Dave's easygoing ways, they worked well together. Sam understood why Charles and Dave were so close. They had formed such a good working relationship that little needed to be said between them.

Once guided toward the lower portions, and with the ground leveling off, the cattle sensed their own way home. Sam and Dave need only follow. Sam pulled out his sweatshirt, T-shirt, and whatever else felt soft, and put it all under his seat.

"Saddle barnacles?" Dave asked.

"Feels like it. Didn't think I would get 'em this far along."

"You can get 'em any time. They're no fun, that's for sure. Go sit in a tub of Epsom salts. Wait till we get back, though."

"I'll do that." Then Sam decided to broach the subject that had been on his mind. "I'm sure you know about the developers wanting to buy up Charles's spread. What do you think?"

"Word does get around. I heard there could be a compromise with a preservation group."

"Yes, it may be one way to keep the spread. Are you concerned you'd be affected if he were to just sell outright?"

"Not really. Well, yes, it would make me sad, of course, but I'd be okay. We Paiutes come from a strong, tough heritage, and we're adaptable to changes."

"I never asked you, are you a full-blooded Paiute?" Sam asked, a bit wary of delving into racial matters.

"Almost. A few invasive species here and there. Actually, I'm related to Chief Numaga from Pyramid. Don't care about my Irish part, but it's being descended from the Great Numaga that's…great," Dave said with a short laugh.

Sam sensed something deep in how Dave had stressed "great" when he mentioned Numaga, then laughed it off as if embarrassed.

Usually, Dave's speech consisted of quick-witted banter over everyday concerns—the nuts and bolts of the working ranch. But his own feelings? Sam wanted to hear more.

Dave seemed to be pondering what he would say, and Sam hoped he would open up and guide the conversation. After a bit of silence, Dave reined in his horse, as did Sam.

Dave took out his kerchief, pulled his hat back, and wiped his brow, as if in preparation. "Your brother is going through what we did over a century ago: having his whole world upended if he were to sell."

"I'm not as ingrained here as he is, but I worry about that, too. But you talked about Numaga. I thought Winnemucca was the Paiute chief around here. I heard about him when we were in school. Don't remember hearing much about Numaga."

Dave looked off into the distance, which was considerable, then said, "Numaga was the war chief at Pyramid Lake. But he was also a peacemaker and a very wise man. Before the silver and gold discovery, whites and Indians lived pretty well together. The whites, even back then, considered the Paiutes to be highly civilized. 'Honest and kind,' as one report put it. But then the gold discovery brought people in from all over the world, and they started to intrude into the outlying areas, looking for ore, settling, destroying the piñon pines that the tribes depended on for food, what-have-you. With that much activity, there was bound to be trouble.

"The Pit River Indians up Honey Lake area were led by the hot-headed Smoke Creek Sam. Unlike the Paiute tribe, they were always causing trouble, and when they did, the whites blamed all the Indians. To them, there was no distinction. There were a few incidents, so a treaty was drawn up with Numaga, who could speak English, to help defuse any situation before it got out of hand. One reporter who interviewed him said that he wasn't just a superior Indian, but a superior man for any race. Powerful words from one whose own race considered itself superior.

"Numaga did the best he could trying to keep the peace, but most of the other tribes were fed up with the whites stealing their food resources, their stock, and generally blaming the Indians for any of the whites' own misfortunes. This one time, many of the surrounding tribes had gathered at Pyramid to formulate some kind of strategy, and were ready to go to war. Numaga tried to persuade them that warfare would be a lost cause, that they should find a way to work and live among them. The other tribal leaders had the greatest respect for Numaga, and listened, but were reluctant to follow his advice. But that's when an incident happened that blew everything out of the water."

"I remember something about a massacre. Is that what you mean?" Sam said, pulling his horse around to face Dave directly.

"It wasn't a massacre. It was a battle. Anytime the Indian wins a battle, it's a massacre. Anytime the whites incite a massacre, it's a battle. Anyway, some whites who were running a way station east of Reno abducted two young girls from Numaga's tribe, raped them, and hid them in a pit in their barn. A group from Numaga's tribe found out about it and went to rescue them. They tried to reason with the five whites who ran the station, but a fight broke out, and the white men were killed. When Numaga heard about it, he knew there was no choice, and told the council to prepare for war.

"Of course, as far as the whites were concerned, it was all the Paiutes' fault. Sure enough, as Numaga predicted, a volunteer army of over a hundred men was formed from the mining towns of the area— Virginia City, Gold Hill, Carson. But they had no training and no competent leader. They just figured they could go out and shoot down any old Paiute they came across.

"Numaga, on the other hand, was a warrior. He knew the whites would be on the offensive, which meant they would have to come into his territory, and he was prepared. When this so-called army went hunting for the Paiutes down near Pyramid Lake, they were met with a coordinated force. The whites panicked, and about seventy of them were killed. Numaga won the battle, but he knew he couldn't win the war. News of it caused a panic in the territory, and, still blaming the Indians for the "massacre," five hundred well-trained army regulars were brought in from California. But, again, Numaga was prepared. He knew the odds were against him, so he got his men to engage the army in a stalling tactic so that he could move the women and children north, knowing the army would be reluctant to follow. Those skirmishes were pretty much a stand-off, but it had its effect, and much of the tribe never returned.

"At the end of that year, 1860, a colonel named Lander, the one they named the county for, and Numaga had a peace summit at Pyramid. The colonel wrote in his report that Numaga refused to speak right away. So they sat in silence for a long time, you know, gettin' sore knees and all. Then toward darkness, Numaga spoke. He explained that the lies of the whites, the broken promises, and the stealing of Indian land and women and stock and the murdering of his people were hard on his heart. Numaga said that it wasn't darkness he was waiting for to speak, but for peace to come to his heart so he could speak calmly—that his hot breath might not burn their ears. Numaga sensed that Lander was a man of truth. He was glad that he had come without promises, and knew he could be trusted.

"After that, there was relative peace in the area, but only relative. A few skirmishes here and there, but Numaga and Lander worked to redirect anger away from blaming sides to going after the people responsible. Numaga knew that if his race was to survive at all, it was going to have to live and work in the white man's world. But it was never the same. The Paiute wars had caused a sensation, and we were all under suspicion after that. The army built a fort, Fort Churchill, to keep us in line. It wasn't really necessary. The tribes had pretty much disintegrated, and those that remained were forced to live on reservations. The whites thought they were being generous giving us land they had no use for. You know, 'where the water don't flow and the plants don't grow.'"

Dave broke his far-off gaze, unscrewed his water bottle, and took a generous swig, then he removed his hat and poured the rest over his head.

"That's a hell of a story," Sam said. "I never knew any of that."

"You were never taught it. You were taught white history, which was written. We had nothing written—not our history, not our gods, nothing. Everything was handed down orally. That was all lost.

"While the warfare had ebbed, the whites took advantage of the decimated tribal lands. Because they had the mechanical technology we didn't have, they could build and live anywhere—and did. They had the notion of owning property, which was incomprehensible to the Indian. Indians belonged to the land and adapted to it. The whites thought it should belong to them, and changed it. Talk about opposites! The whites destroyed their culture, by design more often than not, then expected the Indians, those who survived, to fit into their own.

"Well, the Indian was defeated. He couldn't fit in. He became poor and was looked down upon as lazy by the very race that had made him that way. You can't uproot his tribe and force him to live on a reservation without killing him. And I mean that literally. He was such a part of his land and his culture that he would get homesick to death. He couldn't survive without his land any more than the whites could without their houses and their…things. You know, like that big old clock of yours. It's useless, but it was so important that your ancestors risked their lives to get it here. They couldn't live without the culture it represented. If they had been stripped of their things like we were, they would have been just as demoralized.

"So the Indian became a hanger-on, groveling for trinkets because he could do nothing else. He accepted what the whites expected of him. They stripped him of his vision quests. That was why he took to drink—a poor substitute. When you are ridiculed as a contemptuous half-human, you become one. That's the saddest part of all."

Dave paused and looked Sam straight in the eye. "I'm saying all this because there's a similarity to what Charles is facing now. Now it's developers wanting to take your land, and Charles would feel the loss. Deeply."

Sam shifted uneasily in his saddle, but it wasn't just the saddle sores making him uncomfortable. "You're not saying there's a real comparison, are you? The natives were damn near exterminated."

"Of course not. I'm just comparing one man's situation. All Charles may be able to do is be compensated with money. It wouldn't be enough. We were compensated with reservation lands. That wasn't enough."

"But Dave, you adapted, didn't you? Don't you live a pretty good life now?"

"I do. No question. If I had a white history, like you and Charles, I wouldn't know the other and wouldn't be bothered by it. But I do have that history. It's not a matter of whether we're better off, I think what weighs on us is the culture we lost. It will be the same for Charles if he sells his place outright. So I do see both sides. But I try to follow Numaga's example and judge a man by the man, not his label."

Sam looked at Dave in amazement.

"Yeah, I'm talkin' too much. Well, sorry about that. Just gettin' it off my chest. Can't talk to Charles like this. As a matter of fact, I'm talkin' like Charles myself, aren't I? Hah! When he gets into one of his tirades, I don't counter him much. Wouldn't do any good. I try to overlook his prejudices and look at *him*. He's a good man. Numaga would have understood that.

"But when Charles tells me to look at all the good the whites have done, it does get my hackles up. It's like Indians were stupid or something, like they couldn't survive without the whites, like we had for thousands of years before. When the settlers came trudging across the country, a lot of them were starving and dying while the Indians around them were doing just fine. It was the Indians who had to help the helpless whites. Who was stupid then? We weren't outsmarted; we were overrun by technology and guns."

Sam smiled. "Holy moly, Dave! I never heard you talk so much, or with such passion. You're quite the philosopher."

"Well, I keep it to myself, don't I. I did get some education. I read a lot, like you. But I don't throw it in anybody's face. We Paiutes learned long ago to put on a face of passivity. Of course, whites take that for dullness. We're either the noble red man or stupid, bloodthirsty savages." Looking over at Sam, he laughed. "You can't win. That's why I say Charles is facing a similar situation. He would lose everything of importance to him. Sally said to me once that she thought that clock's big ol' pendulum represented the markings of the new and the renewal of life. But there was no renewal for us. Yeah, I'm pissed. I'm taking a side." He paused before adding, "It becomes a stupid point of pride and honor, I guess. Only wise men really understand, and there's never enough of them around."

"There's nothing stupid about it, Dave. I think honor is just stubbornness, but it's been drummed into our heads that it's a virtue. It may sound righteous and reverent, but it's really meant to force a man to become one with the identity laid out for him. Make him think that the cause is more important than he is. Convince him to die for it, if necessary. I remember a line in Shakespeare where a guy says, 'What is honor? A word…air.'"

"Now who's the philosopher?" Dave laughed. And with that, he wheeled his horse around and started back down, Sam following.

The two continued on in silence.

"Speaking of Charles," Sam said after a time, "have you noticed a change in him the last few days? He was pretty fired up after talking to the other ranchers, and the possibility for compromise, but now he seems to be in a funk."

"Last few days? Hell, he's been, like, despondent for a week now."

"I just noticed it this morning. Why didn't you say something?"

"Not my business. Probably feels he's lost control, what with his bum leg and all putting him out of action. But I figured it's family stuff."

"You're part of the family as far as I can see. And if there's anything bothering you, speak up. Okay?"

Dave nodded, then said, "It can't just be his leg, or his heart, or even the development thing. There's something else going on. Maybe it's the change of life thing. Wait, wrong sex. Midlife crisis—no, old-life crisis—that's it. He's got a case of old-life crisis. Hell, I don't know. He'll snap out of it. Always has."

"We don't snap out of things like we used to. Maybe I'm getting into that old-life crisis myself."

"Maybe we should get him back in the saddle, don't you think?" Dave said. "Not coddle him so much, acting like he's helpless or something. That doesn't help. Needs a kick in the pants. I have some things I can get him to do and make him think he's the one giving orders. Been doing that for years, anyway."

"Good idea. I should give him SOB back. I don't think it was a good idea to borrow him."

"He'll come through. Now, let's move some cows, whatdaya say? And how's your butt doin'?"

"Better now that we've had this talk. I think I'll be standing the rest of the way if you don't mind. And Dave, it's cattle, not cows."

13
Confrontation

Sally came down the back stairs to the kitchen to see Charles sitting at the table, drinking coffee.

"Why did you get up so early?" she asked. Then, lightheartedly, she added, "It's only seven. Just because the coffee timer gets up early doesn't mean you have to."

Charles looked up in annoyance. "You're the second person this morning to ask me why I got up early. Why shouldn't I be up? I'm not helpless."

Not expecting an outburst from her husband, Sally turned with a start. "Of course not, but…"

"Don't tell me. I can relax now with Sam here."

She put her hand on her aching back, trying to massage it. "I don't know why you're in such a huff. You just don't need to worry so much now." She limped over to the cupboard, retrieved a plate, and set it down in front of him. "You don't have to bite my head off." Then, to placate him, she said calmly, "I'll fry an egg and make some toast."

As she peered over at him, she couldn't decipher his look. Was he sorry about the flare-up, or was he even angrier? For all of Sally's sixth-sense acuteness to other people's feelings, the one person beyond her reach was the one she was closest to. Like everyone else, Charles and Sally certainly shared times of frustration, but this seemed different. She sensed a look, not of anger, or even depression, but of resignation.

It had never occurred to her that the great, strong man could have ever come to this.

She was about to add something when Robin could be heard coming down the stairs. Robin was dressed in her standard ruffled morning attire: robe, slippers, and hair that reflected only a few hours' sleep. She looked first toward her mother and was able to blurt out only half-sentences.

"What are you arguing about? Hazel's still asleep. Up all night. Want her to sleep as long as possible. Might be coming down with something." Then, with a little more perkiness, she said, "Hi, Dad. You look like you didn't get much sleep either. Sounded like you were up early, too."

"Humph."

She turned back to her mother, who in turn gave Robin one of those power stares, the unspoken point being: "Don't say anything to your father." Something was going on, and whatever it was, Robin received it quiet and clear.

"Think I'll shower before breakfast." Robin gave a sideways glance at her father while continuing to talk to her mother. "Mom, since I don't need to be at work today, and you have your doctor's appointment at eleven, I'll drive you into town because I want to see if Hazel's pediatrician can see her while we're there. I'll call now and see if I can get an appointment."

"Okay," Sally said.

Robin turned and scooted back up the stairs.

"I guess the boys went out to—" Sally began before being interrupted.

"I'm going into town," Charles huffed. "Have a few people to see." He pulled his chair back and struggled up, trying, unsuccessfully, to hide the pain in his leg.

Sally suspected that he was going to meet with the preservation people, but thought better of asking. She sensed that his pride was under attack and that he was struggling to keep it. Pride can be a fragile thing in a tough man.

~ ~ ~

Three, maybe four cups of coffee had Charles wired as he got off the dirt road and headed down Pyramid Way toward Reno. Because it was his left ankle that was broken, driving an automatic was no problem.

Charles was going to Reno to confront his son, but wasn't sure how he should approach him. *Ease him into what I suspect, give him the benefit of the doubt.* He thought he would let Dan do the talking and not go in with both guns blazing. *There might be an explanation to it all. Clear the air, maybe get him involved with all this, work as a team for once. A father and son collaboration.*

But Charles knew better. He suspected one certain person behind it all. *Just keep your cool,* he thought.

In the recent past, Pyramid Way had been a seldom-used two-lane fast track that went out thirty miles from the Big Little City toward the Indian reservation at Pyramid Lake. Now it was four lanes of asphalt with a stoplight at every housing development—lights that seemed to turn yellow once you were two hundred yards away doing sixty. What once had been a thoroughfare had become a succession of fits and starts on the way to town. It was enough to jangle anyone's nerves, especially in Charles' over-caffeinated state.

He went under the elevated east-west freeway and made a few turns into the commercial center of Sparks, passing by the Sharpenal Building on his right. Reno and Sparks were adjacent towns, and it was often confusing knowing which one you were in. The old joke about Reno being so close to hell you could see Sparks always seemed to get a laugh, at least from strangers.

Charles turned right and into the parking lot of a modest one-story office structure that housed, among other things, the Real World Realty office. *Clever name*, he thought, but he was in no mood to be amused.

Charles knew how fickle the real estate business was, how realtors were forced into playing different roles for different people, trying to imprint themselves onto whomever they were dealing with and changing stripes when the need presented itself. He didn't blame them;

it was the nature of the beast. He just didn't have to like it. In social gatherings, realtors would always put on a show of self-assurance, of being liked and admired by all so as to bolster the feedback of ever-increasing approval. Sadly, Charles thought, it was a shallow performance that had even them fooled. Because the business was a frantic one of emotional highs and lows, it stood to reason that its agents would feel insecure. He remembered a time when a realtor handed him a business card while he was standing at a urinal. They just never quit. And Dan was one of them.

Charles tried to put that behind him. He got out of his truck and entered a building that comprised about a dozen or so gray cubicles. There seemed no real central reception area that could lend the place a sense of cohesiveness, which only reaffirmed to him just how solitary this business was. He had entered a world of competitors who, though thrown together out of necessity, were alone in their efforts.

Charles could see only a couple of people at their desks, and worried that Dan might not be there. Having been there before, he headed down one row and up another, hoping to find Dan in his "office," if one could call it that.

"Dad!" Dan said looking up, genuinely surprised. "What are you doing here?"

Charles noticed the neat attire Dan wore, and guessed that he would probably be meeting with clients later on.

"Just thought I'd stop by, see what you're doing."

"Sit down—wait, I'll go get a chair."

Dan went across the corridor to grab a chair from another cubicle, giving Charles a chance to look around. The one personal item Dan had on his desk was a photo of him and his wife. The rest were sticky notes tacked up on the side walls, and sales pamphlets scattered about sporting photographs of smiling, helpful salespeople. The men displayed that casual but professional look in tie-less sports jackets. The women wore no-nonsense, yet stylish, passive-aggressive garb. (One never knew who you would need to impress.) Despite the heavy makeup and the polished nails, or maybe because of it, they still couldn't hide that not-so-lean and hungry look.

Then again, that was just Charles's take on it. He'd come in with a sack-load of prejudices, and no accounting to the contrary was going to change his mind.

Dan came back with a chair and put it near his desk.

"This is your office?" Charles said, trying hard not to sound judgmental.

"Yeah. It's not much. Most of the time, we're out looking at property. If we have meetings with clients, we use the conference room. I could do all this from home, but it helps to show organization. Don't want clients to think we're small-time."

"Nothing wrong with that."

"Did you come to Reno for business?"

"Well, sort of. I came to see you."

"Really?" Dan said guardedly.

"What do you think about this preservation idea?" *So much for small talk.* Already, Charles was steering this to confrontation, and he wasn't about to let Dan escape with a qualifying answer.

"I don't know. It's an idea, I suppose," Dan said cautiously.

Charles leaned forward in earnest. "But what do you think?" he said, knowing he had his son cornered.

Dan bolstered himself. "I want what's best for you and Mom."

Charles didn't alter his expression. His outward demeanor belied the screaming backflips his mind was going through, but sensing his son's defensiveness, he eased up with a more open tactic. "Well, what's best?" he asked simply. "Do you think we should sell the whole spread?"

"It might be for the best, you know, since you and Mom can't continue working as you have as you get older. If you worked out some deal with that group, you might still be working just as hard. Sell it, and all that would be behind you."

"So, you're in the business," Charles said, letting out more line. "Have you figured out any numbers? Have you talked to anyone?"

"Well, yeah. We've worked out some numbers, and they look pretty good, especially if you were to sell before any of the others. Market's good right now."

"Who do you mean by *we*?"

Dan's face turned red. "Well, you know, we all discuss the value of property here. That's our business."

"But I mean who specifically?"

"Well, I heard that you've met with Reginald and Leland from their realty company. Isn't that right?"

Charles kept his composure. "Yeah, they came by. Who else?"

The benefit of possessing a commanding presence is that people think you know more than you do, and thus volunteer more information than necessary as a hedge against being found out. Charles seldom let on that he didn't know what had been disclosed to him, but just a knowing look or a casual comment could make others assume that he knew it—whatever *it* was—all along. Though it was unconscious to Charles, it could provide more information than one might normally divulge.

But this was his son, not some joker he could play games with.

"Well, I did get a call from Robert Sharpenal asking questions about your spread."

This was the one Charles had suspected. "Who? Turd Bob?" Charles exclaimed.

"He's not associated with those two other guys, is he? That sum'bitch thinks he has everyone fooled. And everyone sees right through him. Hell, he couldn't find his ass with both hands. Only the gullible and desperate look up to him."

Charles was on a roll and couldn't stop himself. "Guy's a man-child. Those are the most dangerous types if you ask me. They get the money to run a big organization, but they don't have a clue what a real business is. All they know how to do is pull strings, bribe, and intimidate. Bet he drives one of those fancy Far-rar-y cars so he can look like a bigshot."

The look in Dan's eyes suggested that T. Bob *did* drive a Ferrari.

"But what does a big organization like that want with the one those other two work with?" Charles asked in a leading way.

Dan was speechless—at least for the moment. But when he looked once more at his father from the angled backlighting of the table lamp, he saw the exaggerated deep lines in Charles's face, and caught a glimpse of the old man Sam had seen that morning. He somehow felt more emboldened.

"Well, Dad, we never talk about it. I think we should. Nobody's getting any younger here, and I think you need to look to your, and Mom's, future. Yes, and Robin's, and maybe even mine, since neither of us have any desire or ability to run the ranch."

Charles, to his own surprise, didn't bluster. His earlier energy was wearing thin, and the exhaustion of that morning was returning. He knew his son was in it for himself, but hell, so was everybody. He didn't want to fight it, but then again, he was not about to let everything he'd ever worked for be destroyed. As long as he had some moxie left, he was going to let Dan know of his decision.

"I'm sorry, Dan. I don't want to give up the spread. I couldn't ever see leaving it, and neither could your mother."

To Charles, Dan did not display the disappointment he thought he would; if anything, Charles sensed that Dan was somewhat relieved.

"I guess I understand, Dad," Dan said, seemingly to his own surprise. Then a lull descended between the two of them. To break that spell, Dan decided to change the subject: "I was kind of surprised when you told the ranchers that they might have the option of putting their lands in the preservation trust. As far as I can remember, you've never seemed concerned about environmental issues."

"Mostly, I see it as a good compromise for us to keep our ranches, and since I was the one who instigated all this, I will be putting our ranch into the preservation trust—if and when it becomes available.

"But for me," Charles continued, "it's also a personal matter. With the trust's stipends and tax credits, it will provide your mom—since she will most likely survive me—financial security, and with Dave, Henry, and Sam working it, it would allow her to stay. That way, you and Robin can continue on with your own careers—I know it might seem selfish of me to be concerned about the ranch's future after I'm gone, but we have to think of your mom."

Charles thought for a moment. "But you may be right about environmental concerns. What I think I'm trying to say is that the land does have its hold on those of us who work and live in it, and the more I've thought about it, the more I realize how integral we all are to the environment—not just with the ranch, but with all of the land we're surrounded by. It's probably one of the reasons I want the other ranchers to go the preservation route. That way, most of our whole area can continue unchanged.

"But there is another angle, a practical one from your perspective in real estate. You know that land ownership is a great asset, and I think this ranch should stay in the family, because, who knows, in time perhaps your sister may want to come back to it. Maybe even you as well. You never know what the future will bring."

As his father said this, Dan was thinking how right he was; land cannot be created or destroyed, only bought and sold, and land ownership, even if it were put into a preservation trust, *would* be an asset.

"But later on, when your mom and I are gone, eventually you and Robin could have the spread worked, or the two of you could go ahead and sell it. And Sam, if he's still around, would probably go along with that; if not, you would inherit his share anyway.

"Of course, being in the trust, it would have to continue on as a ranch—but selling it is certainly doable. Despite all the complaining we do, we do make a decent living off it. All those old ranchers you see at the Farmers Exchange are not the only land owners around here; there are a few younger ranchers out there that have bought and sold their spreads to continue on as ranches—they just don't bother to show up at the hall."

Dan didn't respond while his father was talking, and while Charles had felt relieved that Dan didn't argue over his father wanting to keep the spread, Charles still thought he wasn't getting through to him.

But he *was*.

As he sat there, Charles felt that he had not only disappointed his son, but failed him in some way. He couldn't say what he longed to say: that he was sorry Dan had to grow up in an atmosphere he wasn't geared for; that he should have supported him more in what he really wanted to do. That he was sorry that he was surrounded by all that tough-guy posturing, and that Charles was one of them. Sorry that he hadn't told him that it was all phony BS, that real men don't bluster, only wannabes do. Sorry that he hadn't told him that getting out was the right thing to do, not the wrong thing, and that he shouldn't have felt a failure in doing so. Finally, sorry that he hadn't made the effort to talk with him.

But he didn't say these things. He only felt them.

"Look, Dan," Charles said. "I don't blame you. In some ways, we're all in it for ourselves. When it comes to family matters, they can get pretty contentious sometimes."

"I guess you're right," Dan quietly responded, but had little more to add.

After an awkward pause that implied an end to the conversation, both started to get up, uttering superficialities about whatever trivial subject they could think of, pretending that everything was as fine as before, which, of course, it wasn't. Then would come the goodbyes and "laters" and the pulling away under a cloud.

As it happened, Charles mumbled something to the effect of, "Too bad we couldn't work it out."

Dan decided to pursue it. "What do you mean?"

"You know," Charles said, looking straight at him. "The family being at odds and such. I mean with Robin and her problems and all. It's too bad our family wasn't closer."

"You and Mom had a hard time with her," Dan replied, deflecting the conversation toward the women as the ones who suffered instead of themselves. It was a level on which they might continue. They both sat back down.

"We did. You were away at school when all the trouble started. Or maybe you were already working. It was pretty bad. Your mother suffered a lot over Robin's defiance. She didn't know how to handle it, and so she probably—or both of us—said the wrong things that riled Robin up even more."

"I just remember that she moved out in a huff," Dan said.

"She denied everything we worked for." Charles sighed. "You were never any trouble. You followed your own road, and that seemed to work for you." It was one of the nicer things Charles had ever said to his son.

While the door to communication reopened, the front office door opened as well, and a realtor with two clients entered.

"Morning, Ron," Dan said with a wave. This was responded in a likewise manner as they made their way to the conference room.

"Look," Dan said, "people are going to start coming in now. I just like to come in early—why don't we continue this conversation somewhere else. There's a coffee shop a block from here. Are you okay to walk that?"

"That's fine; it's what my physical therapist wants me to do. I'm afraid I had my fill of caffeine this morning, but I'll let you buy me some pastry, as long as you don't tell your mom."

As they entered the shop, Charles could glean, from all the suits assembled, that these were business people. Unlike Dan's quiet office, this place was noisy, but having found a corner table, it was a good place to continue their talk. They did so for nearly an hour as they never had before, each admitting to their own personal frailties, as well as to their many commonalities. There was a lot to process.

Finally, after some inconsequential talk about this and that, they got up and walked out.

"Us men are a strange breed, Dan. I mean, the way we keep ourselves closed and defensive just makes us stubborn. I want us to be open with each other. And I'm mostly referring to myself."

"Thanks, Dad—I mean for everything," Dan said as they came to the office door, then added: "You may be right: we don't know what the future will bring. I'm sure things will work themselves out when Sam and Robin and I take over the ranch. And by the way, maybe it's time we got to know each other better."

Dan said this in a half-joking way, but Charles could tell he meant it.

"Anyway, I have a meeting to attend in half an hour," Dan said, looking at his watch.

"Let's do this again—soon," Charles said. "I'll even buy you lunch. Later this week?"

"Thursday might be good, but I'll have to see if I'm seeing clients then. I'll call you tomorrow or Wednesday."

Charles's drive back was in stark contrast to the anxiety-ridden drive into the city. Funny how lifted spirits could affect physical wellbeing. The pain of his bum leg felt as light as the burden he no longer carried on his shoulders.

14
Grit

Dan Ellis stood by the window, watching his father drive off. During their talk, he knew his father could see right through him, and it made him feel weak and intimidated. Yet that split-second glimpse of his father's own vulnerability gave him pause. While he believed his father when he said he and his mother would never want to leave the ranch, still, he was concerned about how they could continue working as they had. In any case, Dan decided, then and there, to accept it and help them out in any way he could.

But while their meeting had lifted some weight from his shoulders, several matters remained unresolved. He needed a more complete resolution with his father. As well as their meeting had gone, he needed to open up about his deception. But that would come later. Now he was going to have to bring up some inner mettle, and try to make things right.

First, he needed to talk to his wife. He called to have her come over to his office on her lunch hour and let her in on what was happening.

"Hi, hon. What's up?" Laura said, coming through the door. Then, looking over at him, she said, "You okay? You don't look well."

Laura obviously sensed something was wrong, and decided to let him do the talking.

"I'm okay. Let's go in the conference room so we can talk." He put the delivered pizza on plates, and as they sat down, he began to open up.

"I need to tell you something," he began. "I told you that Dad was concerned about the future of the ranch, and about his wanting to put it in the preservation trust. But I thought he and my mom should just sell it, since they shouldn't have to work so hard just trying to keep it in the family. Since neither Robin nor I have any ability or interest in taking it over, I thought they should do it now before the others so as to get a higher price for it. Well, Dad came by today, and he wanted to talk about it. He doesn't want to sell. But that's not the issue. I have a confession to make. I had some talks with developers…well only one, really—T. Bob. He wanted me to convince my father to sell—to him—so he could develop it. I didn't want Dad to know about it."

"Oh, Dan, behind his back? And T. Bob, of all people?"

"Yeah. I sensed that he knew I was involved with him, probably thinking I was doing it to set us up for a big inheritance. In a way, he would be right. But he wants to keep it, and now I want him to. It was underhanded of me, and I need to make things right for him."

"Oh, dear," she said. But then Laura sensed the guilt he was carrying, and rather than getting upset with him, she realized that she should take a kinder course. "How did he take it? Did you divulge everything?"

"Not everything, but actually it turned out okay. For the first time, we had a good talk; I just didn't fill him in with all the details. I think he knows I want to rectify things—and I will. First, I'm going to cut it off with T. Bob, then open up and apologize to Dad, and hope he accepts it."

"I'm glad. But that still leaves them the problem of trying to work the ranch as they continue to get older."

"That's where the preservation group comes in. Along with the tax breaks and stipends, and Sam's money from his pension and the sale of his house, it will provide them with enough to allow them to stay. But as inheritors, we won't be able to sell it to developers. We could sell to anyone who wants to work it as a ranch of course, but the sale price would be less.

Eventually, after my parents are gone, Sam, Robin, and I will inherit it, and with Sam's blessing we could maybe sell our house and move there in the future. Robin too, if she wanted to. So, what do you think?"

"What does Robin think about all this?"

"Yes…Robin," Dan said pondering. "She…" Just then, the end of his pizza fell on the table, cheese side down.

Laura laughed. "And on this clean mahogany table."

Dan laughed along with her. He went and got some paper towels, and while cleaning up the mess, he said, "As I was about to say: she doesn't know about my involvement, and I don't think she has to; it would be too embarrassing, but she will have a voice since she will also be an owner."

"That would be fine with me. I'd like to see it stay in the family. I like Robin. We got along really well when we were at the lake, but you and I have never been very close to her with her living in Sacramento. Now that she's going to be living here, we should connect more."

"We'll work on that. Invite her over for dinner, and we'll have a talk with her."

"Good idea. Think I would look good in a cowboy hat and overalls?"

~ ~ ~

Dan had told his father that morning that he had a meeting to attend. He did, but not a scheduled one. He was about to confront T. Bob.

Dan entered the elevator of the Sharpenal Building and pressed the top-floor button. When he realized he needed a code, he pressed the three numbers he had seen Leland enter. The door closed, and he was on his way. When it opened, he found himself facing the waterfall, now turned off, and the front desk, now empty. At first, he thought he was by himself until he heard the apartment door open and T. Bob came out.

"Jesus! Dan, how did you get up here?"

"Elevator."

"Shit. Didn't know you had the code."

"It's never been a big secret," Dan said, deciding to mess with him.

T. Bob seemed oblivious to Dan's candor, and continued, "I'll have Jim come over; I want him to be in on this. I want to go over some stuff with you—we may have something. Ah, here's Jim." Putting his arm around Dan's shoulder, T. Bob led them both into his office.

Dan decided to let T. Bob do the talking, and maybe learn something.

"Been talking to a few influential people, one state senator and the Washoe County representative," T. Bob said as he turned to talk directly to Dan. "These reps know which side their bread is buttered on, if you know what I mean. Farmers pay the least in taxes, but the exclusionary bill passed seven years ago keeping those taxes down is coming up soon. Time to make some adjustments. Farmers have been in the way of progress for too long. It's going to take some time and effort to get this new one passed, and I'm going to need your help. You're the smart one in your family. I'm sure once you fall in line," he said condescendingly, "you'll be a big asset."

He seemed disappointed that Dan didn't respond as he thought he would.

"What do you think?" T. Bob added.

From Jim's perspective, being astute to other people's thoughts and feelings, he sensed a renewed confidence in Dan, and also sensed that T. Bob's own confidence was about to get a jolt.

Dan directed his gaze to the window overlooking the mountains. He saw the few structures already there and imagined how they would look impacted. Then he looked back at T. Bob, and instead of the long, drawn-out speech he had planned on the way over, he blurted out the first thing that came to him: "It's not going to happen."

"Come again? You couldn't persuade your father?"

"No, *I* don't want it to happen."

T. Bob lifted an eyebrow. "What? Jim, did you hear that?"

"I heard," Jim said casually as he went and sat on the couch.

"You heard me, T. Bob. You've been pulling my string too long, and it isn't going to happen—the selling of the property, especially to you."

"What the hell are you talkin' about? Why the sudden change of heart? Decided to wimp out on me? Jeez, you're like all the rest of 'em. Can't trust a one. Well, you can't get out that easily, boy. I got your number. You'll never work in this business again if you take this route. And don't think I don't have connections, and not just with the politicians." T. Bob's face was growing redder by the second.

"I want what's best for my family. I told you that before. He wants to keep the spread, and I won't interfere." Dan spoke calmly. "Everyone would know just how you're trying to manipulate the political forces by forcing the ranchers out. Raising land use taxes to make them sell just for your benefit? People don't take kindly to that kind of manipulation."

T. Bob looked at Jim and, noticing his disapproval, tried to contain himself. "Okay. Forget what I said. That was just overreaction. Remember, there's nothing illegal about any of this, just a little pressure in the right places. Everyone does it. But you're threatening me with going public. I won't let you get away with it!"

"I can get away with it. I'm merely threatening to expose the truth. And your politicians? They're very sensitive to public disclosures like this."

The redness returned to T. Bob's face.

"Look," Dan added, easing up a bit, "you have a lot more to lose than I do, and you're not going to take that chance." At that, he pulled out his cell phone that was connected to his office phone's message recorder, just in case.

"Taping this conversation? Not legal! It'll never see the light of day."

"You're right. It is illegal, and I would suffer for it, but not as much as you. As long as you do nothing, neither will I, and it *won't* see the light of day. I'm sure we can agree to that arrangement. You can be ruined, and I lose my job, or we can both continue working, you just not in our area. I think I can count on your support."

"Get out!"

"My pleasure," Dan said as he tugged at his imaginary hat, turned, and walked slowly to the elevator.

When Dan got in it, he stuck his head back around the corner just as the door was starting to close and hollered, "Hey, Turd Bob! Go fuck yourself."

"Jim, he tried to blackmail me!" T. Bob declared, his knuckles pressed into his desk.

"I sensed his reluctance before. I suspect he and his father had some sort of reconciliation. Instead of persuading his father to sell, most likely his father convinced him that he wouldn't. Dan's obviously not going to change his mind, and you might want to think about backing off. I know you, and you would want revenge on him. We've done fine so far, but fighting it, like he said, could put you in jeopardy."

"So that's it?"

"Not necessarily. Ellis, being old, may still sell at some point, but there's nothing more we can do now. All we can do is wait for them to make a move. In any event, we have another project about ready to start. Let's concentrate on that."

~ ~ ~

As Dan's elevator descended, his spirits rose. He felt energized and alive. He felt like his father.

15
Family Council

Now that it had become accepted as a legitimate idea, Charles's preservation suggestion was gaining ground. Once that happened, examples began popping up—some not forty miles away in Carson Valley, just south of Reno. What had been going on under the radar in a short amount of time suddenly became conspicuously apparent to those now interested.

But there was a problem. Because of its more desolate, desert-like nature, the cause for preservation in the north did not carry the same sex appeal of the greener, more historic fertile area in and around Gardnerville and Genoa to the south. Those had been the first settlements in Nevada, and were situated at the base of the sheer, massive eastern face of the Sierra Nevada mountains, which enclosed the whole of Lake Tahoe thousands of feet above. By any measure, it was a spectacular area. Because of its desirable location, the pressure for development was high, but so, too, was reaction against it.

While the buzz of excitement continued to brew, Charles knew he had work to do. To the ranchers, Charles had essentially promised a done deal, but they had discounted, or perhaps had selectively decided not to hear, his warnings that it might not be that simple. For one thing, he still didn't know just how many easements could be bought up. He had to convince the preservation group to take more of an interest, and to do that, he needed to have them meet with the ranchers he knew were supportive.

Charles had been back to his old self of late, due in part to a reconciliation with Dan. But now he felt overwhelmed, so he called for a meeting—this time restricted to his family.

~ ~ ~

Due to his heavy workload that week, Dan had to postpone his lunch date with his father. What he didn't want to put off was to inform his father about his involvement with T. Bob.

Since the family meeting was called for late Wednesday afternoon, he decided to go early that morning and take care of that third, and hardest, phase of his burden.

Pulling up to the house, he could see Charles sitting on the porch, as had become his habit. Dan stopped and sat for a moment, then reached for his Starbucks coffee and got out.

"Hi, Dad."

"You're early. Didn't expect you guys till later." Charles looked behind Dan and noticed that Laura was not with him.

"What's up?"

Dan paused uncomfortably and said, "I want to tell you a few things I should have the last time. Can we walk?"

"Sure. I'll limp, you walk." Charles got up slowly, stepped carefully down the steps, and both men walked away from the house.

"I didn't want Mom to hear us," Dan explained. "I have a confession to make."

"Good. I pretty much know what it is, but I want you to be the one to tell me."

"I was involved with T. Bob. He wanted me to convince you to sell, and I agreed because I thought that would be best. I kept rationalizing that it was in your and Mom's—even Robin's—best interests. But then I had to admit that it would have been in mine, too. It's been haunting me and I should have been open about it, but I wasn't; it was underhanded. Keeping the spread *is* in your best interest. I don't know how to apologize, or even if you would accept it. I hope you believe me. I do apologize—sincerely," Dan said, looking directly at his father.

"I don't expect that it was easy for you," Charles said. "Yes, not being open about it was wrong. But I appreciate your telling me now." He smiled. "Does Turd Bob know?"

"Before you left the other day, I told you I had a meeting to attend. I did, but not a planned one. I decided then and there that I was going to confront him—and I did."

"How'd that go?"

"He got pissed. Threatened this and that if I didn't cooperate. Said I would never work in real estate again, and so on. I let him rattle on until I brought out my phone that was connected to my office recorder, then threatened him back. I don't think he will be a problem for a while."

"Good thinking!"

Dan grinned. "Just as I left, I told him to go eff himself. But in a nice way."

"Even better." Charles laughed.

"So if it's all right with you, I'd like to make amends and help you with your preservation ideas."

"You've got a deal," Charles said as he put his arm around Dan's shoulder and limped him back toward his car. "This will just be between you and me. No one else needs to know."

"Thanks, Dad, but I did tell Laura. I had to," he said as he pulled out his car keys. "Laura and I will be back later for the meeting." Dan got in his car and drove off.

Sally came out just as Dan was driving away.

"What was that about?" she asked with concern in her voice. "They're coming by later, aren't they?"

"Yes," Charles said, continuing to look down the road.

"But—" Sally stopped herself. *If the boys need a private conversation, I shouldn't interfere.*

~ ~ ~

The sun was just beginning to descend behind the mountains as everyone gathered in the kitchen. Sally was making coffee, Dan, Dave, and Henry stood by the sink, and Sam and Charles sat opposite each other at the window that displayed the ever-lengthening afternoon shadows. Robin was sitting with her now two-and-a-half-year-old toddler in her lap and Laura was seated next to her and quietly playing with Hazel.

Charles filled them in about the organization—what he knew and who he and Sam had talked to.

"When Sam and I met with the head of the Carson Valley district a few days ago, they were sympathetic but couldn't promise anything. That's as far as we got. As you know, I wanted to get ranchers from our northern side interested first, because there's no point to any of this if they weren't. Now they are, at least three of them anyway, plus ourselves. We'll need everyone's help to persuade the organization to get more involved. But remember, this is mostly private contribution money they distribute, so that may be an issue. And now that money is getting tight…well, anyway, I know the way I was talking at that meeting those months ago made it seem like they were behind us all the way, but I had to start somewhere. I had to take the chance. But they *are* positively on our side, and would like to work with us. There are a few ranchers in the Carson Valley reluctant to sell their easements, for whatever reason, so we need to show them that there's more willingness on this side. Obviously, they've seen just how devastating these ongoing developments are, and how quickly they're moving north toward our ranches." Charles turned to his son. "Dan, what do you think?"

"T. Bob is always trying to influence politicians into making it harder for ranchers to make a living out here," Dan said. "Raising taxes, interfering with water rights, that sort of stuff. But, hell, because he isn't trusted, I think he may actually be pushing the ranchers more into this deal than toward the developers. Don't know how he can affect the preservation movement, with them still being the enemy and all, but he'll be watching. We may need to warn them about him."

"Trust me, they already know," Charles said with a quick wink.

Sam cut in. "I know you wanted to wait a bit to get more ranchers on board, but the others just may be waiting themselves to see what happens. I think we need to act now and show the organization how serious we are."

"You're right, Sam. I've been sitting on this too long. I'll be the one to call the ranchers because I know them personally, then you and I can meet with them and work out a meeting time with the preservation group."

"It would help to get public support," Robin offered as she hefted and turned Hazel around in her lap. "We could take a photo of one of the mountainsides as it is, then photoshop it with how it would look developed. It's one thing to show an existing development that we can't do anything about, but another to show what a parcel would look like developed. Publicize it, put it in the papers. A lot of people I've talked to about this idea are all for it and willing to act. Also, I would like to go with you two when he meets them. Dan? Could you come with us?"

"Absolutely."

Sally set the coffee cups on the table, put her hand to her aching back, and to the surprise of a few, said, "Well, I'm going to lie down for a little bit. I'm sure I can leave it up to the rest of you to figure this out."

"Okay, Mom," Robin said with a puzzled look. "I have to take Hazel upstairs for her nap anyway. Hazel, say night-night to everybody." Robin rose and tried to wave the child's reluctant hand as she carried her upstairs. "Okay, maybe later."

The discussion continued. "Well, you know me by now," Charles said. "I always make sure there's another card we can play. There's one more scheme out there, but this one's a little more difficult. Instead of giving us stipends, we could still get big tax breaks by putting it into the trust—as long as we work the land."

"Any other thing you're holding out?" Sam asked.

"Nah." Charles smiled back at everyone. "But I didn't think that would be as popular. It's just another option we could use for leverage."

The talk went on for some time, centering on all the possibilities. But in the absence of more facts, the possibilities became speculations, then guesses.

The meeting trailed off from there, with ideas floating around everyone's head.

"Did your mom go to bed?" Charles asked Robin when they took a break. "Is she mad or something?"

"She was just tired," Robin said. "She's been tired a lot lately. When we went for her last checkup, she said everything was fine, so I don't know."

"Guess she doesn't have the same energy she used to. It's the same with me, you know. Old age."

"Oh, Dad—"

"But," Charles interrupted her before she had a chance to say anything, "we all kind of expect her to take care of things like she always has. A lot of things we take for granted, and she never complains. Maybe we should help out a little."

Robin seemed surprised at that. Clearly, she couldn't see her father doing housework of any kind. Of course, that *wasn't* what he had in mind.

"I've been thinking. Maybe you could cut your hours down at work and help your mother more. Maybe just live here full-time."

Robin smiled at her father's innocent comment—innocent because she knew it came from decades past when women were expected to do all the domestic work—once they had completed all their farm chores, of course.

"I'll sleep on it, Dad," Robin said, winking at Laura, who was smiling back.

As the meeting trailed off, Dan and Laura stepped outside and Robin followed.

"So, Dan, Mom said you were here earlier. Said you and Dad seemed to be in a serious conversation. I didn't think you would be involved with this."

With that, Laura tactfully said, "I think I'll go for a walk and let you two talk."

Dan turned back to his sister. "I wasn't, but I am now. Dad needs support. He's doing a lot of this on his own, and however I can help, I will. Maybe you and I could work together on the preservation idea."

"Yes. I want to help him too."

"So what do you think about what he said? Would you be willing to quit your job and move back here permanently to help Mom? The way he put it, it sounded like he would want you to take over her workload."

"I wasn't insulted. I'm past that. What he said was coming from a different time," Robin said, looking off into the distance. "Moving to Reno and staying here a few days a week has worked well for all of us. No reason I can't ditch my apartment entirely and move here full-time, but I'm not ready to quit my job yet. Even though Mom says she can take care of Hazel while I'm at work, it may be hard on her. Maybe two, three days a week. I'll have to see." Looking straight at Dan, she added, "I'm not a kid anymore, have you noticed? Maybe it's time I gave something back. It sounds like you are too."

Dan nodded.

"So we'll try that for a while. There hasn't been a child in this house for years. And, no, I wouldn't let Mom shoulder too much, as much as she would try. She's not the workhorse she used to be."

"That would be good, one step at a time. And another thing: Laura and I were talking—thinking how much you and I, maybe for different reasons, distanced ourselves from the ranch and Mom and Dad. Since you will be spending more time here, I'll make a concerted effort to do the same. As I said to Dad a few days ago, it's about time he and I, and maybe you and I, got to know each other better."

"Well, since Laura invited me and Hazel over for dinner tomorrow night, that might be a good time to start." Robin laughed.

Laura was walking back toward the porch, seemingly mulling something over.

"I was watching your mom while all the talk was going on. She seemed tired. She didn't look well. Is she all right, Robin?"

"I saw that, too…I'll go check."

~ ~ ~

Lying on her bed while the discussion was going on downstairs, Sally took notice of a spider web in the corner of the ceiling. It made her think of the ethereal web of family life, its filaments woven together to a cable-like consistency, ensnaring all within its realm. This made her think about how the family was coming together again—at least with Sam and Robin. She knew that the ranch wasn't a place one could disconnect from easily. It was a conspicuous player in everyone's lives. Few could ever disentangle themselves without effort, or regret. *Then again*, she thought, *Sam did. Well, no, he came back, didn't he? Dan? Who knows? Maybe he and Laura, too—someday.*

Meanwhile, downstairs, the voices droned on.

Sally thought about how they all felt that pull from the land— their discussion about what to do next, what not to do, making plans, all enveloped in a bubble of fear. She closed her eyes as she thought about how hard it was to keep everything in balance.

Living here has always been a fight, she thought. *Like trying to keep a top-heavy ship upright in a storm that never ceases.* Maybe the family was returning as she had hoped, but her own anxiety was in no way lessened. *Why does life have to be haunted with such chronic worry? When does it stop? Only with our last breath? That can't be.*

She opened her eyes again and reconnected her gaze to the web. She no longer wondered about its origin, but felt drawn to it in another way. It all seemed so absurd to her, this concern over worldly things and the problems that need such constant vigilance. *All these possessions that we think of as so important: this house and everything in it, everything we identify as being part of us—the land, even. But they're just part of this outward form we're forced to deal with. Being so preoccupied with this one, maybe there's another side to all this. Could that be who we really are? Is it right here, hidden in plain sight?*

Now she was becoming fixated on the web. The longer she stared, the larger and closer it seemed to become, until all surrounding things seemed reduced to insignificance. The minutia of its miraculous structure, the intricate lace-like strands about its central iris took her whole concentration to the exclusion of all else, including her thoughts.

She couldn't recall what had seemed so troubling a moment ago. Its absence left her with a strange feeling.

Then the thoughts returned, along with the pain. *But for all these things, this order that grabs our attention, something is missing. If only this or that happens, then everything will be fine. How long have we been saying that? Forever. But things are never fine. There is always something lurking, waiting to be troubled over. Why do we never reach that peace we work so hard for?*

Just as suddenly, it came back, the feeling that thought could not define. Just from concentrating on an insignificant web, mantra-like, the whole world seemed to open up. The web was no longer insignificant. It was as important as every large and small thing in the universe, and she somehow felt a part of it.

She wondered if she could let it all go, this attachment to people and things. This accumulating and building up. This identifying with roles and ideas and sides. To be free of past and future.

It wasn't insensibility Sally felt. Just the opposite. She felt an awareness that seemed to transcend everything, even the faith that she had thought of as her strength. She could summon up all her previous thoughts now if she wanted. It didn't matter. She was aware of it all, soaring above it all, understanding it all. What had been so critically important before simply wasn't now. She felt enveloped in the caress of a thousand butterfly wings. And all without reason. That was it, without reason. She felt joy in the moment. *Has this been the real me all along? Is this the other side? It seems so clear.*

Her identity as the caregiver, the rock of Gibraltar—it all slid away to the surrender of an awareness that left only her, not what she had thought of as herself. She knew she could let it all go. Floating, a timeless, sleepless dreaming in consciousness . . .

"Hey, Mom," Robin said as she poked her head through the open door. "You all right?"

Yes. She was all right.

16

Retreat

After four short months, the preservation group had become more interested in the northern section, and with the involvement of many concerned people, including Robin and Dan, greater publicity began to emerge about the consequences of population growth and its impact on resources. Because homes and businesses use far more water than farms and ranches, water availability would be a big issue.

Sides were beginning to brew between progress and stasis, and with big money being what it is, politics being what it is, and population input being what it is, resolution through argument and compromise would take its own sweet time.

So there was a lull in the process, and, because it was July, there was also a rare lull in the workload at the ranch.

Sam decided to take advantage of it.

~~~

After several hours behind the wheel, Sam finally reached the far perimeter of the Black Rock Playa, his truck poised to climb up toward the dirt road above. He stopped, crawled out from the cab, and attempted to straighten himself out. With his back feeling frozen in place, he thought that he should stipulate in his will that he be placed in a sitting position for his eternal comfort.

After unbending somewhat, he looked back at the scene. This great, seventy-by-twenty-mile playa, just north of Pyramid Lake, was actually an ancient lakebed, so flat and vast that one may actually perceive a glimpse of Earth's curvature. This was once part of a sea, but when the land mass rose around it, it became a lake. Then, over millions of years, it filled in with thousands of feet of silt and sand to become the dry, flat expanse that now lay before him. Occasionally, after a powerful storm, an inch or so of water would settle on its surface, providing a glassy sheen and the illusion of what it had once been.

Today, though, the floor of the playa was hard and dry. Sam had set his course from the opposite side and sped across at sixty miles per hour. This gave the sensation of gliding in a speedboat over a smooth lake. The experience of flying so fast without feeling the speed was heady, especially when coupled with the sight of the surrounding mountains that seemed not to move. It was a big place.

Sam struggled back into the cab and powered his four-wheeler out of the loose sand that circumscribed the fringe, then jolted up and turned left onto the dirt road above. He went another twenty miles before turning right and into the beginnings of a narrow canyon. He remembered going by this imperceptible intersection many years ago, and was intrigued by its potential for exploration. The rough road crisscrossed a dozen creek crossings to eventually open up into a beautiful, wide, green valley that sloped upward toward the snowcapped peak ahead.

All the while, he wondered why he was doing this. The protests from Sally, the quizzical look on Charles's face. "What? Are you nuts, going out alone again?"

Sam had gotten plenty of razz from them about his idea to embark on another camping trip by himself. It made no sense to them. Then came the lecture, followed by his solemn promise to stay out of anything larger than a gopher hole. It was bad enough for them to question him, much less for him to have to defend himself with weak reasons that even he wasn't sure about.

"Four, maybe five days at the most," he promised them. Detailed itinerary? Well, a general one, anyway. He gave Charles a map and circled a large area he wanted to explore, and marked a spot where he thought he would be likely to camp.

Charles finally relented and helped his brother finish packing, all the while shaking his head. This time, Sam's Toyota pickup was thoroughly checked out: new tires, fluids replaced, cans of extra gas, oil, and so forth.

Cell phones worked sporadically out there, so communication could be iffy. Still, Sam brought it with him. Charles had given him a survival kit he had made up for himself sometime back—flares that could be seen for miles; rolls of caution tape with black lettering on yellow that could be easily spotted from the air; compass, maps, signal mirror, and strobe light; along with rope, come-along, shovel, and steel stakes to pound into the ground to jack the truck out of tough spots.

Sally and Robin set him up with two weeks' worth of food and water. "You never know," Sally said.

With that, he was off. He refused to look in his rearview mirror, not wanting to spot them shaking their now-collective "what's gotten into him" heads.

Even as he drove away, he felt bad about worrying them. It had been two years since he had deposited himself on their doorstep. Years of life-changing *whatever*. That was one thing Charles and Sally couldn't understand. To them, Sam had returned to his roots, to his home. A little adjustment time and all would be back in sync. But neither had those forty years of completely different life-conforming habits. What was ingrained in them wasn't so much ingrained in Sam. It wasn't that he was second-guessing his decision to make the permanent move to the ranch—that had been made long ago, and for the better. And it wasn't that he was out to prove anything. He was too old for that.

But there was something else, something he felt he had lost in the interim. He wondered whether he had changed in any appreciable way during that time. He suspected that he had experienced a fundamental shift of some sort, but he couldn't quite put his finger on what it was.

Still in searching mode, he felt it would come to him only in solitude and away from the interference of family activity. He needed some clarity, and what better way to find it than to get away from it all.

At the ranch, the one constant was its lack of downtime. Weekends looked suspiciously like weekdays, with a continuous workload that refused to acknowledge timeouts of any sort. Animals had to be fed or milked daily, moved about, and cared for. Irrigation pipes needed to be relocated continually, and so on. The entire infrastructure required round-the-clock maintenance, and it was just another reason he needed a retreat.

Sam figured that Charles didn't mind working full-time this way, as it was his habit to be constantly engrossed in it. When he and Sally had a chance to be somewhere else, even when things could be cared for by Dave and Henry, the sense of duty always seemed to haunt them.

Sam didn't feel that same weight of responsibility. He knew that things could get done without him. But now, with the added burden of dealing with prospects for the spread and its people, he felt that he was becoming more like Charles: also engrossed in this new ranch life.

So now, all this splendor he was witnessing seemed like a metaphor for his feelings. His first thought was that of the back-and-forth movements of the pendulum. *Perhaps that might be too linear,* he thought. *Maybe as a circle, as in the "what goes around comes around" sense. Or even a sphere, where the traveler on the surface has an unlimited choice of direction in which to travel, yet his first step will always set him toward his starting point.* He had hopped from the sphere that was St. Louis to the one at the ranch, though he probably would have characterized it more as a carousel. But, like everyone else, he'd had difficulty seeing the larger picture—microscopically chaotic and unpredictable, macroscopically harmonious to the universe.

Of course, by this time, Sam was committed. He had flown back to Missouri earlier to finalize the sale of the house. It had been up for sale for a while, and his neighbors had been kind enough to oversee it as it sat idle during that time—time in which wounds could heal.

The new owners were as happy to accept the furniture as Sam was to unload it. He then contracted a moving firm to ship all his personal items west to be stored in one of the ranch's outbuildings. No grandmother clock this time around. Before leaving, he met with a few of his old friends over beer to say his last good-byes, and to receive the inevitable envious criticisms.

Sam found a relatively level spot on which to camp in the otherwise up-sloping valley. As soon as he stopped, he took a quick check under his truck for a possible oil leak. Some would have considered that overly cautious—even paranoid. But for the same reason a person might avoid touching a cold stove because he has been burned on a hot one, he considered this action wholly justified.

First, he got out the old, heavy canvas tent that probably dated from the 1950s. It was roomy and large enough to stand in, provided one hunched over, and very much unlike those cramped, lightweight, claustrophobic tents that were so popular with backpackers. Of course, it helped that he didn't have to carry this one on his back.

After setting his cot and sleeping bag inside, he started on the fire pit. Large rocks in a semicircle allowed heat to be directed toward his folding chair and tent. He then set up the old steel A-frame cooking apparatus with the hanging cast iron water kettle procured from the barn, thinking that it quite possibly could have been among the original equipment ferried across the plains. Just another piece of paraphernalia uncommon among modern campers, but he liked the authenticity it gave to the scene. Plus, it was reliable—at least compared to his Coleman stove, which had the peculiar habit of malfunctioning at the most inopportune times. With a full fire blazing from the collected sagebrush, the picture was complete.

With a paper cup of Cabernet in one hand and cigar in the other, Sam sat in his folding chair and waited for inspiration. He looked westward, down through the canyon from where he had entered, and out over the playa to the mountains beyond.

As if to accommodate him and complete the panorama, the sun made a concentrated effort to show off. For the next quarter-hour, various shades of pale pinks and fiery reds played themselves out overhead. One cloud patch would glow in brilliance as another faded, the sun's rays playing a game of leapfrog of ever-increasing intensity toward the horizon, until at last, both the color and the light receded toward darkness.

While that show was folding its tent, another began in the east. A near-full moon began to crest the mountain peak behind him, and a new light added its subtle luminescence to the landscape. It was anticlimactic in a sense, but Sam welcomed the contrast. The moon's softness was suggestive of a Fauré nocturne, unlike the Wagner-like grandeur of the sun's earlier extravagance.

It was a fine sight, but now the darkness forced Sam to get on with his cooking: bacon and eggs in a skillet over the fire, to be served with bread and coffee—all of it authentic, except for the instant coffee that Sam brought along as a sacrificial concession to modern convenience. Otherwise, it was real, honest-to-goodness cowboy fare, just like in the movies.

With his meal on a paper plate, he turned his chair around for this behind-the-scenes second act. He had been looking straight into the fire, and now his eyes had to adjust to the dimness. Slowly, the landscape defined itself into shades of blue-gray and black, with one patch of white shining beacon-like on the snowy peak above. Now it was Mahler's Third Symphony, the great hymn to nature, that came to mind.

Cold also came to mind. While Sam's backside was toasting, his frontside was freezing. So he got up, donned his heavy jacket and cap, and concluded that if the sun had decided it was a good time to retire, so would he. Inspiration would have to wait. When the sun went down at this high of an elevation, the temperature would also, and quickly.

Sam bundled himself in his sleeping bag and was soon comfortable enough. He felt more than a little uneasy, though. The busy household activity at the ranch may have sometimes been annoying with all its noise and scurrying, but at least he could take comfort that there were people around. Here, there was no one. While Sam liked his peace, at least back home, he could count on another's presence to help corroborate his sense of security. *Oh well,* he thought. *Just get used to it. What's a few days, anyway? See what tomorrow brings.*

With the darkness coming on at only a little after eight thirty, he turned over, but he knew that he would simply lie there thinking. Sleep, that sometimes-happy state of oblivion, that longed-for antidote to thought, serves as a welcomed joy the more one ages. But now Sam's mind was working overtime, and he couldn't remember whether that instant coffee was caffeinated or not. *Okay,* Sam thought. *Don't think.*

This, however, reminded him about the problem with the number-two well pump at the ranch. He had changed the brushes in the winding and resealed it; even so, it had blown out the breaker. He turned over and tried to get that out of his mind, and to not think about how the wiring could have been reversed when he reinstalled it, or that it might have been possible to correct it without removing the entire…

He turned over again.

The exhaustion of long hours of driving and the negligible effect of decaf coffee caused him to finally doze off. But trying to sleep in unfamiliar surroundings can work itself onto the mind and into distorted, unnerving dreams. Sam proved the perfect candidate for such a state. He found himself in some poor, small mountain village— Peru or Nepal, trying to convince community leaders to build a members-only tennis club with courts, clubroom, and so on, but he couldn't get his point across because someone was scratching at a door or wall or something. The scratching was persistent enough to pull him half out of his sleep. The visual illusion disappeared, but the noise didn't. Its source was just outside the tent.

A pounding heart now had him fully awake. No animal other than a man could have made such a loud disturbance. *Should I say something?* He could see the moon's spotlight glare through the tent fabric and concluded that it had moved through about a quarter of the sky. Sam guessed that it was about midnight. But time was no concern now. The scraping came again, closer this time.

"Hey!" he yelled with halting breath.

No answer.

"Who's there?"

Again, no answer, just more scraping—this time, a little farther off.

Sam decided that he wasn't going to be terrified about nothing again, like he had been in that mine. Of course, this was not nothing, but he persevered.

Quickly donning pants, coat, and slippers, he burst out with his flashlight shining straight ahead. Nothing. Then he wheeled around, hoping to get the jump on whoever it was, which was, or were, standing right before him. Horses—wild horses, about seven mustangs not seventy feet away. They looked as spooked as Sam felt, but the lead stallion stood his ground as if waiting for Sam to make the next move, which he did.

With the stealth and adroitness of a human evolutionarily distanced from his primitive ancestors for way too long, Sam crept toward them, catching his foot on the steel cooking frame, causing both him and the contraption to collapse in a clanging, steam-forming, catastrophic commotion. His flashlight flailed skyward in light-saber-like fashion, a situation that would have caused a casual observer, had there been one handy, to wonder why someone would think it productive to search the heavens.

Sam was face-down in the dust, and except for the sound of the kettle's steaming water slowly drenching the coals, silence returned. Sam wondered if he might yet regain a certain composure and not scare the horses. But it was too late for that. The lead horse had seen enough of the charade and started to move on, his mares and foals following. The last one gave out a snort that echoed among the canyon walls—one that sounded suspiciously like laughter.

"That went well," Sam said aloud.

He picked himself up and ran an inventory. Bruised elbow, stubbed toe, and the beginnings of minor injuries that would materialize later, including humiliation. He stumbled back into the tent and onto the cot, now with the reassuring knowledge of who his neighbors were.

Mustangs roamed and foraged the remote mountain areas in small packs. Sam figured that it was not likely that this was their first encounter with a human. Either way, wild horses were naturally wary and skittish, and would move off at the slightest intrusion. Phantom-like, they often seemed to appear out of nowhere, framed within a tableau as though a permanent part of the landscape, then disappear just as mysteriously.

Sam slept uneasily through the rest of the night.

The next morning, he went out to pee. Anywhere he wanted. That was the great thing about places like this: privacy was never an issue.

It was chilly, with the wind blowing steadily off the playa. A languid dust devil made an appearance on the flat, swirling and twisting gracefully onto itself, its funnel of dust and sand reaching thousands of feet into the air. Sam's position halfway up the mountain gave him an unusually mesmerizing perspective. But a cool gust of wind proved to be an irritant, and because he did not feel like rebuilding the soaked fire pit, he moved his chair, tray, and stove inside the tent.

Eggs, bacon, and coffee again. No one was there to judge what he made for himself. At the ranch, he felt that he had to follow the eating habits of the household. With Charles's heart condition, the unspoken rule was to eat only what Charles had to eat, which was annoyingly healthy fare that no one liked. Heavy on the vegetables, light on the fatty, salty, sugary, caffeinated good stuff. Sally served as the resident nutritionist, so she pretty much had the final say. Sam had purchased his unlawful eggs and bacon fare only after leaving the ranch for his trip—he was going to make up for lost time.

He started to get out his cooking gear, but feeling drained from the folly of last night, decided to just have some cereal.

Sam went back into the tent and paged through a novel he had been reading, but after a few minutes, put it down and picked up his writing pad. Ten minutes later, he tossed that blank sheet aside as well. *I came here to work things out,* he thought. *Find out what's nagging me, but it's not coming. Tired or not, I need to get out of this stupor and hike around.*

He got up and put on the big duster Charles had lent him, and along with fur-lined cap, gloves, and daypack stocked with water and snacks, he opted to climb up the valley, and perhaps to the mountain top.

As soon as he began, he noticed sporadic horse poop lying about, and wondered if he was following the horses' route further up where they could cross over the ridge on the left.

The road ahead got steeper as he climbed. Soon, it was diverging left and right across the steep mountain face above him, and he could see some structures near the summit. Another mine. *Amazing*, he thought. *Another mine on top of a mountain*. The whole scene gave him pause. Far more rugged and steep than the JE mine, he figured that the amount of effort and expense poured into an operation like this must have been enormous. Just scratching out the now-washed-out road along the steep face would have been difficult enough. And then they would have had to haul up all the heavy mining equipment. *Months of work before they got the first pick into the ground, all without any guarantee of success.*

If history were any gauge, most miners got nothing from it. Sam had once read that the only ones who made any money were the fringe elements, those who sold the goods, lent the money, hauled the merchandise, and overall capitalized on the miners' folly. He figured that miners must have known the odds were against them in almost every way, and yet they persisted, each thinking that he would be the one-in-a-thousand to beat the odds. They could smell it—feel it. Such misplaced intuition had led every one of them to believe they were a step ahead of the others, luck and the deity being on their side. And when they struck out, like they had many times before, the experience became a pathological stimulus, not a deterrent.

It's called a fever for a reason, Sam thought. The pattern of hope undaunted by experience, or the obvious. Today, it would be the lottery, which offered even worse odds.

Sam continued climbing the ever-steepening road. He looked back down from where he had started. The wind had lessened by now, and the sun was starting to do the work for which it was best known out here: making things hot. The duster that had provided warmth and wind resistance had become nothing more than a heavy load. Sam took it off and slung it over his shoulder. He was determined to climb to the top.

Mountaineers understand that a certain distortion occurs when climbing mountains. Looking up, the top always seemed closer than it really is. In trendy parlance, climbers sarcastically call it the "false-encouragement syndrome." Sam, too, was deceived, thinking it would take him less than an hour to reach the summit.

As the day wore on, the sun grew hotter, the slope steeper, and the summit seemingly no closer than before. Frustrated, Sam began to cut the switchbacks. He knew this was a dumb thing to do. It might cut the distance of travel, but the energy output would be compounded.

He stopped and refolded the duster around his waist before continuing. More stopping, more adjusting that useless, heavy coat. Finally, he reached the mine itself, but this time, he wasn't tempted to even peer inside.

The road ended here, so he was forced to cross-country the rest of the way, which was another twenty-five minutes of scrambling over loose scree, then a little bit of snow, then the top.

Mountaineers understand that being a few steps from the summit can be the most transformative. With the certainty of success, and the relief from struggle, it was ironic that those who scaled the more challenging peaks spent no more time at the top than was required for photographic proof.

This peak hardly rose to that level, but Sam felt like he had accomplished something. He placed Charles's balled-up duster on a protruding snow-covered rock and sat on it. The view he had enjoyed from his camp far below had now doubled to expose a new set of desolate-looking mountain ranges and valleys to the east. It was all spectacular, but it also gave him an overwhelming feeling of loneliness. When overcoming a struggle, new feelings often emerge to take their place. In a way, the accomplishment often leads to its own disappointment.

He finished off the snacks and most of the water and got up to leave. The duster shifted from under him and started to roll down the hill, and he had to scramble after it. *Why the hell didn't I just leave it on the trail below and pick it up on the way down instead of carting it all the way here?*

As he descended, he laughed to himself about the old Sisyphus legend that he and Charles had discussed. He knew it was only coincidental, but still, the thought of it got him thinking about how the concentration of day-to-day chores can subvert deeper thoughts. In this case, the struggle to place one foot in front of the other to reach a goal had blocked out all other considerations. He found that this intensity evaporated on the downward trek, and his mind reverted to the old, muddled world. Physical struggles can seem less troublesome than those that can come from freeform, idle thought. *Maybe adventurers avoided that problem by continuously engaging in risky pursuits.*

In any case, the easy descent freed up his mind—not to deeper, burdensome thoughts, but to practical, problem-solving situations. Suddenly, his head swam with ideas about a few projects at the ranch.

His concentration was broken when he caught a glimpse of dust rising along on a nearby ridge. After a few seconds, the picture resolved itself. The mustangs. One, two—no, seven—all of them camouflaged in plain sight, even among the low sage. He continued down the slope, now no more curious about the herd than they seemed to be about him.

He tried to forget the ranch. Even in all this grandeur, the secret attraction of nature didn't call to him like it used to. The landscape seemed to come across for what it was: earth, rolling hills, rocks, sage, and all in the continuing interconnected processes that allowed them to be. It was all so different from how he'd felt when he first arrived. He wondered why.

Sam stopped in his tracks. "Maybe that's what I lost!" he said aloud.

This startled the horses, who, after recognizing the source of the disturbance, returned to their foraging.

The land is not a dream, Sam thought, *but a stage in which life is played out.*

He rounded the last turn in the road, reached his campsite, and spent the rest of the afternoon reading.

After dinner, he retired early. Exhausted from a day of climbing, and with no visits from his ghostly neighbors, he slept soundly.

The next morning was again windy. He tried using his cell phone, but got mostly static. He thought he might have been able to leave a message about his location, and hoped that someone would get it.

After his bacon and eggs, he looked at his map, and with coffee in hand, planned his trip for the day. He decided to go just up the main dirt road some ten miles to Rabbit Hole Springs. During the migration, it had been a famous watering hole along the less-used Lassen-Applegate Trail. Peter Lassen had promoted it in an attempt to get immigrants to settle in his Northern California neighborhood. The beginning of the trail was one that verged northwestward from the Humboldt River route that most immigrants took. The attraction was that it skirted the northern boundary of the troublesome Sierras. Relatively flat, it looked good, but only on a map. It turned out to be the most infamous and dangerous of any of the western accesses, and was later labeled the Death Trail.

Sam followed the dirt road indicated on his map and found what he should have expected: trash, litter, and an old tire scattered around a twenty-foot-diameter manmade shallow pool. A large, rubber suction hose lay half in and half out of the water like some prehistoric reptile unsure of its amphibious leanings. This squashed any idea of drinking from it.

The first two years of the trail's use were relatively uneventful, but in the summer of 1849, everything dried up. At an average distance of twenty to thirty miles between the sparse water and grass resources, and with a greater impact of immigrants, the result was nearly catastrophic. Thousands took the trail that year, and though few actually died on it, the cost to their livestock was enormous.

That year, Rabbit Hole's water supply was limited to little more than a few cups of percolating water per minute. At one point, it was so slow to surface that it had to be sipped through a straw. The next water was a large hot spring at Black Rock, a prominent dark formation at the northern junction of the desert, which lay twenty miles distant across the oven-like playa.

Rabbit Hole's location, being a few hundred feet above the playa, gave Sam, and most certainly the migrants, a clear but demoralizing view of what lay ahead. But for him, it only took two hours to drive there. As he brought his truck off the playa and around the hot springs (pools of water mostly) toward the base of the rock, he came to the only remnant left from the migration: an abandoned wagon sitting wheel-and-axle-less in the sand, a silent testament to the struggles of those who came before.

He headed for the lea of a small hillock he thought he could use for shelter from the wind. To his surprise, he saw another truck up ahead. Glad for the potential company, but cautious about intruding into another man's space, Sam found another spot a hundred yards away and parked.

The other truck was a scruffy-looking old pickup sporting an equally beat-up camper shell. Sam was a little wary about whom he might encounter. He thought that maybe he should head for the next hot spring twenty miles further on. But that would have taken him even farther from the civilized life, from which he was already fifty miles away, so he decided to stay.

His neighbor was obviously not around—probably up on the rock—so Sam settled in. For this day trip, he had brought everything with him but the tent, which he didn't think he would need. More than that, the tent remaining up in the valley had given him a sense of connectedness, the familiarity of a base camp of sorts. It provided the feeling of place and the avoidance of chaotic aimlessness that so often served as the wellspring of insecurity.

He tied the ends of his tarp on the upper corners of his truck bed and spread it out to a couple of poles he imbedded in the sand. That made for a comfortable, shady setting. Then he sat and waited. He didn't have to wait long.

As he had half-guessed, the man who came from around the rock outcropping looked as scruffy as his truck—battered hat over longish hair flowing out like a handful of straw clippings, torn shirt and pants. Behind him, completing the picture, was his dog, a black-and-white non-breed half-trotting, half-limping along. Somehow, the dog looked even older than the man.

As soon as he caught the man's eye, Sam waved. The man did the same on his way to his truck. There is something big in such a small gesture, an insignificant acknowledgment that says a lot in an instant. The upturned palm reveals that you mean no harm, an open door to mutual respect. Sam felt more at ease.

The sun was starting to set. There was no breeze this night—not a breath—and the hot playa would keep the surrounding air warm for some time. Sam looked toward his neighbor, sure that the man must have taken a gander at him. There was a certain protocol when encountering strangers in a desolate location like this. Being the only two people for tens of miles around meant that they both kept themselves on guard, though respectful.

Sam got out his cooking gear and pondered. *Bacon and eggs?* He decided that, yes, what the hell. With some canned spinach, it would be a definite change of diet. He would make overtures to his neighbor after dinner. He soon found that "after dinner" was too late for the canine intermediary, who came over just as Sam had finished eating. The dog acted friendly enough that Sam instinctively reached out to pet him. The dog was only too happy to oblige.

"Dog!" the voice from the truck said. "Get your ass over here!" Then, more resignedly, he added, "Dumb mutt. Don't bother the man."

"He's okay," Sam hollered. "He's no bother."

Since they were parked far apart, conversation would have to be forced. After Sam packed away his stove, he decided to take the opening. He picked up his coat, cap, and at the last minute, reached back into his cooler for a couple beers. So outfitted, he sauntered over.

He found the stranger sitting behind his truck in front of the open camper door. Sam could look in and see a compact but neat setup with a table, a bed, and a shelf of books held in by a wire screen.

"Hi," Sam said. "Sam Ellis. Mind if I join you?" He held out one of the beers.

"Sure," the stranger said, taking the proffered beer. "Richard—uh, Rick." He got up, reached for a folding chair from the side of his truck, and offered it up. "Dog, get over here. Dumb as a post."

The old dog obeyed and came around and sat next to his owner.

"What's his name?"

"Dog. Good enough for him, good enough for me. Answers to it."

Dog seemed to sense that Sam lacked any threat—or any doggie treats, for that matter—and seemed to conclude that future interaction was unnecessary. He lay down and settled in.

"My wife made me get these damn hearing aids," Rick exclaimed, apropos of nothing and pulling one of them half out of his left ear. "Like I needed to hear what she was sayin' all the time. All it does is make everything noisier. Everything's too damn noisy. Just livin' around other people, what with cars and machines and people talkin' and makin' all that racket." Then, apparently thinking that he'd sounded too abstruse, he asked, "You ever notice it?" He looked over for confirmation. "We sure as hell weren't built to hear all that shit. Just a car goin' by is loud. That's why I gotta come out here once in a while."

"Why you wearin' 'em here where you don't need 'em?" Sam replied, falling in with the rough colloquialism of his neighbor.

"This is the only place I ever do wear 'em. It's so's I can hear the quiet. So's I can hear all the little noises. No little noises in town."

"Never thought of that."

"So why you out here?" Rick asked bluntly.

"Same as you, I suppose. The noise I wanted to get away from was of a different kind. Family situations, you know."

"You're not from around here." Rick smiled through gaps of irregular teeth.

"No. Well, yes. Used to be. Lived back east for forty years. Came back. What do you do? You retired?"

"Still workin' my ass off. Work in a car parts store over Fernly. Been doin' that, what, fifteen years now? Before that, well, I been pretty much everywhere."

Darkness came slowly and unnoticeably during their small talk. Rick didn't seem to recognize the Ellis name, as many would have whose families had been here for generations. Sam liked that, as it meant there was no history to acknowledge or defend, no mutual acquaintances to devise a conversation over. Two men unencumbered by bias of any kind allowed for endless possibilities.

Rick got up and reached back into the camper, rummaging through an open cupboard under the bed. He knocked his hat askew on the door frame as he pulled out an old-looking whiskey bottle. He examined his prize, simultaneously tried to readjust his headgear, and stood in minor triumph.

"Fifteen-year-old whiskey," he said. "Sippin' whiskey. Been truck-aged a long time. Don't have much occasion to open it. Suppose this is as good a time as any. I mean, the beer is fine, but I gather you might appreciate this more. Whuddaya say?" Rick hoisted the bottle up, inches from Sam's face.

"Damn fine idea!"

They sat for some time in comfortable silence. As was the case with good alcohol, tongues loosen and acquaintances become intimates.

Rick got up and turned off the dome light in the cab, and with a heaviness, sat back down. Although the moon would be up soon, the darkness was near complete. Their chairs faced Black Rock, and though it was only a few hundred feet high, it looked huge in silhouette. They stared into the darkness, allowing their eyes to adjust.

"Each substance of grief hath twenty shadows," Rick mumbled, not quite coherently. It was enough that Sam could make it out, but not enough to think it called for a response.

Continuing to look up at the rock, Sam caught a glint of something against the black wall, like a pinpoint of light near the top. It couldn't be seen if one looked at it directly, but askance—yes, there was definitely a light emanating from somewhere on that solemn, barren edifice.

"Say, Rick, do you see a light near the top up there? A reflection maybe? Not a star, 'cause it's against the rock. Can't make it out."

"Yeah," Rick said noncommittally. Then, after a pause, he added, "I put it there."

"Really!" Sam decided to quietly wait him out.

"It's a candle. Had two kids with my first wife. Girl and a boy. Boy was headstrong, like me. Lit out when he was sixteen. Didn't get along. The girl, Emily, was my life. We did a lot of things together. Wasn't afraid of nothing. Wanted to go everywhere I went, even after the divorce. She made me clean up my act just by being who she was. Got killed in a car some older kid was driving. Long time ago. Too young for life beyond innocence."

Sam suddenly felt a chill. Could she have been the teen that was killed in that collision with Henry's truck? He wondered if he should say something, then decided not to.

"We liked coming here," Rick continued. "That was before all the sightseers and Burning Man. Used to climb to the top and wait for the sun to go down." He trailed off.

"I'm sorry," Sam said.

"Didn't mean to get maudlin. I just come here once in a while, and if the wind ain't blowin', I set a candle up there. She liked candles."

"It must be hard to live with that."

Rick mulled something over for a time before speaking again. "Grief fills the room up of my absent child. Lies in her bed, walks up and down with me, puts on her pretty looks, and repeats her words. Remembers me of all her gracious parts."

The wheels in Sam's alcohol-muddled mind turned lazily. "Shakespeare?" he asked.

Rick nodded. Then, readjusting his chair, he added, "I only think of her as she was then, a snapshot of one who was young and trusting, so she never changes—never grows up. I can't imagine what she would

208

have become. Probably like most other women, I suppose. But thinking of her in her timeless innocence, that hurts the most."

Rick looked over toward Sam, somewhat sheepishly. "I like to quote Shakespeare—mostly. Most of those books you see in there," he said, stretching his hand out toward his camper shell. "He understood everything. I have an ear to remembering lines. I annoy the guys I work with by quoting him, but most of them are just kids, and kids nowadays, they don't read. They have no patience for wisdom." He took another sip from his plastic cup. "Well, maybe one kid I work with, but he's afraid to chime in when the others make fun of me. Some people think I'm trying to be highfalutin, but Shakespeare's words were for regular people. That's why he's still around. You can tell I'm not cultured much. But then, I don't have to be. I let him do the thinking. All I have to do is read him and make the connections with what's going on now."

After a moment, Sam said, "I kind of did have a reason for coming out here. Just trying to find out where I fit into all this. I'm camped at the base of King Lear Peak, and yesterday I hiked to the top, and coming down, even in all this 'grandeur' I guess you'd call it, I felt like I've lost something since I moved back here a few years ago. Ever since I started working on my brother's ranch, the art and the words come less to me. I don't know, maybe they're no longer necessary. I used to marvel and wonder at the miraculous nature of nature, but not so much now." He paused, then said, "Rick, you've lived here a long time, haven't you? Do you appreciate all this—open land?"

"I'm just used to it. I've lived in a lot of places, mostly in the west. Arizona, New Mexico. Empty places. I couldn't put it into words why I live here either. But I wouldn't want to live anywhere else—certainly not in a big city."

"I like to think back to the original natives," Sam said. "They didn't ponder all this either." Sam stretched his arms out wide. "They wouldn't have survived if they had looked on all this with some kind of romantic swooning. They had to be practical. They probably reasoned only as far as they needed. If they had gone further, they might have lost touch with their world. I think that's what happened to our own people. We went beyond living with that world because we invented our own. Then we got used to it. Maybe that wasn't so bad, but it makes us more observers than participants, and then we try to make sense of it. Can't make sense of an illusion. Always looking, never finding. Participants just learn to work in it, become part of it. Like you, or maybe like I'm gettin' to be now."

"Not so bad, is it?" Rick said. "Maybe it's just a tradeoff, one for the other. But the Indians' way of life was as hard as any white culture. They had their own brutalities and jealousies, maybe just not as far-reaching."

"I guess they both have good and bad qualities," Sam reasoned. "Indians worried about needs; we worry about wants. Once infected with want, there was no going back for them." He leaned forward. "But where does that leave us, Rick? Are we just pawns in this back-and-forth game?"

Rick remained silent.

Sam sat back. "Maybe I should just heed my own advice. The miraculous hasn't been lost. It's being fused into my own practical world without my knowing it. Or is it that maybe we're just getting older and realize we're not getting anywhere. Got a quote for that?"

"What, not getting anywhere, but thinking we should? Well, there's Alexander Pope's *Essay on Man*. I know a couple lines. Wait a minute, okay: 'Man hangs between; in doubt to act or rest. Born but to die, he thinks too little and too much. Created half to rise and half to fall; lord of all things, and prey to all.' Right now, it sounds to me like you just think too little and too much." Rick laughed.

"I do," Sam said. "It makes sense; none of us knows where we stand. You know, it's good to know that people hundreds of years ago were just as confused as we are now."

"You can't tell me they weren't just as smart," Rick said. "Smarter even. People like Shakespeare didn't have any answers. They just said how things were. I think half the battle is knowing that I'm not the only one who feels a certain way. And when you read all these wise things, it makes you feel better."

"Maybe the problem is that we think someone else has all the answers," Sam said. "We're always trying to look to others to tell us what's right. Maybe that's the big scam. Everyone thinks they're alone, when really, everyone's confused. We just bluff our way through. You talked about losing your girl. There's no answer to that. It's not natural to outlive your children. But there it is." He reflected on his own past for a moment. "We never had children. Makes it seem like there's a lack of purpose to it all. Was that our legacy? Are death and non-life the same, I wonder?"

"After you're gone, I suppose," Rick said. "But we can't know the other side. It's like, what were you like before you were born? What's it like to be another person? Just nonsense talk."

"Yeah." Sam had eased into his drink just as much as Rick seemed to have eased into his.

"Well," Rick said, "like you, I think of these things. Don't do no good, of course." He thought for a moment. "Or maybe it does. Otherwise, I wouldn't be trying to find a quote to fit. Hah! 'Patch grief with proverbs.' Shakespeare said that, too."

"You know what that means?" Sam said, making a whiskey-induced revelation. He tried to sit up and turn more directly to Rick, spilling a bit of his drink in the process. "Nowadays, everyone has an opinion on how to fix things, but they don't have the facts. It means there isn't any answer at all. Otherwise, it would have been found out by now, wouldn't it? So…what was I sayin'? Oh, yeah. Only fashions change— not, you know, the other…stuff."

Sam realized that he was starting to ramble, but Rick didn't seem to be paying attention anyway.

"Think I'd better turn in," Sam said. "Gettin' tired. All that driving and such."

"Yeah," Rick said. "Me, too."

Sam got up, a little unsteady, and thanked his campmate for the hospitality. "See you in the morning," he said, heading for his truck.

"Other way," Rick said before Sam got too far.

"Right," Sam said, reversing course.

Once he found his truck, he rolled out his sleeping bag in the back, crawled in, and instantly fell asleep on top of his bag, clothes and all.

~ ~ ~

Morning on the playa. Sam got up. It was late—eight thirty. He scooted out of his truck and looked around. Rick's truck was gone, but he found last night's sippin' whiskey near his chair, half full. *Nice gesture*, Sam thought. He figured it would be some time before he would dip into it again.

He prepared a breakfast of Cheerios and milk. The thought of the usual fare felt unappetizing, and he refused to think too hard on it. Taking a rain check on hiking to the top of Black Rock as he had planned, he packed his gear and headed back toward his more permanent campsite. There would be no major explorations for him this day, what with his headache and all, but he did feel somewhat invigorated at having met Rick.

Sam drove up over the last rise and found his tent safe and sound. He also saw another truck. *Dave?* he thought. It was Dave's truck for sure, but he didn't see him anywhere around.

"Probably out looking for me," Sam said aloud as he stepped out of his truck.

He got his gear out, pulled the tent flap back, and tossed it in.

"Hey," came a voice from inside. "About time you showed up!"

~ ~ ~

"Coffee, Dave?" Sam said as he set two folding chairs around the fire pit and kindled a fire. He brought out an old pewter coffee pot and filled it, set it on a rock, and waited for it to boil.

As they settled in, Sam said, "So, how the hell did you find me?"

"Your voicemail came through," Dave said with, Sam thought, a somewhat disconnected look.

Then he roused himself a bit. "Nice place you got here."

"Fixer-upper. Neighbors are no problem. Didn't see your truck till the last minute. It surprised the hell out of me."

"Well, yeah. Didn't mean to do that. Saw you coming across the flats and decided to relax in the tent. Then I fell asleep. Heard you yammering to yourself again. You're goin' to have to stop that or people are going to talk."

"To themselves?" Sam laughed.

"You didn't crawl into no gopher holes while you were out here, did you?"

"No. Got strict instructions about that. Well, you know I was scheduled to leave here soon, maybe tomorrow or the next day. Why are you here? Not just to check up on me, I hope. You're too late for that."

At that, Dave's subdued manner returned. He picked his coffee cup off the rock, held it in his hands, then put it back and folded his hands again. His lips moved in pantomime as if to will himself to speak.

"Sally's got cancer," Dave choked. "Not good."

17
A Great Dynamo Silenced

High above the great house, on the crest of the nearby hill, lay a rock formation, a natural cairn-like collection of large boulders that over-looked the whole of the JE Valley. When Sam and Charles were kids, they used to play on the rocks and look for arrowheads. Because it was a great place for small animals to hide, it was also a great place for Native Americans to hunt. Now, it was a great place to sit and contemplate.

A lone spectator sitting here on this pleasant early-spring day would enjoy an expansive view of everything of importance. He would see the almost-dry creek bed below, winding its way in and out of the aspen groves, past the barn, and out toward the eastern farmlands to meld in a dreamlike haze toward the misty hills beyond. Or, looking straight across to the hills on the opposite side of the valley, he would see sharply defined gullies exposing the subsurface bones of an earlier epoch that further weathering could little penetrate. Looking left and completing the U-shaped panorama, he would see the high set of wild foothills that sit sentry-like against the northern portion of the Sierras beyond. He would be able to hear the rustle of leaves of the appropriately named quaking aspen, and see their shimmering light patterns as they danced to the tune of the breeze.

But there was no one here this day to bear witness to nature showing off in apparent defiance to the spectacle occurring below.

Below were groups of darkly clothed people milling about the back of the house. One person, now another, would break off from one group to join another, to shake a hand, pat a shoulder, give a hug. A horse-drawn wagon pulled out from the backside of the barn, moving slowly through the crowd and onto the road before stopping at the house. The back door opened as more people came out to join the others. The pallbearers last. Because of the narrowness of the opening, the men carried their burden single file. Once outside, they re-formed and moved slowly toward the back of the wagon, then lifted the casket onto the buckboard and slid it forward.

That was when a wondrous sight caught the crowd's collective attention, along with its breath. Draped over the whole of the casket was the quilt. The oft-doubted and disputed subject of teasing lay there in all its glory. Patterns of the most exquisite colors met the eye. All the pieces melded into a single harmonic composition that radiated outward from its center in a spiral formation that began with muted browns and autumn reds, softly blending into wintery whites and grays further along its journey. Then the light greens and oranges of spring renewal appeared. Lastly, a full splash of reds, dark greens, and yellows of summer circumscribed the whole of its perimeter.

The crowd fell in behind the wagon as it moved slowly forward—Robin and Charles holding on to each other; Dan and Laura behind them. Then came Sam, Henry, and Dave ahead of a very large gathering of friends. The journey was not long. It moved up the road to the family cemetery situated on the far side of the grove of aspen and pine.

Now late afternoon, the once-warm early spring breeze, appropriately enough for the occasion, became a chill.

Receptions after these affairs are often cathartic—an offering of relief to family and friends who, in a more relaxed mood with food and drink, tell stories of the departed. Some interesting, some funny, all loving. But there was no laughter here. It was as if the funeral had followed them into the house to continue its unabated gloom.

~ ~ ~

The idea of Sally's cancerous condition was hard to comprehend. She had sensed that there was something wrong with her, and finally checked in with her doctor. She was referred to an oncologist, who discovered that she was already in stage three of the disease. At first she refused to admit it, then delayed disclosing it to her family, mostly because she knew that everything would change, that her whole world, meaning her family, would turn topsy-turvy. Indeed it had, for once it was revealed, everyone was focused on her care.

She and her doctor both knew that it was more serious than she wanted to let on. As with most uterine cancers, it was spreading quickly, meaning there would be a declining survival rate as time went on. But because Sally was in her oncologist's care, her doctor was not going to give up without a fight.

And so the family members experienced the scenario that has touched so many. There were consultations with other doctors and discussions about the options and procedures she would have to endure. Although she had an innate sense that the disease would be terminal, Sally agreed to go through the chemo-radiation process. The treatments were not for herself, but for her family. She wanted to give them hope in what she believed to be a hopeless situation, and didn't want to counter their initial involvement. They needed to engage themselves in the process as though they could somehow affect the outcome.

At first, Sally tried to continue with most of her chores as was her habit, but because of the treatments, she tired easily. Robin took temporary leave from her job to stay there and make the meals, and along with Henry, Sam, and even Charles, do the washing, clean the house, and above all, bolster her with encouragement. Laura and Dan came often after work to help out. Even Sally felt a ray of hope, but as time wore on, it became an agonizing pattern of good days/bad days as she continued to find herself in a bind between wanting to let go and a family who didn't want her to.

Fighting went against what she wanted for herself; she did not want to impede the disease's inevitable course with what she sensed to be false detours. So there were sleepless nights fraught with exasperation, and the worry which no words could temper. Her oncologist was still cautiously hopeful because she knew that Sally had courage. Indeed, she had—the courage to let go.

Sally could see the anguish in her family, and especially in Charles who, despite the positive attitude he and the family tried to exhibit, reluctantly began to understand the inevitable outcome. Sally understood that the things we impose on the terminally ill, out of love, is burdensome to all involved, that praising those who combat terminal conditions with courageous determination, who fight to the bitter end, believing, literally, in the legacy of heroics, was tearing at her family.

"Don't give up, Mom!" Robin pleaded. "I'm not going to have you quit." Harsh words from a loving daughter wanting to do right.

Eventually, Sally received the painkillers she needed. She felt that to suffer through pain was absurd. Yes, the drugs would bring the end closer, but that was all right. As Sally's life began to drift away, so too did all her worldly cares that had once seemed so important. While everyone else was emotionally engaged and agonizing, she began to feel a detachment from family and friends, as though they were somehow being pulled from her.

How odd, she thought at the time. She didn't feel the longing and yearning for them that she could see in them for her. She knew that it was not wrong to think that way, for it was not a contraction she felt, but an expansion—an expansion and depth that grew to envelop not just those select few, but everyone. It grew to envelop the world as one.

So this is what it's like, was her final thought. Like dust scattered in a whirlwind, she folded within herself to peace.

~ ~ ~

It had been eight months since her initial diagnosis, and now a week since Sally's funeral. On a late afternoon, the family gathered in the living room, the mood still mournful. They were talking quietly among themselves when Sam noticed it first.

"Sure seems quiet, doesn't it?" Then, looking up at the grandmother clock, he added, "Is it only three thirty?"

"No, it's about five," Dan said.

"The clock stopped!" Robin exclaimed in surprise.

That got everyone's attention. The absence of the loud ticking was now apparent. Except for periodic maintenance, the clock had never ceased working in all the years it stood there. Now conspicuous in its silence, it was as if a great dynamo, one central to the power source to the entire ranch, had been stilled.

For it to stop near the time of Sally's death was just too coincidental, too eerie. A chill went through everyone as though some mysterious, meaningful event had taken place.

Dave, who had been sitting on the couch, leaned forward, and with index fingers to lips from folded hands, effected a thinking mode. "Well, I think it's a sign," he said slowly, pausing while everyone waited for the profound pronouncement, "that maybe someone should take over Sally's job and wind it back up."

For the first time in months, Charles smiled.

18
Negotiation

It was now September, and over four months since Sally's passing. For those who were close to her, the mourning period may have abated somewhat, but for Charles, its shadow was unrelenting.

Sam was sitting on the porch sipping the last of his morning coffee when Robin drove up and stopped at the house.

"Hi, Robin," Sam said as she got out of the car.

He walked over and opened the rear door. "And hi to you too, Hazel," he said to her as he undid the belt of the child's safety seat and led her out by the hand.

"Hi, Unca Sam," Hazel, now three and a half, said with a big grin.

"Come on up, Robin. Charles is still asleep. So how did your dad's appointment go with the doctor yesterday?"

"Naturally, he told me he was fine, but then I had a chance to talk with the doctor alone, and he wasn't so positive. He's got him on more heart medications, blood thinners and such, but he was also concerned about the grief he knows Dad's still going through. He thought it could lead to other problems. Being seventy-two doesn't help."

"I think all the anguish and depression has to have an effect on his body. He's suffering the most, Robin, and it's more profound than he'll admit. Even after all these months, I haven't seen much sign of recovery. I know you're doing the best you can, and I'm glad you're moving here full-time. It'll be a big help to him, and to all of us. Your mom—I think we're just now realizing how central she was to this operation. She left a big hole."

"Yes," Robin said, looking off in the distance. She then looked straight at Sam, but went silent for a moment. "It wasn't all that long ago that Mom and I had a reconciliation of sorts. I should be grateful we had it at all." Then she recovered, smiling. "I'm glad you're here, too—*Unca* Sam. I know life has to go on, but I feel like we've fallen off a cliff or something." She took Hazel's hand and looked around. "Dave and Henry can still run things, but it won't be the same. I hope I can be of some help."

"You already are—"

Before he could continue, a pickup came out from behind the barn and stopped near the porch, Henry driving.

"Henry's helping me move the last of my things I left at Dan's house—we have to leave in a few minutes. I'm taking Hazel with me, of course. Wouldn't want you and Dad to go into a panic if she starts crying. Hazel, go over and see Unca Henry now."

"Another Unca? I'm starting to feel pushed aside," Sam teased.

"She has enough love for a lot of Uncas—Unca Sam!"

Henry got out and picked up Hazel, swinging her around a couple of times before putting the child's seat in the truck. He lifted her in and fastened her seatbelt, Hazel laughing all the while.

Robin looked at the interplay between the two. "Sam, after all that we've gone through, Henry hasn't said much about Mom's passing. Dave was pretty open about how he felt—but Henry?"

"You're right. He must have been affected; after all, it was Sally who took care of him after the accident. Did he hide his grief because he didn't think he was part of this family?"

"Oh, my. After all this time." Then, Robin said with determination, "I'll have a talk with him. Okay Sam, gotta go." She headed for the truck.

Charles limped out just as Henry and Robin were pulling away.

"Morning, Charles."

"Sam."

"They're going to get the rest of Robin's things at Dan's," Sam said. "How do you feel today?"

Charles ignored the question. "I'm calling a family meeting for later on this afternoon. Dan will be coming by. Haven't told Robin yet, but she should be back by then. I want to go over our plans for the future."

"Have any ideas?"

"Yes. I want you and Dan to help me sell off the property."

"But—"

"Sam, I'd like you with me. Of course, we'll hear what you and Robin and Dan think, but I'm pretty sure that's the best course for the two of them."

For a moment, Sam stood in a state of shock.

~ ~ ~

Late that afternoon, Charles, Sam, Robin, and Dan were sitting at the kitchen table. No small talk.

"I want to make this simple," Charles began. "The effort to keep the ranch was for Sally's sake. With her gone...well, I think it's time we make the move. I want to know what you think, but I think it best we sell the property."

His words were met with absolute silence.

"Dan, what do you think?"

"I thought we had this worked out, Dad," Dan said hesitatingly. "Don't you think while we're all still in, well, a grieving period, that we should wait a while before making such a big decision? I like the preservation idea, but...well...I guess you have the biggest stake here."

"Robin?"

"I agree with Dan. You know, I might get used to being here. I think we should wait and see too."

"I know what you're saying, but your mom's imprint is everywhere— in the house, in the fields. I don't know if I could handle staying here without her. Now, if your mom were alive, that would be different and we could go on like you and I talked about, Dan. But on top of that, I have to accept, as I'm sure you do, that my own health isn't so good."

"Dad!" Robin said.

"You know it's not a minor issue. I'm old and won't last forever. You two have your own lives to consider."

"I'm here for good now, Dad. I can take care of you!" Robin said with tears welling up her eyes.

"I know you can, and I appreciate that, but that's not the point. By selling the land, I—all of us—will be able to live in comfort anywhere. Now, I'm two-thirds owner, and with Sam's blessing…" here Charles looked over to Sam for confirmation.

Sam shrugged at that comment and did not argue against it, but when he peered over at Dan and Robin, he saw the look of despondency in them both.

Charles did not see that, and continued, "We'll make arrangements to sell. We can make good money from this. I'm also going to make sure Dave and Henry will be cared for. I want you to think it over."

All of them sat in semi-paralyzed shock.

Robin heard a noise coming from Hazel's playroom, wiped her eyes, and went up to check. This gave Charles a chance to talk to Sam and Dan.

"Now, Sam, I don't know how much you know about T. Bob, the developer."

"A little."

"Dan, there's no need for you to face him. We'll work with Reginald and Leland, since it's their agency we're dealing with. I want you to get some numbers—high numbers we can work with. We know that T. Bob is desperate to get this place and will pay well above market value. It would also help if he thinks we're reluctant to sell, or that there might be some competition."

Dan said with a sigh, "I did not see this coming, Dad, but if the two of you are in agreement…I guess I understand." Then after a long pause, he added, "I'm afraid I have to leave in a few minutes. I'm closing out a sale tonight. You know, T. Bob will be ecstatic knowing you're thinking of selling, and if the country is headed toward some sort of financial bubble, as a lot of us think, this would be the right time. I'll call Reginald and set up a meeting—if you want me to."

"Yes, could you?"

"Of course. I'll start on that right away."

"You do that. We can all meet with them. Wait. Actually, I may want just you and Sam to meet them. Call me. I'll depend on your expertise, son."

When they were alone, Charles brought Sam up to speed about T. Bob without divulging Dan's prior relationship with him. No one else needed to know how deeply involved he had been.

"Thanks for not arguing against the sale, Sam."

Sam moved his chair around to face Charles directly. "Remember when I told you about that mine I explored? The one where I found a grave in a side tunnel that seemed purposely dug for it?"

"Yes."

"Later on, while trudging toward the highway, I pieced together what I thought might have happened. In their shack, I discovered things that only could have come from a woman's hand—curtain rods, scraps of wallpaper. The operation looked like it would have taken two men to run, and I figured she may have been the wife of one and maybe sister or something to the other. I think she was the one buried there—otherwise, they wouldn't have gone to all that trouble. And they certainly wouldn't have continued to mine it. I think they must have been so despondent that they just sealed it up and left."

Charles seemed to ponder the comparison. Then, with a strained look, he said, "I know what you're saying, Sam. I know how they must have felt. Thanks for understanding."

~ ~ ~

"I've got him!" T. Bob said to Reginald and Leland in his office. "Getting that property out of the hands of the most influential holdout will set me up big time!"

"What with his wife dying and all," Reginald said, "and with him being old, he might be desperate. No one to inherit the place. His son can't run it, and certainly not his flaky daughter."

T. Bob nodded. "We'll lowball the bastard!"

"Give us a number we can work with."

"Okay. Try seven or eight million."

"And the maximum?"

"Hmm. I can go higher, depending. Maybe eleven-five."

After the two left, T. Bob called James over the intercom to come to his office."

"I heard," James said as he walked through the door. "I think you might be a bit hasty, and letting your emotions dictate what you want to do. Whatever price they might agree on, it will be high, no matter what. Now that this preservation thing is getting publicity, environmental issues, including water concerns, are gaining support. Because they know which way the wind blows, your politicians have already begun to hedge their bets and are easing up on their support for wholesale development. Not only that, but there is a lot of talk about a financial bubble that we may be headed for. Just sayin'."

"I hear what you're saying, but if I can get my foot in the door by buying up the Ellis spread, and have it developed quickly, we should be ahead of that so-called bubble. Then we'll be set for further development when the financial climate improves. I want you to get the ball rolling on those preliminary designs we started on."

"It's your funeral," Jim said sarcastically as he bolted out of the room.

~ ~ ~

"Got the call from Reginald," Dan said to his father and Sam over the phone. "Naturally, he's agreed to having a meeting."

"Where should we meet?" Sam asked. "Certainly not in their office. Here again?"

"I think so," Charles said. "They may balk at that and try for a neutral location. A restaurant is no good. Noisy, and they may try to push drinks on you. No, have it here again. They don't need to know about my general health. When they do come, give them an excuse for my not being here. I know, tell them I had a meeting with the preservation group. Show them we have options. I don't want to be here and say something they could latch on to."

"Good," Dan said. "That'll make them think we're not desperate. That's important."

~ ~ ~

It was late morning when Reginald and Leland drove up. One car this time, and having learned their lesson, they apparently left the car vent closed. Sam and Dan decided to wait inside and make them knock on the back door.

"Play poker, Sam?"

"Chess. I'll let you do the bluffing. Ready?"

Sam waited a bit after they heard the rap on the screen before he opened it.

"Hello, Leland," Sam said to Reginald.

"I'm Rege."

"Right."

"Glad to see you again. Oh! Hi, Dan," Rege added in surprise. "Haven't seen you in a while."

"Let's sit outside," Dan said. "Coffee?"

"Sure." Rege, who was obviously going to do the talking, said, "Where's Charles?"

"He wanted to be here," Dan said, "but he had a meeting with the preservation people. He left it to us to work out a potential plan, if the numbers look feasible."

Rege and Leland looked at each other but didn't give anything away.

Sam came out with four cups and a thermos of coffee, and put it on the patio table. "Help yourself."

Reginald didn't hesitate to dive in. "First of all, I—we—want to express our condolences to you two, and to Charles, over the passing of his wife. It must be hard on all of you."

"Thank you for that," Sam said. "It has been hard, but we're recovering."

"I guess her passing made Charles think about the future, and maybe made him reconsider selling this spread."

"Well, actually my brother and I had been thinking about this for some time, even long before we met you that day. We're just looking at options we might pursue. Selling it—at the right price, of course—may be a possibility."

Rege effected a knowing smile, but Sam refused to respond in kind.

"If you don't mind my asking, are you part owner, Sam?"

Land ownership being public record, Sam knew that Reginald was feigning ignorance.

"Yes."

"It must be difficult to not have heirs to pass the land to. Selling it before it's too late might be the best option."

"Sam is an owner, and Robin and I are the heirs, Rege," Dan said with some exasperation. "And Robin has expressed interest in taking it over. Actually, she's rather upset at the possibility of selling it. But who knows? I may scrap my own vocation and get interested myself. By the way, Sam here has been working the ranch for some years, just as he had in the past."

Just then, as if on cue, Robin, Dave, and Henry came up the drive and stopped at the barn. Getting out, Robin, dressed in overalls and her mother's hat, waved, then talked to Dave as though giving him instructions.

"That's her," Sam said. "We may have a bit of a conflict, but we'll talk to her about it."

"Money talks," Leland blurted. Then, realizing his gaffe, laughed. "Just kidding."

Sam could see why Rege did all the talking.

"Okay," Dan said. "Since I'm in this business, I know the game. The numbers game. We all want the other side to come up with a number first, but I know what this spread is worth and know who's desperate to buy it. So here it is: twelve and a half million. This is not a negotiable number. Tell your boss that."

"That's pretty steep. Don't think it would go."

"Then so be it."

Rege seemed taken aback by Dan's decisiveness. And so, just as quickly as it began, the "negotiation" was over.

Hesitating, Rege said, "We'll work on it and give you an answer."

They walked to their car and left.

Robin came over to them. "Did I look in charge?" she said, smiling.

"Perfect," Dan said.

"Do you think he'll go for it?"

"I know the bastard. It's well above what he wants to pay, but not so out of line that he won't. He has the mind of an adolescent. He'll fear being left out."

"Well, my act may not be that much of an act," Robin said as she looked around. "I could get used to this. There's probably a little bit of Mom in me."

"It'll be a loss to all of us, Robin," Sam said, "but the money will help us take care of Charles. It may not be too long before we need to put him in a care facility. A good one."

Just as Dan started toward his car, Robin went to talk with him. "Dan—is this really happening? It's just dawning on me that we will never be part of this place again."

"I'm feeling that too," Dan said with concern. "But I do believe Dad when he said he couldn't live here without Mom. When Sam said we might eventually have to put him in a care facility, I just now realized how fast things are changing. Because neither of us have any interest working here, or even if it were put into the preservation trust, we would still have the full-time job of overseeing it. Either way, it would still most likely have to be sold."

"Dad may be thinking he is doing this for us, but as far as I'm concerned, we're doing this for Dad."

"Good point. But what about that preservation idea?" Dan said. "Obviously that option is out for this ranch if Dad sells it, yet he's the one who instigated this idea. The other ranchers might not take too kindly to that—might even make them lose initiative."

"Hmm, I see what you mean…but maybe not. There has been a lot of sympathy for him after Mom died, and many probably understand why he is doing this. But since there are a lot of new people involved in the preservation movement now, most of the ranchers are seeing it as a way to keep their spreads. In any case, I'd like you and I to get more involved and help them out; Dad would like that."

"Another good point. You know, sister, you and I could make a good team."

"It's about time. Mom always wanted to pull our family back together."

~~~

"Charles wasn't there," Rege said to T. Bob. "Left it to Dan and Charles's brother to dicker with us. They were pretty adamant. Almost take it or leave it. I don't think they're in any mood to compromise. From what I gather, his daughter might want to fight selling it, and may want to take it over herself."

"Can't trust a woman," T. Bob said. "But that just may have been a ploy to let us think they're not desperate."

"Don't think so," Leland said. "We saw her out there directing the workers."

"That's a big chunk of money. That traitor Dan knows what it's worth. He knows that I know it would set up a domino reaction with the surrounding ranches. Then he goes and sets a high figure, but not so high I wouldn't try to grab it." T. Bob paced over to the window. "I'll have to get more funding from the family," he mused, "but it can be done. Go back with another offer. Everybody compromises. We're going to build nothing less than a new city. I won't be stopped now."

~ ~ ~

After two months of real negotiating this time, the parties agreed on twelve million, and the contract was signed.

Sam and Charles knew it would be some time before permits could be issued, so it was stipulated that the family could stay on the ranch a maximum of eight months, allowing them time to secure other living arrangements.

~ ~ ~

Two months later, Robin called Sam in a panic.

"Sam!" she hollered over the phone. "I think Dad's had a stroke! Seems paralyzed on his left side. Ambulance will be here in a few minutes. Where are you?"

"Reno—I was on my way to Dan's office," Sam said. "Want me to come there?"

"No, we'd just be passing each other. Meet me at the hospital. Get them prepared."

"Okay. I'll call Dan and have him meet us there."

"Ambulance is here now. Meet you at emergency."

~ ~ ~

"It couldn't have been a heart attack," Robin said to Sam in the waiting room. "He's confused and can't talk or move his head much." She spotted her brother rounding the corner. "Dan! Thank God you're here."

"How's Dad?"

"Stroke, I think."

"Yes, it was a stroke," the doctor said, having overheard Robin as he entered the room. "I don't think any blood vessels were ruptured, which is good, but he'll be disabled for a while. I'm hoping it's only temporary. I can't give you anything definite on recovery. Now, he can't talk yet, but I've seen this before, so don't be too alarmed. He will improve, but by how much we don't know. Considering his age and heart condition…well, that might complicate things. All we can do is wait. He'll be here for a while, and we'll keep him fully monitored, of course."

They all went in to see him. As with many who have had a severe stroke, this strong man looked disordered and sickly. His eyes were open and he tried to speak, but couldn't.

Robin held his hand. "Don't try to talk, Dad. We're here to help you. The doctor says you're going to get better."

Charles blinked his eyes in recognition.

She smiled at him. "You rest. We'll be back to see you in a bit."

Once they were outside the room, Sam broke the silence. "If he doesn't improve substantially, like being able to feed himself, we *will* have to move him to a care facility."

"You okay, Robin?" Dan asked.

Robin tried to hide her tears. "How much do we have to take? Mom's gone, and now Dad…"

"I know," Dan said, putting his arm around her. "We'll get through this."

~ ~ ~

Several weeks later, Charles did recover enough to sit up and converse somewhat. Even so, he was in no condition to return home.

During the next month, he showed no improvement beyond his initial recovery. It was decided, as Sam had predicted, to move him to a high-end care facility. Charles didn't fight it. He did not want to be a burden to Sam and Robin. Dan, after the agreement was signed, and knowing they had to move out in a few months, had early on been looking for a house for Sam, and found one in Carson that was near the care facility. Sam bought it outright, using a portion of his one-third share of the payout.

Once Charles was moved to that facility, Sam convinced Robin that she and Hazel should stay with him at his new home for the time being. And so, for the first time in its long history, JE Ranch sat vacant.

Whenever Sam went to visit his brother, it was hard for him to see the look in his eyes. It reminded him of the look of resignation he had seen that one morning outside the house, and then again before Sally's demise. He sensed that the stroke, coupled with his grief, may soon have its ultimate effect—that Charles may not last for much longer.

While Charles still had his wits about him, he wanted to talk to his brother before it got too late.

"Sm. Damn it. SAM!" Charles blurted through his semi-paralyzed mouth as he tried to sit up in his hospital bed. "Want to make sure things taken care of before I'm gone."

"Don't try to sit up, just lay back," Sam said. "You seem to be getting better, Chuck."

"Don't pat-ronize. Stroke will probably happen again. Want to comm…talk while still can. Need to go over things. Steve Bryant, our tx…TAX advisor came. He knows a good attorney that can help me update my will for Robin and Dan. And you need to get your own affairs in order."

"You're right. I should have done that sooner."

"Call him and work it out. And want you to know, Sam, how much I appreciate you being here. Sorry about losing…ranch, but all for best for Robin and Dan. And thanks, by the way, for saving my life at the lake…fifty years ago."

"You remember that?" Sam asked, sounding surprised. "Well, I had to. Otherwise, Mom and Dad would have made me take over the ranch. But really, I appreciate being here. It's helped me more than you will ever know. And we made the right move selling the spread, though we all feel a sentimental attachment to the ranch."

"Did we make wrong decision?"

"Not at all. It took a while for it to sink in, but we're all good with it now. Since Robin is living in Carson with me, she's now back full-time at her insurance company. Told me yesterday that they wanted to promote her to assistant manager. Not only that, she and Dan are starting to become active within the preservation organization to help the other ranchers."

"Good for her. She gets more like her mo…mom every day."

Sam pulled a chair over and sat closer to the bed. "But there's something else. A crazy long shot that some of us have been thinking about."

Charles listened patiently as his brother filled him in on what he was thinking.

"You're kidding! You think? Well, thanks for thinking of that, anyway. Some, uh…sometimes life makes such a big jump—brings you right back where you started." Charles smiled, or at least he tried to.

~ ~ ~

Like Sally, Charles was ready to let go. In anticipating his own demise, he had added a provision to his will to give a handsome portion of his share to Dave and Henry, who had accepted an offer to work at Ray Wheeler's spread. Robin and Dan would receive the balance.

Three months later, Charles had another stroke, more devastating this time. Though he could nod his head, he was no longer able to converse; it was hard on everyone. Robin placed some of Charles's personal items where he could see them. Among them were his well-worn hat and Charles's and Sally's wedding photo. Dave and Henry would occasionally show up just to talk to him about their problems working on the Wheeler spread. Of course, they were doing just fine, but figured Charles wouldn't mind being favorably compared to working for another rancher.

Charles continued to fade, until eventually, his life force stopped. Unlike with Sally's unexpected and relatively quick passing, Charles's death did not come as a surprise, as his health concerns had begun years before, and continued throughout his current illness. He had been pampered with continual love from his family, as well as from the many who knew and admired him. He had actually come to like it.

19

The Storm Abates

As Dan, Robin, and Sam had suspected, the quick sellout left T. Bob unprepared, and he went to work resurrecting his previous preliminary plans into detailed plans—his Sharpenal Spring Valley Terrace project, or as Dave thought it should be called: "Turd Town."

After four months, T. Bob's completed plans were sent to the planning commission for approval, but by that time, Robin and Dan were now deeply involved in the preservation movement, and helped promote publicity concerning litigations over environmental impact laws. Because people in power were becoming aware of the growing number of environmentally friendly voters, the final approval was for only a scaled-down version of the development. Not only was he short on cash after buying the spread, investors like Fred Banks, whom he had once counted on, were balking at investing in a project that would not justify the handsome return T. Bob promised.

But T. Bob was determined. Having mortgaged everything he could, and with more loans from the family in Chicago, bulldozers finally descended on the ranch, and portable fences of orange plastic went up.

Then a new issue came up. With only family members present, Charles had been quietly interred next to Sally at the family cemetery. No one in T. Bob's organization sensed a problem—except for Jim. Though the cemetery was far enough away from the proposed development itself, it was still on the property, and Jim was worried that potential buyers might express reluctance to buy in. He informed T. Bob, who made a rash decision—a bad one as it turned out—and tried to get a ruling to have the family plots relocated.

But the ruling came down: the cemetery could stay. So Sam, Robin, and Dan decided to have a second, more formal service on the ranch and made preparations for many of Charles's friends to attend. This attracted a lot of publicity that T. Bob could do nothing about.

"Our crazy idea just might work," Sam told Dan and Robin. "Time may be on our side."

The backhoe, ready to pounce on the ranch house like some *Tyrannosaurus rex*, had sat idle all that time, and would soon become as impotent as its fossilized ancestor, for just as Dan had predicted, the recession hit. Even if the money were there, the investment would not bring the return T. Bob counted on.

T. Bob's family, major stakeholders in this development, were more than a little concerned. They refused to pump in more money, and requested that he return to Chicago for "consultations."

T. Bob was facing bankruptcy. In order to pay off his debts, he had to sell off everything: house, car, his office building. He got less than anticipated for it since it needed major remodeling in order to undo its conspicuous extravagances and convert it to a profitable office structure.

And, of course, he had to sell the ranch. Only one anonymous buyer came forward for that. Since no developer wanted to touch it, it was only valuable as a ranch. The offer came in at two and a half million, and was accepted.

And so justice, in its own peculiar way, was served.

~ ~ ~

The bulldozers on the ranch retreated. The fencing and signs promising a fabulous future for all came down. The house and grounds were left in their original condition to await the new owners.

Moving trucks came to the house, unloaded their contents, and left. The next day, a new Ford pickup pulled up to the back door of the still-standing great house, with an older red Toyota truck following. The man emerged from his truck, went around the other side, and opened the passenger door to take the hand of a now-five-year-old little girl. They stood for a few minutes, surveying the surroundings in awe, then went up the back porch and unlocked the door.

"Do you want to start it now?" Robin asked Hazel as she opened the door for her daughter.

Hazel was excited about the grandmother clock her mother had promised she could start. She looked enthralled as she gazed up at its overwhelming size.

"Open the glass door to the pendulum, honey," Robin said. "That's right. Okay. Now pull it to one side—lightly now. Then let it go. Not too far."

Hazel did as told, then watched, rapt, as the pendulum moved back and forth, making a loud ticking sound.

Robin slowly and carefully set the time by turning the hands. After looking over at a smiling Sam, she bent down to her daughter. "This clock has been in this house since it was built over a hundred and fifty years ago. It was owned by your great-great-great-grandmother, then your great-great-grandmother, then great-grandma, grandma, and now me. Someday, it will be yours to hand down to your children."

The reverent tone in Robin's voice did not appear lost on Hazel, who looked upon the object as something worthy of veneration.

"You sure you have enough greats in there?" Sam asked.

Robin smiled at Sam. "No, but close enough."

"That clock makes me think how time has flown by these last four years."

"Funny, to me, it seemed to drag," Robin said with a twinge of sadness in her voice.

"Probably because of Hazel," Sam said. "Five years is an eternity to her. That's all she's ever known. Strange how time seems different to different people."

"Yeah," Robin said absently. "So, you ready to move back home?" Sam's face tensed in mock surprise. "Ready? I already have!"

~ ~ ~

Sam sold his house in Carson, and had, along with Robin and Dan—each with their own third payout—bought into the property equally. And just as Sam had once been absentee owner, Dan would continue in much the same way with his ownership. He would have no involvement with the ranch's workings or finances, but they all wanted to keep the spread in the family. As Charles had once said: "You can never tell what the future will bring."

Robin had wanted Dave and Henry to quit working the Wheeler ranch and return to the JE, but she was unsure how to approach them. She had a speech all worked out to entice them, and if unsuccessful, induce them with some guilt by reminding them of the handsome payout they had received from Charles's will. She went to the Wheeler ranch one afternoon when the owner was away, walked up to Dave, and opened her mouth to say something.

"Thought you'd never show up," Dave said. "Have a few things to finish up here and Henry and I will be there tomorrow. Wheeler already knows."

~ ~ ~

One balmy evening, Robin and Sam were sitting on the back porch, having their coffees.

"I'm just sorry that Dad wasn't able to see us get the ranch back in the family. He would have been so thrilled."

Sam took a sip. "One of the last times I talked to him, I told him that there might be a good chance of getting it back. I might have been a bit optimistic—but why not? In any event, it really cheered him up."

"Well, now *that* cheers me up," Robin said as she turned around to look at the house. "Isn't it funny, this house has a complete wraparound porch, and we only use the back door. Do we even have a front door?"

"I think I remember one." Sam laughed. "Isn't that the way with old houses, though? Fancy parlors that no one uses, and funky kitchens where people spend most of their time. I guess function is more important, especially on a working ranch like this one." Then, musing somewhat, he went on, "You know, you said once you thought there was a lot of your mom in you. I think there is."

Robin nodded. "So where do we go from here, Uncle Sam?"

"After all these years, Sam is fine. Hazel can still call me Unca Sam, though. But where to go from here? Now that the dust has settled, you and I need to go over a few things, and I just want to get this out of the way. I'm going to pass on my interest in the property to you only, making you two-thirds owner, and you and Dan will divide my finances. Dan already knows this, and he's okay with it. I've already had my will worked up, so it's all settled," he said with finality.

"Sam! I am not ready to go through this again!"

"Don't worry, I expect to be around a long time. My health is actually quite good. Unlike your father, I don't have that history of backbreaking work. That, and the anguish of always trying to make ends meet probably took a toll on him.

"But that's not all. Since you will be around longer than me, I want you to be the controlling factor in running the ranch, just like your parents were when I lived back east and wasn't involved. Of course, I am involved now, but with your energy, I think you and I can make this work."

"Sam," Robin said, leaning forward in her chair. She then relaxed and added, "Well, okay, I guess I know what you're saying. Our roles will work themselves out as time goes on. I'm just glad my brother and Laura are helping out with the financial and legal paperwork for us. Nothing like having a couple of professionals in the family."

"I've got Dan working on setting up a family trust for the four of us," Sam said with a slight snicker.

"Four? Hazel wouldn't be involved."

"I don't mean Hazel. I'm kidding, of course; it would just be the three of us. It wouldn't affect the trust, but eventually you may want to get married."

"To who? Some cowboy only after my money?"

"Why not? You women have been doing that for ages. What about Henry? Nice kid, hard worker, make a good stepfather for Hazel."

Robin laughed so hard she could barely get the words out: "Now there's an idea!"

"What's so funny?"

"Henry has his own boyfriend…or didn't you know that?"

"Oh."

"You've seen him here a couple of times. Henry told me they might live at his place in town, but that might be too far away. I told him that he and his friend could live here—actually I insisted, but we'll see how it goes."

"What do you think Dave thinks about that?"

"I'm sure he knows about it. He does come from a history of upheavals, so I doubt he is too troubled by it. And anyway, as far as I'm concerned, me getting married is way on down the road."

"It still wouldn't hurt to have a man around for Hazel."

"Like you and Dave and Henry and Dan aren't enough? She'll have plenty of male role models. You can be assured they will all dote on her. But if you are appointing me to be the controlling factor, I do have some ideas I'd like to run by you," she said with a gleam in her eye.

"I'm listening."

"This old house has been structurally remodeled over the years, but I think it's time for a major interior overhaul. Don't you? And while we're at it, maybe tear down that old cinderblock bunkhouse and build a couple of decent log cabins for Dave and Henry. That way, we could keep our extended family together. And speaking of my brother and Laura…"

"We were?"

"Laura has expressed some interest in her and Dan living here, maybe in the future sometime. What do you think?"

"Fine by me. But this old house big enough?"

"It sure wouldn't be, since they are now expecting—twins."

"Really?"

"They put off starting a family until they felt financially secure, which of course, they now are. We'll just build them another house."

Sam, realizing just how confident Robin was, leaned over toward her and said, "You are energetic, aren't you?"

Wearing her mother's hat, Robin leaned back in her chair and smiled.

20
Renewal

The JE Ranch was now back in business, with most of the remaining characters in place.

With his payout, Dan started his own real estate firm. Bucking the trend, he made sure his salespeople were honest and aboveboard. Because the recession was thankfully minor and coming to an end, his venture was beginning to bring in more business than he had ever thought possible.

Sam and Dave and Henry would continue to work the land, and Robin, after quitting her job, soon began to assume the responsibilities her mother had. Whatever the future held for the entity that was JE Ranch, she would be in line to serve as the conscience and essence to the lives of its people.

But running the ranch wasn't her only interest. She wanted to continue with some interests her father had.

One evening, Robin decided to attend one of the ranchers' meetings at the old hall. She was dismayed to see the poor condition of its members, and the hall itself. In her talks with some of the members, no one seemed to blame Charles for selling the property after his wife's death. But while several members had opted to go the preservation route, she could see that the organization had been treading water and was looking for direction since her father's passing.

Not one to be concerned with crashing this good-old-boys club (emphasis on *old*), Robin decided to jump in. After all, she was

Charles's daughter, an energetic woman who wanted to do right. She soon began to gain, grudgingly at first, the respect of its members. She let them in on a few ideas for enlivening the organization. More by default than anything else, she took over her father's role as president.

First, she wanted to re-emphasize the preservation idea her father had started, and get more of them interested. As an example for others, she and Sam and Dan put their property into the trust, with no stipends other than the tax breaks it would reap. She thought this would loosen up preservation money that could help some of the other ranchers.

She also wanted to get some new blood into the organization, and made it a point to convince a few of the younger ranchers, and those in the southern area, to attend the meetings. Next, she urged several of the wives, and their daughters, to get engaged in the association, knowing that more of the ranchers' sons would follow. Being attractive herself didn't hurt in that regard. But in the spirit of compromise, she saw no problem with the old-timers' need to hold their occasional men's-only drinking fests.

Then she got some local politicians back into the mix. She had several of them come to the meetings of the newly renovated and decorated hall to impress upon them the organization's importance to the community. She wasn't about to let her father's objectives falter.

Robin had a lot on her plate. She had not only taken on a leadership role in the ranching community, but had a preservation agenda to attend to, a ranch to run, and a child to bring up.

For Hazel—now six and precocious—might one day become a handful once she was old enough to set out on her own adventures. But her savvy mother, unlike the innocent and trusting Sally, would be prepared. She made sure that Hazel's first-grade friends, along with her new cousins, would be welcome to come over.

Slowly, it seemed, the Ellis family was beginning to grow again.

Given that they had received a generous share of the inheritance, Dave bought himself the most tricked-out, fire-engine-red pick-'em-up truck. He attached a pair of longhorns to the hood as an ornament, thinking he might become a magnet to not a few women in the area. That was just fine with him.

But a culture born out of necessity cannot always be created out of intention, and for some, initiative may be lost. Fortunately for Dave, the foundational work ethic was ingrained in him, and, despite his generous payout, he continued working as he had. Henry would likely follow in his father's footsteps; quiet, steady, and personable—he would stand a good chance of watching life's outrages pass him by.

Then there was Sam. He was only too happy to let Robin take the lead. He just wanted to get back to work, now with the luxury to pursue some ideas he had. First on his list was to replace that pesky well pump. Then he would go about devising a solar project that would make the ranch energy independent. It would take a while to restock the herd, to get the fields plowed and planted, but they had the money and could get additional labor whenever needed.

Sam was now about the same age his brother had been when Sam had deposited himself on their doorstep five years before. Perhaps he, too, would follow the same path into old age, though just as likely not. *We do seem determined to consciously avoid the mistakes of others*, he thought, *though often to tread into new and untried mistakes of our own.*

In any case, he would continue to think, ponder, and question, as was his wont. Just as with the prophets of the past, he suspected that the desert held great secrets. But they were called secrets because a mind dependent on reason could never penetrate them. So the answers would continue to elude him, even when he had found them.

As had those who came before them, Sam and Robin would try to mold the land for their own uses. But as the original natives understood only too well, the land's deep and far-reaching roots, predestined as they were unconscious, would just as likely mold them to the land's own needs.

And within the old house, the great mechanism would continue to mark the passage of time. Its pendulum movements, from one position to the next, would portend the unpredictable nature of progress and return, and deep within lay the rumblings and disturbances of a thousand meanings.

For some, the passage of time will evoke regret as they continue to ignore the eternity of the present that surrounds them. For others, time merely gives meaning to change, and will ride its current and allow it to take them where it may—to the new, and to renewal.